**MIKE RIPLEY** has twice wo...                    ...h
Award for comedy crime and his *Angel* novels have been
optioned by the BBC. He has written for television and radio
and is the crime fiction critic for the *Birmingham Post*, as well
as co-editor of the *Fresh Blood* anthologies which promote new
British crime writing talent. He lives with his wife, three
children and two cats in East Anglia.

# FAMILY OF ANGELS

## Mike Ripley

**ROBINSON**
London

Constable & Robinson Ltd
3 The Lanchesters
162 Fulham Palace Road
London, W6 9ER
www.constablerobinson.com

First published in Great Britain by
HarperCollins*Publishers* 1996

This edition published by Robinson,
an imprint of Constable & Robinson Ltd, 2002

ISBN 1-84119-509-X

Printed and bound in the EU

A CIP catalogue record for this book is
available from the British Library

10 9 8 7 6 5 4 3 2 1

FOR

Tim Coles, because it's about time.
About time he destroyed the negatives.

And for Big George,
Who took me to Hackney for the first time.
Under duress. In a Volvo. Bastard.

## NOTE

The odd (very odd) Angel reader will recognize material here drawn from the first Angel short story *'Smeltdown'* published in *A Suit of Diamonds* (Collins Crime Club, 1990).

I am indebted to Tim Coles for advice on how to steal an aircraft. My agricultural consultants prefer to remain anonymous. None of them have ever appeared on *Gardeners' Question Time*.

M.R.

# Chapter One

'This is one hell of a place to pick for a family conference,' said my father. 'Couldn't you have put your mind to it and found somewhere really inconvenient?'

'You're a busy man, Dad,' I said with a smile. 'I thought I'd come to you and save time. Now stop moaning and pull up a beer keg and sit down.'

I nodded towards a steel keg of lager and he grasped the hand holds in the rim and manoeuvred it out from behind a gas cylinder so he could straddle it as I was doing. Our knees touched briefly.

'Not much room in here,' he observed.

'No, it is small,' I said, 'considering the volume of boozing done here.'

'Mostly the hard stuff, of course. This will be just the beer cellar, I suppose. Funny, I've never been down here before. Not that I come down this end of things much at all.'

'Well, you wouldn't, would you?'

He looked at me to see if that was supposed to mean anything.

'You got in without trouble?' he asked, but he wasn't really interested in the answer. He was watching the closed circuit TV monitor in the corridor.

'No problems,' I said honestly.

'There should have been,' he said, but almost to himself. He was totally distracted by the TV screen now, squinting over my shoulder to read the text on the green background. 'You still living in . . .?' he asked vaguely.

'Hackney. Yes.'

'Still driving that clapped-out old taxi cab?'

'Yes.' Next question.

'Kept up the trumpet playing?'

'Yes.' Get on with it.

'Women?'

'Please.'

He almost smiled at that. At least it took his eyes off the monitor.

'Don't suppose we can actually get a drink here, can we? I could have arranged lunch if you'd let me know when you were going to turn up.'

His left hand wandered to a metal cask of beer which had been tapped and stillaged on its belly, a white plastic tap protruding from the end connected to a plastic pipe which disappeared up into a hole in the ceiling. He moved aside the bar towel which was draped across the cask so he could read the legend engraved in the metal: PROPERTY OF YOUNG & CO., WANDSWORTH.

'Your message said it was important, so I thought I'd pop round straight away.'

'I said it *might* be important. I didn't say it was urgent. Who was it, by the way,' he said slowly, 'who took the message this morning?'

'Someone I share the house with.'

'She sounded quite pleasant. Said she had no idea you had a father.'

Thanks, Fenella. I owe you one.

'If I thought for one minute you were interested, Dad, I'd say you were fishing.'

'You're right,' he said, flicking a thread of cotton from the knee of his trousers. 'I'm not really interested in what you get up to. It's probably better that I don't know. Your one great strength, Fitzroy, is that you have always shat on your own doorstep and not mine, and long may you continue to do so.'

'Thank you for sharing that with me, Father.'

He stroked his chin like a man checking the closeness of a shave. He had once, in his youth, sported a beard which would have got him a backstage pass at Woodstock. I'd seen the photographs. Black and white, of course.

'Whereas your brother . . .'

Here it comes.

He put his hands on his knees and flexed his fingers as if inspecting his manicure.

'I was waiting for the smart remark,' he said in a voice which brought back memories of a dozen schoolmasters.

'I try to pick on people my own size,' I reasoned. 'Finbar is, and always was, too easy. It would be a shame to take the money.'

'Hmmmmm,' he hummed, moving from schoolmaster to headmaster in one fluid tonal shift.

I was not going to let him provoke me, no matter how bad the wind-up. And the wind-up was coming, that was for sure.

'Still not talking, then? It must be – what – four years or more?'

I made a point of looking at my watch.

And kept looking.

Eventually, he went for it. Most do.

'Is there some time pressure on you? Got to be somewhere? Left the cab on a meter?'

I looked up slowly.

'No, just bored.'

He ground his teeth. It was petty, I know, but most of the really satisfying things in life are.

That was something I had learned from my father.

'I thought the whole thing had the ring of Greek tragedy to it,' he charged on. 'Two brothers, one girl. Brother meets girl, gets engaged to girl, girl goes off with other brother. Classic recipe for a family feud.'

'Only if the family is called Addams, Father, or maybe Manson. It wasn't that big a deal.'

'My dear boy, I've dined out on this story, allow me to embellish it. There was poor Lavinia, jilting her betrothed at the church . . .'

'Her name was Lucy, Dad, and it never got anywhere near a church.'

'It was announced in *The Times*.'

'No, it wasn't. There was a very rude personal ad in the *Daily Mirror* on Valentine's Day and everybody was doing it that year.'

'Look, it's my story, let me tell it my way. Two brothers torn by lust. A house divided. Never would they speak to each other again . . . Just a minute, this isn't Greek, this is Victorian melodrama.'

'It wouldn't make a daytime soap,' I said, cool as I could.

11

'You're probably right,' he pretended to concede. 'What *did* happen to you and Lucy?'

'It lasted about a month then she legged it with a commodities broker from the City. I never could give her the skiing holidays she'd been used to.'

'I take it you got over her?' I wasn't sure whether this was a probe or just a conversational link.

'More times than Finbar did,' I said, watching his face.

'That doesn't surprise me,' he said instantly. 'I always knew you could look after yourself.'

I had to, I thought, but I didn't rise to the bait. I'd been here before and arguments down this road were best won like fights: quickly and by whatever means to hand. Afterthoughts and recriminations were, like return bouts, almost invariably anticlimactic.

'Have you seen your mother recently?' he said, changing tack.

'Not for a while. Have you?'

He ignored that and went for the diversionary move.

'It's her birthday next week.'

'I know that. I don't forget them,' I lied.

'Give her my love, won't you?'

'Of course, if you really want me to,' I said cautiously. 'When I see her next, that is. Whenever that is.'

'I just assumed you would be seeing her before I did,' he said far too casually.

No, I wasn't going to fall for it.

'Why should you assume that, Father?'

I fell.

'So you could ask her if she knew where Finbar was.'

His eyes wandered to a box of soft spiles – the small, fat wooden pegs they use to vent casks of beer – and he reached to pick one out, examining it as if it was the most wondrous thing in the world.

'Why should I go and see Mother to ask her where my dear brother is?' I said, trying to remember the breathing exercises.

'Because Finbar's gone missing.' He finally made full eye contact, but kept his face as straight as a judge's death mask.

12

'Haven't you heard a word I've said? Do try and keep up, Fitzroy.'

When people ask me, and they do, if I have ever minded being named Fitzroy Maclean Angel, they rarely believe me when I say no, not at all. I have a good explanation to hand in that I say my father was very impressionable and the week I was born, he'd just finished reading *Eastern Approaches* by Sir Fitzroy Maclean. And I was very happy to live with that, especially as, the next week, my dad took *Mein Kampf* out of the library and things could have been different, to say the least. And it has come in useful in that I can ring the changes and be known – to different people in different places – as Roy, Fitz, Mac, Roy Maclean (Mastercard), F. M. Angel (Visa) and even (once) a new jazz-based commercial radio station, Angel FM. Most times, though, people want me to say it was a real handicap and got me bullied at school and nowhere with women. So I lie and tell them that if it keeps them happy.

Finbar was different, and in more ways than just his name. I never could work out where my parents got Finbar Miles from, and we both cursed them at different times and for different reasons, for giving us the same initials, although I think Finbar overreacted to that American Express bill and I did pay him back eventually.

Being the eldest, Finbar was expected to take over the family farm. Being Finbar, he thought this an excellent idea and it never occurred to him to question it. He went off to agricultural college like a lamb and bullshitted his way through to some sort of qualification in farm management which, as far as I could see, included a free pass to every Young Farmers' dance ever likely to be held anywhere and introductions to a legion of women who did not have names and were only distinguishable by the colour of their 4 × 4 off-roaders and their personalized number plates.

Finbar loved it and he had the future Mrs Finbar Angel all lined up for when he graduated. (She was called Sookie, I think, and she came with an Izuzu Trooper, a red 2.5-litre job with built-in CD player. Only done 9,000 miles. Nice motor. I'm pretty sure her name was Sookie. Maybe Susan. Or was it Alice?) But what he had not expected was the gift of a farmhouse, which our father announced at the wedding reception.

Now, the family farm was no Ponderosa but then again, there is no such thing as a small farm in Suffolk. As smaller, neighbouring farms had been subsumed over the years, the property included at least three derelict farmhouses. It was one of these – Windy Ridge – which was to be Finbar's wedding present. The only catch was that the newlyweds had to move there straight away as Father was selling the main house (and a fair chunk of land) to pay off his debts. Oh yes, and to finance his divorce as he and Mother were separating and he was going to move to London full time to set up a new home with his physiotherapist, Miss Dido Temperton.

Before the bride and groom or the bride's father or the best man (both of whom were supposed to be making speeches) could react, my mother stood on a chair and threw her hat in the ring. It was a perfect, and perfectly amicable, solution, she told the wedding guests. Now the children were off her hands, she could concentrate on her career as an artist and Father would be very happy in the capable hands of Miss Dido Temperton, about whom the popular press had been both ill-informed and unfair.

After that the reception went downhill, although the band I had put together for the party afterwards did a couple of good sets and, come to think of it, we never did get paid. But the centre of attention was my parents and the attendance of a couple of 'society' hacks made sure the news made most of the papers the next day.

No bride likes to be upstaged at her wedding and so Finbar and Sookie/Susan/Alice (whatever) got off on the wrong foot. This was compounded by the news that they were not going to live in the west wing of a Tudor manor house (as my father had a cash buyer already lined up) but in a dilapidated farmhouse which had been uninhabited – by humans, though not by turkeys in the run-up to Christmas – for thirty years.

I never knew the exact timing, but within weeks rather than months of the happy couple returning from their honeymoon, Mrs Finbar moved to London and set divorce proceedings in motion.

I helped Finbar make Windy Ridge habitable, mixing cement,

installing electricity, securing the roof and even trying my hand at plumbing, as he was strapped for cash but determined to make a go of what was left of the farm as Father had made him manager.

After I had moved on I still stayed in touch with him, even visiting from time to time. Hence the incident with Lucy, since when, not surprisingly, things had cooled somewhat.

About six months after Finbar's wedding (by which time the solicitors were already on the case), Father left Miss Dido Temperton following an incident in a (then) fashionable restaurant just off Piccadilly to which the police had been called. I knew because I read it in the newspaper.

Two years after Finbar's wedding – in fact, just about the time he was celebrating his divorce – I got a handmade Christmas card from Mother which told me that she had been studying origami and was living in an 'artists' community' on the Essex coast. As I opened the card I accidentally tore the movable Star of Bethlehem, which was supposed to rise over the nativity scene she had watercoloured, no doubt ruining hours of concentration.

I wondered at the time how she had got hold of my address as I hadn't told anyone. As they say, you can run but you can't hide.

But the point was that while Mother and Father might disappear up their mid-life crises and I might choose to lose myself in Hackney, so far all we were doing was behaving in character. The Finbars of this world simply didn't go *missing*.


'Finbars don't go *missing*, Father. Well, maybe they do, but only in the sense of missing between the barbecue and the drinks table, or missing as in "he's been a long time finding the toilet". But not *missing* missing, as in no one knows where he is and nobody's seen him for a couple of months.'

'Ten days, actually,' he said softly, while clearing his throat as if to cover the words.

'Ten days? That's not even the hangover from an Eighteen to Thirty Holiday. How long would I have to disappear for before you let the bloodhounds out?' I snapped, meaning: before you noticed.

15

'You're different, you can look after yourself. It's just as you say; it's so out of character, something must be wrong.'

He was avoiding eye contact again, studying a spare white plastic beer tap as if it had been invented by Leonardo da Vinci. It probably had.

'It's because Finbar runs the farm, isn't it?' I tried, looking for an angle. 'There's something wrong with the farm, is that what it is? Finbar cooked the books or something? Run off with the profits, has he?'

'Oh, come on, Fitzroy.' He flared slightly, a reaction at last. 'You know Finbar wouldn't know how to start to cook the books and there's precious little profit to run off with these days.'

'That's right, I was forgetting. There's no such thing as a rich farmer, is there? So what's he done then? Screwed up his set-aside quota from the Common Market?'

He gave me his best scathing look. We were out of the head-master's study now and on the barrack square.

'It's called the European Union now and some of us take it very seriously. Anyway, Finbar has a deputy manager who takes care of most of the business and Ineson hasn't noticed anything amiss.'

'Ineson? Old Godfrey Ineson? Christ, he's not so much a name from the past as a smell.'

'He's salt of the earth is old Godfrey, don't be chopsy,' he said peevishly. 'Anyway, it's not him, it's his son Barry and he knows what he's doing.'

'And Barry doesn't know where Finbar is?' I pushed. 'Doesn't know where to look?'

'He says not. It was Barry who rang me to ask if I knew where Finbar might be. Said there were orders to send out, things to buy . . .'

'Sheep to plant and corn to shear?' I offered helpfully.

'Yeah, OK.' He grinned faintly at that. 'I'm about as much a real farmer as you are. But Finbar seemed to enjoy it. He really liked the life.'

Because you told him he would from a very early age, I thought, but didn't say it.

'Could you ever see Finbar working in an office?' he pitched, clutching for straws of sympathy.

'What's an office?'

16

'You know what I mean.'

'OK, put it this way. It's not that Finbar's elevator doesn't go to the top floor, it's just that when he gets there, he doesn't notice the doors are open.'

He managed to keep his face straight.

'That's cruel, but probably true. But no one could say that of you, could they? That's why you've got to go to the farm and find out what's happened to him.'

Now it was my turn.

'Hey, come on, Dad, wake up and smell the petrol fumes. That's a ridiculous reason.'

'He *is* your brother.'

'I've only your word for that.'

'And your mother's.'

I pretended to think for a second.

'Nope, she never owned up to Finbar. Not to me, anyway.'

'Look, he's family.' Pleading now. 'You can't just walk away from a family problem.'

'Watch my feet.'


Of course you can walk away from family problems. In fact, my Rule of Life No. 4 is: Family problems? Run, don't walk. I know, I had been taught by experts.

And the strange thing was it seemed to work. Had we, as a family, had any closer contact over, say, the last ten years, then all of us would have been up on attempted murder charges, or one of us would have been facing a mass-murder charge. Or, alternatively, I could have got away with it and be living in the nearest country with drinkable beer and no extradition treaty. (Must check out where that is.)

I used to tell people that my family had a policy of respecting each other's space, and this was long before the Californian shrinks made it a buzz word diagnosis. Then, more recently, I put it down to my parents being prototype members of Generation X, or early Zippies – technocrat ravers – ruled by spontaneity and a love of living for today.

Then I realized we just probably didn't like each other very much and didn't have that much in common. None of us gave much of a monkey's about any social pressures to remain a tight-knit group and there were no economic ties to bind us. So why not go our individual ways? After all, we could always send Christmas cards.

And one of these Christmases I would get round to it.


'Oh, come on, Fitzroy, family is important,' said my father, looking over my shoulder again at the TV monitor.

'Forgive me if I'm totally underwhelmed by that, Dad. I don't seem to recall us sitting round the fire roasting chestnuts and making our own entertainment. In fact, your idea of quality time was showing me how to work the VCR.'

He narrowed his eyes. 'My, my, do I detect a chink in the armour there?'

'Yes, but not mine. I can sleep nights. If family is so top of mind for you, then you do something about it. You started it.'

'No, I –' he began.

'Yes, you did, you slept with Mother,' I cut him off. And all for the sake of a sly one-liner, when really I should have been more alert; and listening.

'OK, I get the picture,' he said as if conceding. 'You won't go and find Finbar for the sake of the family. That right?'

'Yup.'

'Then will you do it to put your mother's mind at ease?'

'Is she worried?' He wouldn't meet my eyes. 'She doesn't know, does she?'

'I'm not sure. She might know where he is and there may be absolutely nothing wrong.'

'And you'd like me to ask her?' I offered sweetly.

'You'll go and see her?'

'Nope.'

He hardly paused in his mental shopping list of bribes. We had done family loyalty and motherly love, so mercenary ought to be coming up soon.

'I'd make it worth your while if you were to take a few days off and go and snoop around in Suffolk. Are you busy at the moment? Anything on you couldn't moonlight from?'

He looked at his watch, but he wasn't timing my answer.

'Nice watch,' I said. It was a Rolex, or looked like one.

18

'A gift from a grateful Middle Eastern government for services rendered,' he said automatically, as if rehearsed.

'Aren't you supposed to declare things like that?' I asked innocently.

'In that case, it's a ten-quid fake from a bloke with a suitcase on Oxford Street.' He'd rehearsed that too. 'Would a couple of hundred buy some time out of your busy schedule?'

'Why not save your dosh and give her a call?'

'Three hundred, then.'

'Now I'm getting really suspicious, Father dear. Why won't you call her?'

I half wished I was interested in the answer rather than just the baiting process.

'She's not on the phone,' he said lamely.

'Oh, come on, there'll be a number somewhere. A neighbour, a local pub, something. In case of emergencies.'

'If there is, I don't have it.'

'Then go and see her yourself. Christ, you could be there and back in a morning.'

'I can't,' he said quietly. Then, faintly: 'I daren't.'

Ah, here comes the emotional blackmail tactic.

'And what on earth are *you* frightened of, oh wise, grey owl of a father?' I smiled.

'Your mother, of course. And less of the grey,' he came back. 'You see, I'm thinking of getting married again.'

'So we can scrub the "wise" bit as well.'

'I knew you wouldn't understand,' he said without batting an eyelid. 'The problem is, your mother won't either.'

'Let me guess why.' I mugged it as if I had to think hard. 'Is it because her replacement is rich and beautiful?'

'Oh dear, so cynical so young,' he tut-tutted.

'Well, thanks for the "young", anyway.'

'No, I meant you've been cynical since you were young. But, I'm afraid, that's part of the problem too.'

'What is?'

'Your mother's replacement, as you so elegantly put it. Yes, she's rich and very beautiful, but she's also young.'

'How young?'

He took a deep breath. 'Young.'

'Come on, how young?'

'Twenty-four,' he said, looking at the ceiling.

'Hell's teeth, Dad, be afraid; be very afraid. Mother will go ape-shit.'

'Tell me about it,' he exhaled wearily. 'I'm under enough pressure as it is and I really couldn't handle her on the war-path.'

'Yes, I can see that, Dad,' I said sympathetically.

He brightened. 'So you'll go and see her?'

'Oh no, I'm far too busy,' I said smugly.

He glared at me. If looks could kill I would have had flesh wounds.

But before he could say anything, a bell rang out, echoing around us and down the corridors. It was an electronic ring rather than the metallic clatter of a fire alarm. But then I knew it was not a fire alarm.

Father unglued his buttocks from the beer keg and stood up.

'Sod it,' he said. 'I've got to go and vote.'

# Chapter Two

The Red Lion is probably the nearest pub to the Houses of Parliament if the traffic system round Parliament Square doesn't get you and provided you can fight your way through the massed ranks of tourists camcordering Big Ben.

Taxi-driver legend has it that an American couple stopped a cabbie there once and the male tourist asked if Big Ben was the clock on the famous tower or a bell inside it. The cabbie said it was actually the bell and so the American turned to his wife and said: 'There, I told you so.' And then the wife said: 'Now let's ask a woman.'

I dodged through a crocodile line of French schoolchildren (you could tell they were French because of the chic with which they dressed, plus they were all smoking Marlboro) just as it started to rain. I wanted to get to the bar before they decided to take shelter, even if it meant elbowing a couple into the building rush-hour traffic. Hell's teeth, they were on holiday; I'd just had to talk to my father. My need was greater than theirs.

The pub was filling up nicely for the pre-evening crush, mostly junior officials from the Treasury across the road who had got trapped there without coats or umbrellas by the rain and couldn't get back to their offices. Not that they would dissolve or spoil their hair gel or anything, it was just that if they turned up with damp spots on the shoulders of their suits, someone would notice and clock how long they had been away from their desks. The really professional afternoon drinkers always leave a spare jacket over the back of their chair to give the impression that they are somewhere else in the building. It's a trick often credited to share dealers in the City, but it originated in the Civil Service years ago.

I ordered a pint of Tetleys from the Australian barman and before he had pulled it, a large bourbon with ice as well. He raised an eyebrow at that, but said nothing. I didn't blame him, two-fisted drinking in the afternoon had been out of fashion for some time. But then, *his* father was probably in Australia.

I carried my beer away from the bar over to the window shelf and searched through my jacket for the cigarettes I had known I would need. I lit up and exhaled, watching the smoke cloud back from the window, obscuring the view of the mews down the side of the pub. That suited me fine.

Unfortunately, I could not help but notice the reflection of the small, swarthy, unshaven character who had materialized behind my right shoulder. But then, if I hadn't been smoking I would probably have smelled him.

'Hello, Taffy,' I said without turning round.

'Angel? It is you, isn't it?' The voice was a put-on croak, meant to give the impression that he was in imminent danger of death by raging thirst. 'You couldn't spring me for the price of a pint, could you? I am totally threadbare, Angel. Threadbare. Me luck's gone completely and I've got no job, no prospects and no invisible means of support. I've been 'anging about here for . . .'

That was the trouble with Taffy Duck. He couldn't keep his mouth shut if you put superglue in his lager.

'Taffy, shut it and I'll put a glass in front of it. What do you want?'

'Hey, thanks, Angel, that's being a gent, that is. I'm at the end of my tether, I can tell you. This is not my year, this isn't. I've been down before this but I reckon this time . . .'

'Taffy, I'm either going to the bar or just going. Now name it.'

'A large brandy would slip down a treat, my friend,' he said quickly.

'You decide the drink, I'll decide the size. And I ain't your friend, Taffy.'

Taffy Duck was one of those people you really couldn't remember where or how you met the first time. The only thing you do know is that you regret it happening.

He was a driver. Nowadays, he drove trucks or coaches, usually with scant regard for tachographs and regulations about the amount of time spent behind the wheel. But originally, as he would tell you at length, he was a train driver on the London Underground and one of the few who had experienced three 'one-unders'. Most drivers are moved on to other lines after a suicide and if they experience two, they are usually transferred to other duties. Taffy Duck had gone through three and had only

22

six other tube lines to be jinxed on when he decided to quit. Or maybe he was pushed before he jumped. He had been off the rails – some would say literally – and on the roads for five or six years but he never tired of expounding his theories about how (never why) the 'one-unders' do it.

He would tell you how, after the first 'one-under' had thrown themselves in front of his Central Line train, he had insisted on driving with the cab lights on. This way, potential jumpers could make eye contact with the driver and, maybe, think again. Of course, you could argue that making eye contact with Taffy Duck was a good way of strengthening your resolve and going through with it.

Then he would get obsessed with the technicalities of jumping on to the line. How it was the electricity current which killed you, not the voltage (25,000 volts). Personally, I attributed a lot of fatalities to being hit by a moving train (300 tons), but what did I know?

I didn't even know how he got the name Taffy Duck. It sounded like an anagram in a Welsh crossword, but as far as I knew he was born and bred south of the river in Woolwich.

'Put this in your face,' I said, handing him a single brandy before he could start talking again.

'Oh God, that's a lifesaver, Angel,' he moaned, sipping his drink. 'I'm threadbare.'

'Yeah. You said.'

'I did? Well, I don't mind admitting I'm rock-bottom depth-charged on this one, mate. Yer health.'

He waved the glass in front of his face. If he'd shaved today, Gillette owed him an apology.

'I haven't been this barrelled since I had that one-under at Mornington Crescent. Did I ever tell you about the blonde tart who . . .?'

'Yes, you have, Taffy.' The Mornington Crescent incident had been his third one-under and he'd tried to sell his 'devastated driver' story to the tabloids.

'But what's "barrelled"?' I had to ask. Sometimes I should trap my tongue in a door.

'I'm scraping, mate, scraping the barrel. Scraping for every scrap of food, scraping for a job, some dosh, the rent money.

Reduced to poncing drinks and the odd smoke off of old friends.'

His eyes fixed pointedly on the cigarette I was stubbing out.

'I'm not an old friend, Taffy,' I said, ignoring him.

He licked his lips, the fumes of the brandy going some of the way to nullifying his breath. There was probably a very interesting experiment in binary gases going on inside his mouth.

'But you've never seen me this low, have you, Angel? Not this brought-down?'

Now that was a tricky one because, to be honest, I hadn't noticed any difference from any of the other times I'd had the misfortune to run into him. If I wasn't careful, I could hurt his feelings here.

'Oh, fuck off and ring the Samaritans, Taffy. I hear they have slack afternoons. Don't ponce on me, I've got my own problems. What are you doing here, anyway?'

'On the lookout for a job, that's what.'

He stared at me as if that was the most stupid question in the world. I stared back at the most stupid answer.

'Dressed like that?' I pointed at his greasy overcoat (wool isn't naturally that shiny unless it has been very badly treated) over a faded blue-striped shirt. 'Jesus, Taffy, this is a good pub. They have standards. That coat alone would get them prosecuted under the Food Act or whatever it is which says you shouldn't poison people in pubs.'

'Not here, Angel.' He waved his empty glass some more, thinking I might have missed it earlier. '*Here.*'

He indicated through the window and out into the wide open world of Parliament Square.

'What?' I played dumb. 'The House of Commons? Shit, Taffy, I always thought you had to be elected to get there. I never knew you could just turn up on the lump and get a job. What do they do, come out at seven o'clock every morning and say: "We need you, you and you; sorry, lads, rest of you come back tomorrow"?'

He swayed back on his heels at that, then narrowed his eyes.

'Are you gonna buy me another drink?'

'No chance.'

'Then you're fucking weird. I always thought so. I was after driving work, with the tour buses. They all come here.'

He was right about that. All the open-top see-London bus-and-coach parties congregated outside Parliament at some point.

'I was trying to tap up some of the drivers, see if there was any openings, like. Had to resort to touting for business, since my last job went belly-up.' He looked down into his empty glass expectantly. 'Last week, that was.' He sighed. Loudly. 'Through no fault of mine.'

'God, I'm pathetic,' I said, taking both our glasses to the bar for a refill.

'So anyway, I was driving this tanker . . .'

I hadn't the heart to say I'd only bought the second drink to *avoid* the story. I just drank some more beer and even gave him a cigarette and aimed for his nose hair as I lit it, but he hardly paused for breath.

' . . . tanker of diesel. Contract job, from Harwich and there's this caff out there in Essex, place called Spaniard's Corner. 'Course, it's not a corner as such, just a roundabout turn-off off the A12. Anyway, it's always been known for a good breakfast nosh and it opens at five in the morning so you can't argue with that . . .'

I counted the raindrops on the window. Then I looked around and confirmed my theory that he was emptying the pub. Then I thought about the odds on me winning the National Lottery before he finished talking. And then how those odds could be improved if I actually bought a ticket.

' . . . bag over me head and sticky tape round me like a fucking Christmas parcel and they were legging it with the keys and the next thing the truck turns up in Epping two days later, empty. Now where's the bottom-line bleeding logic in all that, eh?'

'I'm sorry, Taffy, I wasn't listening. What did you just say?'

'I know it's tricky to comprehend,' he patronized. 'I mean, where's the sense? Where's the logic?'

'No, Taffy, I didn't say I didn't understand you, I said I wasn't listening to you. Now run that last bit by me again.'

'It's like I said. Who'd go to the trouble of hijacking a tanker-load of diesel, just for the diesel? I mean, the diesel's worth, what, twelve grand retail, but the truck and the rig are seven or eight times that, yet they turn up empty two days later. Who'd go to all that trouble to pinch some fuel?'

'Pensioners with central heating? Look, Taffy, I know I'll regret this, but start again, will you?'

I did. Regret it.

He had been hired as a relief driver. He had hitchhiked out to Harwich with a pair of false delivery plates under his arm, which usually guarantees a free ride in a car belonging to anyone in the motor trade. Picking up the tanker was no problem and, because it had been recommended as a good nosh spot for drivers, he stopped off at a café (caff) at Spaniard's Corner for his lunch (dinner).

After his Cornish pasty, chips and beans plus a couple of slices of white bread (though I did plead to be spared the details), he felt the need, as you would, to visit the toilet block between the caff and the adjoining garage.

Halfway there, he was tackled behind the knees and before his forehead had bounced off the tarmac, a plastic shopping bag was whipped over his head and insulating tape had secured his hands behind his back. Thus trussed, he was picked up and unceremoniously dumped behind an industrial wastebin, more tape securing his feet together.

His pockets were gone through, the tanker's keys removed and a few minutes later he heard a diesel engine start up, followed by the kick-start of a motorbike.

He hadn't noticed a motorbike, of course, but when the police arrived and questioned one of the waitresses in the café, they placed two guys in leathers and helmets parked twenty feet from Taffy's tanker whilst he was stuffing his face. Beyond that, nobody had seen anything worth commenting on.

However long the police had held Taffy – and in most people's opinion it couldn't be long enough – he was back helping with their enquiries less than thirty-six hours later when his tanker was found in a lay-by near Epping. And there was the mystery, as the tanker was intact, undamaged and unvandalized; just empty. The hijackers had left a £90,000 articulated tanker rig (probably cleaner than when Taffy was driving it) at the side of the road, but had relieved it of its cargo of 33,000 litres of diesel fuel, retail value, about £12,000.

So who needed free diesel so much they were willing to risk

a hijacking in broad daylight, possible charges of assault (though in Taffy's case they would be reduced to justifiable homicide), and the problem of dumping a rather large truck and rig without being noticed?

Not only who had the need, but who had the facilities. I mean, 33,000 litres of diesel can't just be syphoned off into the fuel can you keep in the garage for the lawn mower. And that amount of fuel would cut a very big lawn. Say, a field.

Which got me thinking of my allegedly missing brother, the farmer, and things agricultural and the answer to Taffy's problem seemed so obvious it would be churlish not to share it with him.

'Well, that's a stonker, Taffy,' I said cheerfully. 'It's a puzzler, that's for sure. Got me stumped. Sorry, but you're on your own on this one, I gotta go.'

Just as I said it, most of the remaining afternoon light from the window was blocked out by an exhibit from the *Guinness Book of Records*. (Largest dinner jacket ever made category.)

'The boss wants to see you, Taffy,' growled the dinner jacket.

The man inside the dinner jacket had no neck and thin blond hair swept back from a receding hairline into a ponytail. Taffy and I together, side by side, were narrower than his shoulders. His nose had been broken more than once and his left ear looked more like a sun-dried tomato than a piece of flesh.

Why was he wearing a dinner jacket? Why was he wearing white cotton gloves and a dinner jacket? Why was I wondering? Why was I still in the pub?

'See you around, Taffy,' I said quickly, putting my empty glass down carefully on the window ledge.

Taffy wasn't saying anything, but his lips were moving. Shaking, actually.

'Wait,' said the dinner jacket to me. Then to Taffy: 'You owe the boss an explanation, an' he wants it now. Who's he?'

'Angel. He's Angel,' Taffy croaked, his mouth dry and not from the brandy either. 'I was tapping him for a drink, that's all.'

'You bin talkin' to him? Telling him things?'

He seemed bigger and nearer, but he hadn't moved.

'Time of day, time of day, that's all,' Taffy whined.

I held up my hands, palms out. Even dogs are supposed to understand that.

'Hey, I got to go, guys. Leave you to it. Got to be in Hackney by six o'clock,' I said without much conviction.

'Give you a lift,' said the dinner jacket, looking at me without blinking.

I blinked rapidly to show him I wasn't kidding. I really was intimidated by him. It didn't seem to make much of an impression. Maybe he'd failed Body Language at school.

'Look, er . . . thanks, but there's no need for me to put you out.'

'No problem. We're going to Hackney anyway. You're coming wiv us. End of.'

That was a nice touch. No 'let's think about this' or 'what options do we have here?'. Just: 'end of'.

'And you' – he raised a white-gloved index finger and Taffy's knees began to quiver – 'you 'ad better have your story ready for the boss, or you are cruising for one seriously bad bruising. I've wasted my afternoon off looking for you, touting round minicab companies and coach stops. Do you think I liked that? Dressed like this?'

The gloved hand waved regally to indicate the dinner suit, the straining bow tie and the white frilled shirt.

'Did anyone say anything to you?' I asked before I could stop myself.

'No, they didn't,' he said in a carefully measured tone. 'Do you want to?'

'Not me,' I said quickly. 'Hey, I'm grateful for the lift.'


Outside, he had an ageing Volvo saloon parked on double yellow lines under a sign saying 'No Waiting At Any Time'. We were within sight of the Houses of Parliament and opposite a citadel of government offices. We were so close to Downing Street, you wouldn't need a bottle to launch your rocket. Every other pedestrian should have been a copper or an MI5 man. They probably were. They probably thought it was an MI5 operation.

The dinner jacket pointed at the rear door of the Volvo and

Taffy got in first, sliding over the seat so I could follow. The door slammed shut and the dinner jacket walked around the front of the car to get to the driver's door.

When he was as far away from me as he was going to be, I made a grab for the door handle. Nothing happened; the bastard had put the child locks on.

By the time the dinner jacket had positioned itself behind the wheel, and the suspension had righted itself, my hands were back in my jacket pockets.

When he started the engine and moved off into the traffic, I hissed at Taffy out of the corner of my mouth: 'What the fuck is going on?'

'If you hadn't got me chatting,' Taffy hissed back, 'I'd've shown that pub a large proportion of leg and been well away by now.'

'What?' I almost yelled at him.

'I only popped in the pub for a piss,' he said, all aggrieved. 'You can do that there without the bar staff seeing you.'

He was right about that, it was one of the pubs on every pro driver's list of rest stops, where you could get to the Gents toilet without passing the bar. There were other well-known ones, like the Pontefract Castle in Wigmore Street, and the Chiv wine bar opposite, and Dirty Dick's in Bishopsgate . . .

'Taffy, that's not what I asked, you old tart. Where are we going?'

'Hackney,' he hissed, like he'd been caught smoking in church.

'I gathered that. Who are we going to *see* in Hackney?'

We were rolling along the Embankment by now, passing the Tattershall Castle, the floating pub and another pit stop for the desperate driver if really pushed.

'The boss, like Domestos said,' Taffy whispered.

*Domestos?*

'Taffy,' I said quietly and slowly through gritted teeth, 'who is this boss person and why are we going to see him? And give me a straight answer or your head goes in the ashtray.'

'The boss. My boss. The guy who gave me the driving job. The guy who owned the diesel what got syphoned. Donald McCandy.'

Oh, bugger.

'Big Mac McCandy?' I croaked.

'Not to his face,' said Taffy as if he was giving tips on etiquette.

Double bugger.

I leaned forward and talked to where the driver's neck would have been if he'd had one.

'Any chance of dropping me off at Amhurst Road?' I asked politely.

The dinner jacket stretched out his left hand and turned the Volvo's radio on. Loudly. It was tuned in to Classic FM and they were playing a Beethoven sonata.

It seemed to soothe him.


I don't live in Amhurst Road; quite the opposite direction, in fact, in Stuart Street.

I had lived at number nine for more years than I probably should have, but I had a good arrangement with the landlord, Mr Nassim Nassim, which involved the occasional odd job, a pegged rent and no questions asked about the fact that I shared Flat Three with a psychotic cat called Springsteen. When Mr Nassim had informed me, very politely, that he had a 'no pets' policy, I had pushed him into my minuscule kitchenette, where Springsteen was eating his sixth meal of the day, and said: 'You tell him.'

When I let go of the kitchen door handle so he could escape, he agreed not to press the point and I never again complained about the size of the kitchen. He had proved there was room to swing a Nassim.

Before I had moved to Hackney, I had lived south of the river in Southwark until a sort of accidental explosion had destroyed the place where I hung my hat. But even down there I had heard of Big Mac McCandy.

Like most of London's would-be gangsters – and, for that matter, the Metropolitan Police – he was not a Londoner by birth. Yet the stories about him could have fitted the profile of any of the famous East End villains of yore, apart from the mindless sadism and casual violence, that is. He was said to be kind to animals, probably kind to his old mother as well and legend had it that he had subsidized a street party in Hackney to help celebrate the anniversary of VE Day.

I had no idea if any of it was true. I had no real idea of what he did, if he was any sort of gangster at all. He probably put his occupation as 'Company Director' but that didn't exactly narrow it down. All I knew was that in saloon-bar gossip in pubs east of the City, his was a name which, if mentioned, was mentioned with respect.

I had never met him and I had certainly never crossed him.

I would have been quite happy to have kept it that way.


The dinner jacket piloted the Volvo alongside the river until we got to Tower Hill, then he struck north up through Whitechapel and Bethnal Green. He knew enough short cuts to avoid the worst of the traffic but the journey still took the best part of an hour.

I was regretting leaving my own set of wheels – a delicensed Austin taxi, the quintessential London black cab – at home. I had thought it a wise precaution given that parking around Parliament Square is a nightmare and that meetings with my father usually involve vast amounts of alcohol. (Usually to help forget the meeting rather than during it.)

If I had risked bringing my trusty cab Armstrong, then I would not have met Taffy Duck and not been facing whatever it was I was going to have to face. It was something else I could blame on my father, but the thought was of little comfort.

The dinner jacket never said a word all the way to South Hackney, though I had gathered from his reaction to the radio that he had a weak spot for Scarlatti and a grudging admiration for Duke Ellington's version of 'The Nutcracker'. So he couldn't be all that bad.

Taffy Duck hadn't so much talked as muttered to himself more or less the whole journey. He seemed to be rehearsing his story, over and over again, never quite convincing himself. Either that or he was praying.

The Volvo pulled off towards Victoria Park and I was taking bearings should I get the chance to run for it, when we turned left into a side street and pulled up.

We were outside a snooker club called the Centre Pocket. On

the door and the two blacked-out windows were designs of red snooker balls racked into their triangles. A sign on the door said there were ten tables inside, but for members only. Above the door was the standard liquor licence statement saying that it was 'licensed for the sale' of alcohol, but there was no clue as to who held the licence.

The dinner jacket levered itself out of the car and walked round to my door. He opened it and grunted: 'Inside.'

While Taffy was sliding across the seat, still muttering, I made one last attempt to befriend the dinner jacket.

'I've got it,' I smiled, nodding towards the dinner suit and the white cotton gloves. 'You're going to referee a snooker match.'

He screwed his face up until he looked like a slab of cement suddenly puzzled by the meaning of life.

'No,' he said. 'Whatever gave you that idea?'

# Chapter Three

The sign outside had lied. There were only eight tables in the club and all were occupied, mostly by young lads not old enough to drink but all dressed in smart/casual mode as if they had just come from a photo-shoot for a mail order catalogue. I was glad to see them there, honing their skills, showing dedication to the sport, working hard for their big break which could bring them fame and fortune. Face it, they could have been knitting tea cosies for all I cared. They were witnesses. Surely nothing too bad was going to happen in front of them.

Then I saw the figure sitting on a high stool at the bar and I remembered all the times I had been wrong before.

I took a desperate comfort from the fact that he seemed to be set on giving Taffy a hard time and ignoring me.

'Nice of you to drop in, Taffy, it's been so long and that's not good for management-employee relations, you know. All the books say that, an' all the management-training videos as well.' There was a burr in the accent like the edge of a razor blade. 'Constant interface, that's what's called for. Or so they tell me. And that, Taffy me old son, means that management must make itself accessible and the workforce – that's you – should be where we can bleedin' well find you.'

He had not taken his eyes from Taffy, nor had he raised his voice. But Taffy was shaking. I was delighted to have been relegated to part of the furnishings.

'And who the fuck is he?'

Wrong again.

'He's Angel. He was subbing me for a drink. He's an old pal. We used to drive together. He hangs out round here. We were just chewing the flannel when Domestos turned up and gave us a lift . . .' Taffy's words tumbled over each other.

He paused only when McCandy reached for a drink from the bar. I hadn't noticed it before; an incongruous V-shaped crystal glass containing a bright green liquid, crushed ice and a short white straw. How could you miss a crème de menthe frappée in a Hackney snooker club? Because I had been looking at his hands, that's why. He wore gold rings made out of half-sovereigns on both hands, something which always disturbed me. (Rule of Life No. 85: Never trust anyone who wears rings made from coins. If they do it because they think it's fashionable, then they have appalling taste. If they do it because they can double as knuckle-dusters, keep clear of them anyway.)

'What did you say his name was?' he asked Taffy in between sips of green.

'Angel. Roy Angel, Mr McCandy.'

Taffy had to pick now to start telling nothing but the truth. He never had in court.

'My name's Donald McCandy,' he said, putting his glass back carefully on the bar. 'And that's Domestos, another of my workforce.'

I didn't say anything, I just nodded to show that I had heard him even if I had not understood. He seemed determined to stress that he was management and he had employees. I couldn't follow the logic. Fair enough, no one referred to 'gangs' any more, they were 'crews', and the younger crews who dealt in soft drugs and illicit raves, were staffed by 'drones' to do the leg-work. I had no idea where he was going with the personnel management doublespeak.

'Don't you want to know why we call him Domestos?' he asked casually. 'You know, like the lavatory cleaner?'

I knew where he was going with *that* one, and I wasn't stupid enough to respond, so I simply shook my head and gave him a brief shrug of the shoulders.

Taffy, of course, couldn't resist it.

'Because he's thick and strong, like it says in the adverts?'

I didn't see exactly where Domestos hit him – it was some-where behind his right ear, I think – but I heard it. I winced almost as much as Taffy did.

'The other answer is that it's because he kills all known germs,' said McCandy conversationally, 'and that doesn't nor-mally get a slap. Then again, sometimes it does. Still, the rest of the evening's our own now, isn't it?'

I didn't like that one bit.

'Don't I know you, Roy?' he said, looking at me for the first time. And I didn't like that at all.

'Don't think so, Mr McCandy. Can't say we've ever met.'

Was that deferential enough? Behind us, the young hopefuls were still playing snooker and taking no notice of us. The sound of the balls clicking against each other sounded as loud as the last tickings on a time bomb.

'Just because we haven't met doesn't mean I don't know you,' McCandy observed. 'There's lots of people know me but I've never met them.'

The Director of Public Prosecutions for one, I thought, but kept it to myself.

'I'm sorry, Mr McCandy, but I don't know where it was we didn't meet,' I croaked limply. 'If you see what I mean.'

He took it in his stride; he was probably used to invoking gibberish in people.

'In one of my pubs,' he said thoughtfully.

'Hey, Mr McCandy, I met Angel in a pub this afternoon.'

We both looked at Taffy pityingly, then McCandy came back on to my case.

'You were playing in one of my pubs – leisure units I'm supposed to call them now. Dirty Nellie's, was it? No, the Silver Dollar down in Poplar. Mexican Night last year during Pub Week. Chilli hot enough to take your head off and piss-poor imported beer with a slice of lime stuck in the top. You were in the band that night. You were in the band playing . . .'

'Trumpet?' I offered.

' . . . that tuneless, crappy mariachi music,' he finished.

I remembered it as a financial disaster, as I had loaned my share of the band's wages to the bass guitarist and never seen him since, and also because I had broken a basic rule of life by going into a pub with 'Silver' in the name.

'Nice pub, Mr McCandy. Good gig,' I said.

McCandy turned on Taffy again.

'Thought you said he was a driver?'

'He is, honest.' Taffy steeled himself for another knuckling from Domestos. 'That's where I first met him.'

'I used to drive gear for a rock band,' I explained, because I wasn't going to let Taffy. 'He drove a back-up truck on part of a tour once. I've not worked with Taffy since. And if I'd never seen him again since then, I wouldn't have lost sleep about it.'

McCandy took another suck on the straw in his crème de menthe.

'So this meet today, what was that about?'

'Pure, unadulterated shitty bad luck on my part. He saw me before I saw him coming.' I took a deep breath and went for it. 'And I've never driven a petrol tanker in my life.'

'So Taffy here's been discussing our little industrial problems, has he?'

'Of course he has, Mr McCandy. You know Taffy, he could blab for England. You need a staple gun to shut him up when he's on a roll.'

I heard Domestos shuffle closer behind me. Either he was making a note of my idea or I was cruising for a bruising, as he'd put it so pithily back in the Red Lion.

Taffy couldn't stand this slur on his character any longer and thought it time to open the case for the defence.

'I only like mentioned it to Angel because he lives on your patch, Mr McCandy, and he keeps an ear to the ground. He might have heard something. And' – it was almost as if a lightbulb had lit up above his head – 'because he drives a cab. A diesel cab.'

He almost sang the last phrase, but thankfully McCandy didn't seem too impressed.

'And I've got a diesel Mercedes, Taffy, but not even the wife putting her foot to the floor could get through 33,000 litres of juice this regularly.'

He was being very reasonable about it all suddenly. Bad sign.

'Would you have a use for that much diesel, Roy?'

'If I did, I'd make sure it wasn't nicked from you, Mr McCandy.'

'So I've got nothing to worry about with you two, then?' He was looking at his drink now and I wondered if it was a signal to Domestos behind us.

'Taffy's too stupid to steal from you, Mr McCandy. I'm not stupid enough.'

He thought about this for a moment.

'Good answer, Roy.' He waved his right hand and a barman I hadn't noticed before glided up to him. 'Set me up again, Julian.'

The barman, a young, clean-cut type with a double stud in his left ear, didn't exactly break into a sweat to serve the boss. Boss and, I guessed, owner as well.

'Certainly, Mr McCandy,' he said quietly, 'but it's Justin, not Julian.'

McCandy seemed to ignore him. He muttered 'Whatever . . .' and then shot a look towards Domestos.

'Friend of Nigel's from uni-bloody-versity,' he sighed. Then it was back to business. 'So you're a bright one, are you, Roy? Then you tell a thick old bugger like me what you would do with two tankerloads of diesel.'

'Two?' I said, showing an interest before I could stop myself. 'Have I missed something?'

'Same thing – 'xactly the same thing – happened to Ferdy Kyle,' Taffy blurted out. 'Ferdy was driving for Mr McCandy here and he had a tanker nicked at a transport caff near Chelmsford, few months back.'

'That's why I had to hire Taffy,' said McCandy philosophically, 'because Ferdy hasn't exactly healed yet. Well, not fully. And I never thought lightning would strike twice like it did. Two tankers lifted from pit stops on the A12, both turning up a couple of days later dry as a bone. Doesn't make sense to me. Two nearly-new tankers? You'd have thought there was a market for them somewhere, I mean, there was a time you could make a few notes exporting JCBs.'

I tried to look as if I didn't know what he was talking about, but I had been well aware of a spate of thefts of JCB mechanical diggers and bulldozers, mostly from farms. After a quick respray they were transported to Harwich or some other east coast port, usually at night, and stashed into a container ship bound for some underdeveloped and unsuspecting Third World economy. Until the insurance companies got together and realized there were a lot of similar claims all from roadwork gangs or farmers within an easy drive of the coast, it had been a relatively simple crime. Before then no one thought twice about locking something that big and that heavy, which normally moved at no more than ten miles per hour. It all just went to prove the old adage: If it ain't nailed down, it's mine.

'The tankers were just dumped, were they?'

Why was I showing an interest? I knew it would end in tears.

'Both left bone dry but otherwise clean as a whistle. Not even the radio nicked. Just emptied then left locked and parked up in the street.'

'Where?'

His eyes narrowed and I thought it might have been a question too far, but then I was only making conversation.

'The first one was Potter's Bar. Taffy's was found in Epping.'

'Easy exits from the M25,' I muttered.

'So what?' McCandy flashed back.

'So maybe nothing. Were the tankers yours?'

'Hired.'

'But the fuel was.' He nodded agreement, curious now. 'So where would you put it?'

'I run a garage down in Hornchurch,' he said, misunderstanding.

'No, not where *you* would put it, but where would someone else put it? Who uses that much diesel and has somewhere to stash it so it wouldn't look out of place?'

He shrugged a shoulder half-heartedly.

'A garage, like mine. Where the fuck else would you hide 66,000 litres of diesel? Hide under cover of daylight. Keep your stolen Christmas trees in a forest. You think I haven't thought this through? It has to be a garage, it's obvious. End of.'

So why was he asking me? Why buy a dog and then not bark in the night yourself?

'How about a farm?' I said nervously.

He thought about that, quite seriously if the way his eyebrows joined together was anything to go by.

'Inside the M25?'

'Sure.' There were indeed farms inside and outside London's great orbital drag, or there would be until they widened it again. 'But it's more likely outside, but with easy access. Loads of places in Essex or Hertfordshire.'

'Hang on a minute, agricultural diesel has a dye in it, doesn't it? It's coloured so nobody can use it. It's a tax thing.'

'You're absolutely right. It's dyed so you can't sell it in your garage and I can't use it in my cab, but who cares if a farmer uses the undyed stuff in a tractor or two?'

McCandy looked at his drink, then at the young barman who was showing him the back of his neck while polishing a glass with a dingy tea towel.

'I knew Angel would come up with something,' Taffy blurted out. 'I told you he keeps an ear to the ground, Mr McCandy, didn't I? He knows stuff.'

'Shut it, Taffy,' McCandy growled. 'I haven't even started with you yet.'

For once Taffy did shut up. And so did I.

'Do you know any farmers, Roy?' McCandy asked quietly without looking at me. He seemed more concerned with the barman and whether him turning his back on the boss was a firing offence. Firing Squad, that is.

'Not in Hackney, Mr McCandy,' I said truthfully.

'Hmmmm.' He tapped a fingernail twice on the bar. 'OK, Roy, I hear what you say. Good talking to you. I'd get Domestos to give you a lift home, but he's got a snooker match to referee.'

'But he . . .' I started before I could help myself.

McCandy grinned. 'What? Told you he was playing oboe at the Barbican tonight, or going to dinner at the Guildhall with the Chancellor of the Exchequer? He does that. It's just his little way of getting over his natural shyness.'


As soon as I hit the street outside the Centre Pocket, I turned right and legged it across Victoria Park Road and into the nearest pub.

I ordered a pint of strong lager and change for the cigarette machine. Then I ordered a second pint and by that time my hands had stopped shaking so that I hardly spilled any of it.


I made my way home to Stuart Street by a devious route, partly to pick up a Cajun chicken takeaway from Hackney's latest ethnic franchise, and partly to check whether I was being followed. I had no reason to think it was other than paranoia, but that was a good reason in my book.

I looked up and down the street before diving for the door of number nine, key in hand. Once inside, I leaned back on the door and did the deep-breathing exercises the magazines recommend for panic attacks before job interviews or when opening a tax demand.

I turned my head so I could see the communal house phone on the wall. There was a yellow Post-It sticker stuck to the receiver. Its message, in green ink, read: 'The man who said he used to be your father rang again. He sounds very tall. Is he? Love, F.' And just to make sure I knew it was from Fenella, she had drawn a teddy bear face in the bottom right-hand corner.

Fenella and her partner, Lisabeth, had lived in the flat below mine for as long as I had been at Stuart Street. They had kept themselves very much to themselves until the recent Gay Pride rally in Victoria Park. Lisabeth had returned wearing a 'Lesbian Avengers' T-shirt, which was fine by me except that I think she really should have treated herself to the Xtra-Large size. Once I saw it, and knowing where she'd been all day, I thought: that's it, they're finally coming out. But then Fenella had staggered in, weaving in the wind from too much white cider, and she'd been wearing a 'Bears 'R Us' T-shirt. Since then, she had adopted teddy bears or bear faces as a sort of personal logo and I'd never actually dared to ask her why.

She had recently taken a job as a telesales girl for a mail order clothing company. Apart from asking customers whether they preferred Loganberry or Kalahari (because their first-choice colours, Merlot and Oyster, were no longer available), she didn't have a lot to do and the job was obviously boring her stiff. Hence, she played games trying to guess the physical features of the callers. Most of the punters were women, so she would try and guess what they looked like in the clothes they had ordered. With the men, she had only progressed as far as height, but she had to guess it from the tone of their voice and before they gave her their inside leg measurement.

Hence the reference to my father on the Post-It note, which I ripped off the phone and screwed up before dropping it on to the floor. I didn't give a thought to littering up the hallway, because that was now Mr Goodson's patch.

The Mysterious Mr Goodson, as we called him, lived in the ground-floor flat and was something, though not a lot, in local government. We rarely saw him, and there were specific times when we never saw him, like days, nights and weekends. But occasionally he would emerge from Flat One and answer the phone for us (though no one ever rang him) or pay the milkman, or announce something which he thought we all should be interested in. He had done just that earlier in the year, saying solemnly that as a 'clear desk' policy had been introduced in his office, he was now taking responsibility for the ground floor of the house and would keep it in order to help him be more self-disciplined at work.

So we let him. If he had been hinting that maybe we should each take a similar responsibility for our part of the house, then it was a hint we failed to take.

The other residents of the house, Inverness Doogie and his Welsh wife Miranda, lived in Flat Four above me. As I unlocked the door to my flat, I heard their door open and close. I checked my watch to find in horror that it was only just after six p.m. Doogie would be on his way to work as a late-shift chef at a West End hotel.

I let my door swing open just to see if Springsteen was lying in ambush, then turned to buttonhole Doogie as he clumped down the stairs. One of these days I would ask him why a chef like him had to wear such heavy-duty kicking boots. But then, as his main hobby after cooking was streetfighting, perhaps I'd leave it.

'Wotcha, Angel, you old reprobate. Pissed already?' he greeted me.

'No, I'm not,' I said indignantly. 'Not yet, anyway, stick around.'

'No time to enjoy myself, me old mucker, some of us got to go to work, you know. 'Nother day, 'nother half-dollar.'

'Hold up a minute, big fella, I want to bend your earhole for a minute. Sit down.'

I plonked myself down on the top stair and patted the dusty carpet next to me.

'A wee minute, then, that's all. I'm on Baked Alaskas tonight.' He sat down and sniffed with professional curiosity at my bucket of Cajun chicken.

'Good choice, Baked Alaska. One of my specialities. Got me through university.'

Doogie gave me one of his killer looks.

'I know I'll regret this, but how did eating Baked Alaska get you through college?'

'Not eating it, cooking it. Usually about two o'clock in the morning. Every bloke there tried to impress the women with dope, or booze, or philosophy, or their music collection. I was the only one who could show them how to put ice-cream into a red-hot oven and get away with it. Knocked their socks off, it did.'

Doogie nodded appreciatively. 'Aye, it would. And the rest of their underclothes as well.'

'That was the general idea. I owe it all to Len Deighton's *Action Cook Book*. Great book. Had diagrams, so you knew what to do.'

'But now you're down to takeaway buffalo wings, is it?'

I levered the polystyrene top from the carton and offered him a piece.

'Cajun chicken in hot sauce, with a side order of Tabasco. Want one?'

'I'll pass. Did you want to say something or are you just gonna go on trying to give me an inferiority complex?'

I took a bite of a chicken leg and felt the Cajun sauce immobilize my lips almost immediately. I put the bucket down behind me on the landing and waved the chicken in the air at him.

'I want to ask you something, Doogie, but don't take it personal.'

'You'll know if I took it personal, when you wake up.'

Yeah, yeah. I'd been threatened by professionals today.

'Do you have a father, Doogie?'

''Course I do. Everybody does. Only thing in life that's certain is that somebody fucked your mother.'

'I wasn't thinking so much biologically, as, well, parentally. I mean, would you do something for your father even if you didn't want to do it?'

'Aye, sure I would. That's what sons are supposed to do.'

'Even when it's something your father could do himself, but just doesn't want to?'

'Aye. Why not?'

'Even if it involves the rest of the family and the family business?'

42

'Och, the bastard,' he said softly. 'No offence, Angel. Is he offering money?'

'Yes.'

'However much, it's not enough.'

'Thanks, Doogie, that's good advice.'

'Do you want some more?'

'Sure.'

'You're going to need another carry-out. Your cat has just nicked your dinner.'

I turned towards my flat to see Springsteen's rear disappearing inside. The bucket of Cajun chicken was empty.

'Dinna worry,' said Doogie, starting downstairs. 'He'll bring it back when the hot sauce gets on his whiskers.'

'No, he won't,' I said with a sigh. 'That's his favourite bit.'

# Chapter Four

Next morning, I remembered just in time that I was supposed to be at work. But as the job in question was providing a backing track at Danny Boot's recording studio in Curtain Road, punctuality did not actually come with the job description.

Turning up at Boot-In Sound Services before noon was regarded as being keen. Arrive before ten a.m. and they assumed you were a burglar.

It was one of the dafter jobs I had ever done – musically, that is. The two latest crazes in the middle-of-the-road music scene were Gregorian chants and slushy pop ballads done Aztec fashion on the Pan Pipes. In both cases, these were the sort of tapes you would find in the glove compartment of company-owned Fords (sales representatives and below) or even smaller Audis (area managers and above), and which the Fashion Police should have the power to confiscate in on-the-spot style checks. But in the best tradition of British 'me too' marketing, everyone was cashing in on the act, trying to churn out cheap versions which magazines, supermarkets and garages could use as giveaway incentives.

Danny Boot's studios were ideally equipped to remix, edit and mass produce to order, making a decent profit as long as they could avoid paying any royalties to big names and as long as the supply of slightly substandard cassette tapes from Thailand didn't dry up. But on the plus side, the profit enabled Boot-In to keep going and provide the occasional new and original band with a launching pad.

I had no one to blame for this job except myself, as I had acted as talent spotter for Danny and even helped out at the live recording sessions for 'Canticles from the Hymnody of St Fulgentius of Ruspe', a title Danny had thought up himself, working on the theory that in this market, the longer the title the more authentic the product. He had also designed the cassette-box inlay with a cover illustration of a group of hooded monks tramping across a desolate, grey landscape. The concrete-coloured background and the positioning of the eight monks walking purposefully towards the camera suggested that Danny had been more than a little influenced by the poster for *Reservoir Dogs*, but no one felt mean enough to point this out. I had also somehow managed to forget to tell Danny that the recording was not actually a gang of monks, but rather a group of lay-brethren from a Church of England retreat in Dorset, supplemented by some regular members of the local church choir and the local pub's darts team. I had also forgotten to tell him that the fact that three tracks needed a solo trumpet fanfare as backing (on a Gregorian chant?) was part of my 'fee' for discovering the act. It had totally slipped my mind that one of the leading lights in the St Fulgentius retreat, was the brother (even if not an actual Brother) of probably my oldest living friend.

'Oi, Angel, I've just had that chopsy Irish monk on the phone again!' yelled Danny Boot as I tried to sneak across Boot-In's open-plan office. 'He's asking about discounts for bulk sales. And what sort of a name for a monk is Gary?'

'It's because nobody can pronounce Gearoid,' I answered automatically, pronouncing it correctly as 'Garrodth'.

'So what do I tell him? We're waiting for you, you know. Just how much longer are you going to tie up my studio?' Boot was shouting at the back of my head by now.

'Last track going down today, Danny,' I said over my shoulder. And it would be, just as soon as I thought of something to play.

Boot-In Sound Services had two glass-fronted soundproof studios leading off the main office, the whole shooting match built into the upper floor of a terraced house tucked behind Liverpool Street Station. It was one of the most ghostly parts of London, with few other businesses around, virtually no residents and very little through traffic. Boot had made a good job of it, I suppose, but he could never get over the fact that the credit line on all his productions would read 'Recorded at Curtain Road, EC2'. Still, there was a time when nobody had heard of Abbey Road.

I had a sound tech called Kevin working with me on the 'Canticles' and it had taken me most of the first session to straighten him out. He had assured me that he could 'digitalize' my single line melodies after just one take, however many split notes or fluffed tones I blew, into a class-finished product. I explained to him, as gently as I could, that as the grand total of my musical input on the project was probably two minutes' worth, we could actually do the job in one session, half an hour tops. As both of us were being paid by the session, up to a maximum of three, it made more commercial sense to string it out.

Kevin sat in the control booth and came through on the intercom as I was unpacking my ancient B-flat trumpet.

'In your own time, Angel,' he squeaked. 'Once through for balance then we'll put one down. I don't want to hang about too long today. Boot's got something else lined up for me.'

'Take the work while you can, Kev,' I said into the mike which dangled from the ceiling. 'Anything in it for me?'

'Not unless you can play the Pan Pipes.'

'You're kidding.'

'No, straight up. He's got this idea for a compilation of Rolling Stones ballads done on the Pan Pipes, called "Inca Rock".'

I paused in applying lip salve and gave him my best pitying look through the glass screen.

'Do the Rolling Stones know about this?'

He held out his arms like an Indian god in the universal buggered-if-I-know gesture.

'It pays the rent,' he said lamely.

'Try squatting,' I said.

I limbered up with the opening bars of 'West End Blues', hitting most of the right notes, if not in the right order. Kevin did not seem overly impressed.

'Was that it?' he squeaked over the tannoy.

I ignored him and took a single crumpled sheet of music out of my trumpet case. It was a twenty-four-bar melody simply called 'Fanfare' ripped from an old school music/hymn book which I had picked up at an Islington jumble sale. Speeded up, it sounded suspiciously like 'Hail to the Chief', but slow and with a touch of echo, thanks to Kevin's electronic control box, it would do.

'Got it,' announced Kevin, 'and by the time I'm finished you'll sound like you were playing in the cloisters of a fourteenth-century Sicilian monastery.'

The idea of moving to a Sicilian monastery began to appeal

suddenly as Danny Boot rapped on the glass of the booth. He held a mobile phone in his hand and pointed at it, then at me.

'Are you taking calls, Mr Angel, or should I just carry on acting as your answering service?' he sneered as I opened the door.

'Who is it?' I whispered, meaning: Who knows I'm here? There was nothing odd about ringing Boot-In on a mobile, all the phones in the place were mobiles. Not surprising, really. Boot had enough computer buffs on the payroll and one of them, if they were capable of digitally remixing me, must be capable of cloning the odd phone number so that some other mobile owner gets the call charges. (It's reckoned that you can get away with this for about three months.)

'How should I . . .?' Boot started, then simply tossed the phone at me. 'It's your father,' he said, turning on his heel.

I stepped back into the recording booth and let the door hiss closed, then drew my thumb across my throat until Kevin signalled that he'd cut off the microphones.

'How many times have I told you not to ring me at work?' I shouted into the mouthpiece.

'Very good, Fitzroy, very amusing,' my father said drily into my ear. 'Have you thought over my proposition yet?'

'How did you get this number?'

'Some girl at your flat gave it to me, the one who's not at work today because it's her day off. She sounded nice. Tried to sell me a striped Oxford shirt. What sort of a colour is "Jacaranda", anyway?'

'It wouldn't suit you. You're too tall.'

'Yes, come to think of it, she did ask me how tall I was.' Good old Fenella. 'But have you?'

'That's for me to know and you to wonder . . .' I started. 'Oh, sorry, I see what you mean. No, I haven't thought it over because there's nothing to think over. I said "no", didn't I? I don't want to debate about it. No negotiation, no discussion. End of.'

I should have added 'No Surrender' but it would have been wasted.

'Look, I'll give you five hundred – call it a late birthday present.'

'Which birthday? To make up for the tricycle you forgot last time?'

'Oh, don't be such a big girl's blouse, Fitzroy. All I'm asking you to do is go and see your mother, for Christ's sake.'

'Well, *you* won't.'

'I can't. It would be too difficult. You know that.'

'So you want me to do your dirty work for you?'

'She'd be delighted to see you, you know that. What harm could it do?'

'If she decides to shoot the messenger, quite a lot . . . Hang on a second.'

Something made me turn to the glass screen between the sound booth and the main office. I saw Danny Boot grinning all over his face and Kevin, sitting on the edge of Danny's desk, biting a hand to stop himself giggling. The rest of the staff of Boot-In were all looking in my direction, too. One of them had written 'Take the money' on an A4 notepad and was holding it up to me.

'I've got to go,' I said into the mobile and switched it off. Then I looked up at the microphone in the ceiling and yelled: 'You bastards!'


I packed my horn back in its battered brown case, snapped the locks and walked out of the sound booth with as much dignity as I could muster.

'I've got your wages for you, Angel,' said Boot, offering an envelope and trying not to smirk.

'Thanks, Danny. Do the same for you one day.'

'Hey, come on, man,' he tried, still grinning. 'We all thought it was really touching, your dad ringing you like that.'

'Yeah, well, Danny, at least mine is allowed access to a phone,' I snapped.

'Hey, hey, don't be so uncool. We really did think it was kinda sweet, your dad waiting outside and phoning first.'

I must have looked at him as if I had just seen him crawl from under a stone. He seemed to be used to it.

'Can I have that again, with subtitles, please?'

Danny's expression turned to genuine surprise.

'The guy outside in the suit. The one sitting on the bonnet of your cab, using a mobile. One of the girls spotted him just as the phone rang . . .'

By that time I was over near the window, peeping down into Curtain Road.

There was indeed a man leaning against Armstrong, but it was not my father. Not unless he'd put on about a hundred pounds, had his neck compressed by a lift landing on his head, and was on his way to referee a snooker match. He was punching a number into a mobile phone and having trouble making his fingers fit.

'I'm out the back way, Danny,' I said, already walking towards the fire exit. 'If anybody asks, I left an hour ago.'

I didn't have any faith in Danny's willingness to cover for me, and I couldn't really blame him if it was Domestos asking the questions. His basic bad attitude would almost certainly mean that he would say I had only just left and that suited me fine.

I jumped the stairs four at a time. The fire door took a shoulder charge to get open and then I was out in the parallel street to Curtain Road. The first side street brought me back on to Curtain Road, about twenty yards down from where I had parked Armstrong.

Domestos's Volvo was parked two cars in front but there was no sign of him. I gambled that he had gone inside and was making his way up to the studio. Danny wouldn't delay him long, so I didn't hang about either.

I strolled briskly up to Armstrong, unlocked the driver's door and stashed my horn in the luggage space and got him fired up first time.

I was about fifty yards down the road when, in my mirror, I saw him emerge on to the pavement. He was looking down the road in my direction but he wasn't waving or shouting or throwing bricks or anything. Good sign. If he wasn't in a hurry, it might just give me a few extra minutes. I had no doubt that he knew where I lived, and he probably knew the back streets as well as I did, so I would not have long.

I took the direct route home, down the Hackney Road, and when I got to Stuart Street I was sorely tempted to leave the engine running. But then I thought no, I wanted Armstrong to be there when I got back, so as usual when parking in Hackney, I locked all the doors and counted the wheels.

Once inside number nine, I raced upstairs and banged on the door of Flat Two as I passed. By the time I was unlocking my door, Fenella had appeared.

'What have I done now?' she asked automatically.

'Nothing yet. Feed Springsteen. If anyone comes looking for me, I've gone to the country for a few days. Feed Springsteen. You don't know where I am or when I'll be back. Feed Springsteen. If you run out of cat food, go to the shop and buy some. If my father rings, tell him I've gone to see my mother. Feed Springsteen. I haven't left a number because there isn't a phone where I'm going, not that you know where it is. Oh, and one last thing: feed Springsteen.'

They accuse Suffolk of being flat and they usually point out that it is one of only two or three counties in the country without a university. Sometimes they add that the reason there is no graffiti adorning the Ipswich Town football stadium at Portman Road is because the local supporters haven't yet worked out how to use spray-paint aerosols. None of these things is really true, but such stories were commonplace in the late eighties when it was fashionable for the successful stockbroker to have a weekend cottage on the Suffolk coast (well, the locals didn't need them, did they, not at those prices?). The literary scene got in on the act with 'writing weekends in the country' and for a time there was a constant convoy of Volvos heading up the A 12 on Fridays and back down again on Sunday evenings. Hundreds of column inches in the so-called 'lifestyle' sections, which should be called get-a-life sections, of the quality papers were dedicated to the joys of the weekend countryfolk and Suffolk found itself in the frame. At one point, the coastal village of Walberswick suffered under the alias of Hampstead-on-Sea, but then both the stock market scene and the property market deflated like a pair of balloons two days after a party. The invasion beach head receded and Walberswick scurried back into anonymity.

I got a good run through the east London sprawl and Armstrong set off at a steady chug up the A 12, weaving between the container lorries and commercial vehicles heading for the ferry crossings at Harwich or Felixstowe. Every petrol tanker I saw made me think of Big Mac McCandy and every transport café I passed, of a trussed up Taffy Duck.

The feeling that someone else had worse problems was a comfort but I refused to tempt fate and stop at one of the roadside cafés when my stomach told me loudly that it was lunchtime. Instead, I pulled off the dual carriageway and found a pub in the village of Stratford St Mary where the landlord served me a low-alcohol lager and a dish of lasagna and hardly raised an eyebrow at the black London cab parked out front. Perhaps he thought it did something for the image of his pub. Perhaps he would give me a free drink or three to park it there regularly. Stranger things had happened.

But it did make me think that Armstrong wasn't exactly the most inconspicuous vehicle to be driving around the East Anglian countryside in. All his advantages in London, where he was part of the wallpaper, counted against him here. Hot-air balloons were more common around here than black cabs.

Still, I convinced myself, all I was doing was visiting my brother's farm and then playing the dutiful son act and dropping in on my old mum. Where was the harm in that?

What was left of the family estate was based around the village of Earl Shelton to the west of the Tunstall Forest. The village school had long since closed, as had the church, although churches are 'made redundant', not closed. But I was happy to see that the Old Crown pub still survived, albeit in need of a coat of paint and the fact that the outdoor skittle alley had been replaced by a children's playground with a plastic, smiling tree which would have given Tolkien nightmares.

The village appeared deserted; no one gardening or strolling in the summer sun, no one buying or selling anything, trying to make a buck. A passing alien from a distant galaxy might assume the population to be out in the fields, toiling on the early harvest. I knew they were all indoors watching the afternoon soap operas on TV.

Finbar's farm, Windy Ridge, was about three miles out of the village and a mile from the road down an unmade track. It wasn't on a ridge, if anything it was in a dip between two gently rolling hills cropped with what looked like barley from a distance. The barley wasn't moving much, so you could say it wasn't windy either. To be honest, none of us ever knew how it had got the name.

Technically speaking, Windy Ridge was a farm*house* rather than a working farm. It had outbuildings for cows and pigs, but I had never seen beasts there in my time, and in any case, most pig farming in Suffolk is now done outdoors. You can see huge fields from the road with tube-like tents in neat rows and the pigs rooting around in their own personal space. From a distance they look like United Nations refugee camps, except the facilities are probably better.

I bounced Armstrong up the track towards the house, a late-nineteenth-century brick and plaster building with a slate tile roof, a window in each corner and a door in the middle. It looked normal enough, if deserted, with all its windows closed on what was turning out to be a hot afternoon. Nothing stirred. It was like they used to say in the old westerns, maybe it was *too* quiet.

But what had I expected? I had been told that Finbar wasn't around, that was why I was here. And I had known not to expect any livestock as the farm business was purely arable over a network of fields, some here around Windy Ridge but others owned or rented up to twenty miles down towards the River Deben. Maybe I was just spooked because there were no vehicles around; no cars, no tractors, no rusting hulks of agricultural machinery. What sort of a farm was it without at least three unlicensed and dangerously unserviced vehicles?

I parked Armstrong at the side of a Dutch barn, the only new building on the farm I had noticed, which sheltered a dozen or so huge bales of silage, each wrapped in bright yellow plastic. As I got out and peeled off my aviator sunglasses – not a fashion statement, just the best for driving in – I realized that I had parked so that Armstrong could not be seen from the road to the village or even the farm track unless almost level with the barn. Old habits die hard.

The front door was locked and locked solid with a Chubb lock too big and too modern for the varnished pine door. The down-stairs windows were also shut tight and had had deadbolts fitted, from the look of them, fairly recently. So Finbar was getting more security conscious; but then, 'thorough' was never Finbar's middle name.

I strolled round to the back of the house, which opened on to a small courtyard of ancient, cracked concrete slabs. Surrounding it were old and decrepit dairy buildings from when the farm had run dairy cattle. Most of the roofing was gone and the split doors were rotted and swinging off their hinges. They were full of exactly the sort of junk you would expect to find: old tools, a rusting bicycle, a workbench bent out of shape, empty petrol cans and half-empty cans of paint. But there was no sign of a spare key or any obvious jar or bottle which could hold one.

When Finbar and I had modernized the place, we had always left a spare where either of us could find it whatever time of night it was and however smashed we were. Obviously some old habits did change.

The back door, although by no means as sturdy as the front, was also locked and, by leaning on it, I realized it was bolted too. I considered forcing it, but only for as long as it took me to notice that one of the small fan windows above the kitchen window had been left propped open.

There was a water butt with a wooden lid nearby and by kneeling on it I could open the quarter window to its full extent. It was almost an open invitation to a burglar, and something which would have negated any insurance claim back in London. But that only gave an opening of about four inches by six, which meant a burglar would have to have arms about five feet long to reach the lever catch of the main kitchen window.

No problem. On the rusty bicycle in the old dairy there was an ancient bicycle pump and with the handle extended, it gave me the reach I needed. I hooked the lip of the pump handle over the window latch and tugged. Hey presto. Easy as falling off a water butt.

As I made to hoist myself in through the open window, I flung the pump casually towards the cowsheds, where it clattered among the other rubbish. But as I was squeezing my shoulders through the opening, I heard a second crash as something metal fell over. And then, while kneeling on the windowsill, buttocks flagrantly pointed skywards, there came the distinct sound of breaking glass.

Once I had climbed over the sink and stood on the kitchen floor, I stared across the yard at the cowsheds but there seemed to be nothing else to hear. The chain reaction I had started appeared to have run out of steam.

A quick scoping of the kitchen didn't tell me much. There were no half-eaten meals on the table, no coffee bubbling on the hotplate. This wasn't a Marie Celeste situation, this looked like somebody who'd gone on holiday in a slight rush.

The fridge, however, revealed six pots of yoghurt which were four days past their eat-by dates and an open pack of pepper salami where the remaining slices had curled like old boot leather. There were also two cans of Stella Artois which were nicely chilled, so I helped myself to one.

I popped the can and sipped as I moved through the house.

There was a pile of mail on the floor by the front door. The postmarks went back just over a week but mostly they were circulars from agricultural suppliers or bills for the gas or electricity. One was from Finbar's Visa card company and I felt a chill on my neck to see it addressed to F. M. Angel. I stuffed that one in the back pocket of my jeans and went upstairs.

One bedroom had been in use and although Finbar had treated himself to a double bed, there were no signs that he had shared it recently. The bathroom contained only male soaps and cosmetics, but there was no sign of a razor or a toothbrush.

That made me look through Finbar's wardrobe, but it was a waste of time as we were so out of touch I wouldn't know what was likely to be missing. There was a shiny blue blazer on one of the hangers and I took it out and tried it on. It had a breast-pocket badge which told me that Finbar still retained (or pretended he did) his membership of the flying club over at Shelton Green where we had both obtained our private pilot's licences as teenagers. (I had actually got mine before I started collecting driving licences, another thing Finbar held against me.)

The blazer told me nothing except that Finbar had probably put on a few pounds since I had last seen him, but it was whilst I was preening myself in front of the wardrobe mirror that I turned to the window looking down over the back yard.

And I froze.

54

Walking slowly out of the cowshed where I had thrown the bicycle pump, was Chuck Berry.

I tore off Finbar's blazer and ran downstairs to let him in.

'You're still alive,' I said, trying to sound sincere.

He flicked me a look through his one good eye and strode into the kitchen.

'I know it's probably a sensitive subject, but let's face it, you must be getting on in years now. I never thought I'd see you again, really I didn't.'

He ignored me, choosing to stand facing the fridge instead.

'And I just know you're dying to know how your number one son is getting on, aren't you? Well, Springsteen's doing just fine. He took to the city like a . . . like a . . . duck to water.'

I had hesitated because I suddenly remembered the time my mother had built a duck pond at the old house. It had taken Chuck Berry exactly one month to kill and eat the ten original duck residents. Two of them he'd taken while swimming. But maybe his memory wasn't so good these days. As far as I could guess he must be sixteen or seventeen years old.

He waved his thick black tail just once. I knew the body language.

'Fancy a yoghurt?' I asked, opening the fridge.

I opened three different flavours for Chuck Berry – it was always Chuck Berry, never just Chuck – and left him sniffing the pots.

Finbar had converted one of the front rooms into an office. The desk had a small computer set-up surrounded by piles of papers, mostly invoices paid and unpaid, circulars from the National Farmers' Union or copies of farming magazines and advertisements for chemical fertilizers. Farmers probably got more junk mail than anyone except doctors.

There was nothing I could see which might tell me where Finbar was. Perhaps there was something in the computer but I wasn't prepared to abandon my basic computer illiteracy and waste half the night trying to guess Finbar's stupid password just to read his tax returns.

I rooted through the desk drawers and found more invoices, some estimates for building work, a load of paperwork from the European Commission on agricultural policy, rules, grants, regulations and more rules and then I found something really interesting.

However many bills had piled up by the front door and however many of the invoices on the desk were unpaid, a statement from a garage in Colchester told me that Finbar had recently taken delivery of a new BMW Series 5 Touring. Nice car, but not one to turn up in to the small claims court.

That left just the answerphone and I had been resisting the temptation to hit the playback button ever since I had entered the room and seen the red light flashing by the digital display which told me that there were five messages waiting.

I finished my can of beer and found a pencil in the general desk mess, ready to write down any vital clues on the back of Finbar's Visa bill envelope.

The answerphone was a good one, with a computerized voice which told you the day and time of the messages. Messages one and two were social notes, the first from someone called Ken saying he would be down the Old Crown that night and the second from a female called Kate who demanded his presence at 'a bash' at 'the club' in Woodbridge. I hoped neither of them were still waiting.

Messages three and four were from our father. The first one crisp and businesslike asking Finbar to get in touch. The second, two days later, saying:

'Look, Finbar, I've had old man Ineson on again. What's going on down there? Give me a ring, for God's sake.'

On neither message did he say who he was. Well, why should he? We both knew the voice, even if we sometimes forgot the face that went with it.

The last message was dated just the day before and the voice was vaguely familiar, although slurred rather than deliberately disguised.

'Finbar. It's me. Where the fuck are you? They're coming.'

I stared at the answerphone for a while without doing anything.

Chuck Berry came into the office to see what I was doing. He wandered around bumping into the furniture and I knew how he felt. Then he sniffed loudly and made his way upstairs, shedding long black Persian hairs as he went.

I reached for the phone and dialled 1471, wondering why they never thought to do that in the detective shows on television.

# Chapter Five

You dial 1471 and the phone tells you the number of the person who last called. In the case of Finbar's phone, this came flashing up on the display unit and it was a local number and one I recognized.

The system is perfectly legal and is known as Call Return and it is said to have cut the number of malicious calls by twenty-one per cent since it was first introduced. The trouble is that the really dedicated obscene phonecaller (or when lover calls lover and doesn't want to be traced by a spouse) knows that you can have your number withheld simply by dialling 141 before you call.

I dialled the number the phone had displayed and it was answered on the third ring, but not by the voice on Finbar's machine.

'Ineson Agricultural. Hello?'

I'd got the right number, but I'd got the father not the son.

'Hello, Mr Ineson, is Barry around?'

'No, 'e isn't and who would that be 'oim now speaking to?'

If there was one thing I remembered about old Godfrey Ineson, it was his ability to put on a really good Suffolk accent whenever it suited him and it usually suited him when a pay rise or a round of drinks were in the offing.

'It's Fitzroy, Godfrey, Fitzroy Angel. You used to call me Young Mister Angel.'

'Only when you were a kid and your dad was around, and that wasn't often. We used to call you the Little Randy Bugger down the pub. Come to think of it, you take after your . . .'

'Yeah, thanks, Godfrey. Listen, I was trying to get hold of Barry to see if he knew where Finbar was. I'm up at Windy Ridge and the place is deserted.'

'Has been for over a week. Someone in the village said they's seen a taxi goin' to the farm. Should've known it would be you.'

I might have known I couldn't get home unseen. These people miss nothing.

'So is Barry around?'

'Like I told your father, Barry don't know where Finbar's gone. He's been worrying himself sick lately.'

'Can I talk to him, Godfrey?' I tried.

'You could if he was here, but he's in Harwich this evening. I'm not, though.'

'Not what?'

'Not in Harwich. I'll be in the Crown tonight. In about four minutes' time, to be precise.'

You just can't fight the Country Code, can you?

'I'm on my way, Godfrey.'


I left the kitchen window open in case Chuck Berry wanted to get out, though the last I saw of him he was shedding hairs all over Finbar's flying club blazer and looking as if he was settled for the night. If he got hungry he could nip out and kill something. I should have noticed when I arrived that it was almost too quiet because there were no sparrows nesting in the eaves and no pigeons lurking in the Dutch barn. In his prime, Chuck Berry had been able to influence the flight paths of migrating birds.

For a man I had never known to wear a watch, Godfrey Ineson had a great sense of time, and timing. He was not only in the pub before me but was draining the last of a pint of Adnams as I walked in.

'My round, I suspect,' I said.

'Let's not fight about it,' Godfrey agreed. 'Welcome back, young Fizzer.'

I was grateful that the Old Crown had only just opened and that Godfrey and I were alone with a sallow-faced landlord I didn't know, who wore an expression that suggested his dinner was getting cold.

'I've really missed being called that, Godfrey,' I said as I paid for our beer. 'It brings back so many happy memories.'

He caught my tone. 'So what do they call you up in London, then?'

I was tempted to ask him if he wanted a list, but I settled for: 'Roy.'

'Oh, well,' he sighed and pointed his beer towards a table near the window.

Godfrey couldn't be much over sixty but he had the puckered leather complexion of a man who had worked outdoors all his life and who would probably look no different when he was eighty or ninety. He and his son Barry were self-employed farmworkers. They didn't own any land themselves, they hired out their expertise and machinery and Windy Ridge was probably one of four or five farms they worked for. In the winter, they would pick up work from the County Council, cutting hedges, gritting roads, even snow-ploughing. Old Godfrey alone, even though retired now, had forgotten more about the Angel farming interests than Finbar and I and our father would ever know.

'You staying at Windy Ridge?' he asked once we were settled.

'Hadn't planned to,' I said between sips of Adnams bitter, a beer that came close to my definition of the perfect pint. 'Place is locked up and deserted.'

'How did you get in then?' Sharp as a sickle, old Godfrey.

'Kitchen window was open,' I returned his serve.

'Did you leave it open?'

'It's OK, Chuck Berry's in there on guard.'

'Then pity the poor bugger who breaks in. That cat was born mean and it lived wild for two years to my knowledge before your mother took it in. Since she left, he's just got meaner. I still reckon it was him took out my pair of ferrets three year ago. The new vet insisted on an autopsy and said –'

'An autopsy? On a ferret?' I had to head this one off quick. I had a feeling it was a story best heard when drunk and I still reckoned I had some driving to do that evening.

'It was a new vet in the district. Young lass, seen too much television. She heard about my ferrets getting picked off and said she wanted to do an autopsy on what was left of one of them. Silly little bitch said it must have been a gin-trap what killed him, then a fox or something had chewed up the body. But I knew it was that bloody cat from the way he looked at me.

'Anyways, a coupla months later, Finbar takes him for a booster shot or something and the new lady vet says, "Here, nice pussy," – which was just what Finbar was thinking – and the next thing you know she's in an ambulance heading for Intensive Care and the local Blood Transfusion Unit has to double its quota for the month. You took one of his spawn, didn't you?'

'Yeah, but I was lucky, I got the quiet one of the litter.' I made a move to change the subject, conscious of the rapidly declining level of his beer. 'But it's your offspring I was after, Godfrey. I wanted to talk to Barry to ask when he last saw Finbar. We're getting worried about him.'

''Bout my Barry? Nothing to worry about there. My Barry can take care of himself,' he said too quickly. Then he gently lifted his empty mug and tapped it on the table.

As I stood up to get him a refill, I said: 'Yes, but Finbar can't.'

I waited at the bar while the landlord filled Godfrey's glass, noting that there was none of the effete London habit of a fresh glass every time round here. Stick with tradition and to hell with the health regulations.

'That's only because your father never gave him the chance to,' he said as I returned, nobly resisting another drink myself.

I was surprised at what he said and knew it was a subject not a little fraught with potential aggravation. But still, I rose to the bait.

'What do you mean by that?'

Old Godfrey savoured his beer almost as much as his moment.

'Your father laid it all out for Finbar, you know. He smoothed paths, set up deals for Finbar to take the credit for, made sure he had the right connections in the county. And always he was subtle, never pushy, so it looked like Finbar had come up with the ideas himself. Lots of opportunities, lots of favours called in. Even when he left your mother, he made sure Finbar had a head start with Windy Ridge – an' he could've got a fair price back then.'

'So how is that not giving him a chance?' I asked, genuinely puzzled. 'It sounds like he had lots of chances but never succeeded with any of them.'

'Ah!' Godfrey almost twisted his tonsils getting to the punch-line. 'But he was never really allowed *to fail*, either, was he?'

I began to realize that an evening with Godfrey definitely required a serious drink; such as a bottle of whisky with the top off.

'And you' – he was on a roll now – 'you're supposed to go around bleating that you never had those chances.'

'I didn't need them,' I said quickly.

'Exactly. You . . . didn't need them.' He ended lamely when he realized I was agreeing with him. He then perked up again. 'It was fairly bloody obvious that you could look after yourself from Day One. Just like that cat your mother took in – Chuck Berry, if that's any sort of name. Once you could walk and feed yourself, you weren't reliant on anybody.'

'Is this pub licensed for psychiatry?' I asked the landlord, who was cleaning ashtrays at the bar. He shrugged his shoulders and disappeared into a back room. Maybe he had gone to check.

'You can laugh, young Fizzer,' Godfrey muttered.

'I try to, I try to.'

'But don't ever mock the father-son bond, even if you don't need it. My Barry knows he can always turn to me if he ever needs my help.'

Now there was a curious piece of information to volunteer.

'Are you sure?' I asked seriously.

''Course I'm bleedin' sure. He's my flesh and blood. I'd do anything for him if he was in trouble.'

'No, Godfrey, I meant are you sure *he knows*?'

And for a full two minutes, that shut him up.

'Where is he, Godfrey?' I prodded gently.

'He's gone out. He's in Ipswich for the day.'

'You said Harwich on the phone.'

He gave me the squint he usually reserved for the bead on the end of a shotgun.

'One of the two. He's been going there a lot lately – on business, of course.'

'Whose business?'

'Well, not yours, for a start.'

'OK, OK,' I calmed him. 'That was out of order, but I only wanted to know if it was anything to do with Finbar.'

'It moight 'ave,' said Godfrey slowly, drawing on all his East Anglian vowels to give himself thinking time.

'Truth is, I haven't seen Barry since yesterday morning and he's hardly said a civil word to me for a month now.'

'And that's unusual, is it?' I put my sincere face on – the one that tugs at the muscles under the ears – just in case he misunderstood.

'Oh, yes. When I retired and let Barry take over the business, he used to come and chat a lot about work problems. Ask advice, that sort of thing. Seeking my valued opinion, as you might say. Then, about a year ago, he started to get really thick with Finbar and went all secretive. I don't know what's going on any more. Not with the business, not with my Barry; nothing.'

'Did he work for Finbar like you used to work for my father at the old farm?'

'No chance. Windy Ridge couldn't support him full time. It could hardly support Finbar.'

So where had the new BMW come from?

'Barry helped out at seeding and harvest,' Godfrey went on. 'And he and Finbar went fifty-fifty on some rented fields and set-aside, but it couldn't have been more than, say, twenty per cent of his time.'

'And what did he say when Finbar went missing?'

'Nothing, that was the trouble. I'm sure he knows something but he wouldn't talk to me about it. I heard in here' – he gestured vaguely around the pub – 'not from Barry. An' when I put it to him, he went all huffy and tried to brush it off. I knew there was something up, so I rang your father.'

He looked at me full on.

'I knew your dad would care. He's sent you to find him, hasn't he?'

'Yeah, something like that,' I said. And the price was going up by the minute.

'I knew he'd be worried. And I knew he'd get the family out to help. Good family ties always come through.'

'Absolutely,' I agreed. 'Let me get you another beer before I go.'

I stood up, wondering how best to handle my role as the vanguard of our family's crusade.

'By the way, Godfrey, do you happen to know where my mother lives?'

It took me about forty minutes to drive to Romanhoe, across the county boundary into Essex and over towards the coast. I had been there once before, which was probably more than the Romans ever had.

Technically it was a port, but it didn't have a harbour or anything and was actually a good five miles from the sea by water, although only two as the crow flew. It took its name from the dubious historical claim that Roman trading ships waited there in the curve of the river until a high tide gave them enough clearance to make it upriver into Colchester. The one bit of the story I believed was that the Romans had never actually come ashore there. Not a single Roman artefact had ever been found there, despite the surrounding area being so stiff with archaeological trivia you could trip over it. But then I had always rated the Romans in the common-sense league.

The road in – there was no road out – snaked downhill for over a mile and ended in a sort of town square with three sides. The fourth side was a concrete hard sloping into the river (if the tide was in) or thirty feet of thick black mud (if out). The really posh houses had bay-window views of the river and private yacht moorings. That was the Quay, which also housed a real tourist trap of a pub called the Black Buoy and an authentic ship's chandler's store.

In the side streets off from the Quay there were the less picturesque pubs the locals used and there was even a station still in operation (and, of course, a Railway Tavern) for those adventurous enough to commute to London one way, or those desperate enough to risk a day at the Clacton seaside the other.

The railway line formed a natural boundary between the 'old' port and the 1930s 'town' which had developed ribbon-like along the one access road. Whatever industry the old port had made its money from – timber, coal, grain, whatever – that had long since gone. The sixties had seen an invasion of hippies and artists who had turned the place into a nest of craft shops. Some had stayed on, still hippies but better businessmen now, and newer generations had followed. Every useless gift you would never want to give anyone was for sale. Candles either too pretty or too hideous to ever light; corn dollies; models of someone else's idyllic country cottage; soft toys; pottery; hand-carved light-pulls; organic honey; wooden fruit; brightly coloured wooden jigsaws which spelled out the name of your children in the shape of a pig; more key rings than a prison inspector would need; and paintings.

So many paintings. Watercolours, oils, pen and ink, hand-coloured prints. And all, or almost all, of the Romanhoe water-front and the yachts and private pleasure cruisers which had usurped the brown-sailed Essex coastal smacks and the long-forgotten fishing fleet.

There was a certain vampiric quality to it all. The resident artistic community made a living (OK, not much of one) from images of a defunct working port in which they would not have lived when it was a port, or from jolly sailing scenes featuring the yachts of rich incomers whom they despised as 'weekend sailors'. (Actually, the real locals referred to them as 'cloth-cap admirals' and were quite happy to sell them ship's stores, paint, beer, fish and chips, you name it.)

Old Godfrey had put mother's address as five, Station Street, one of a terrace of eight late-Victorian cottages overlooking the railway line and the approach to Romanhoe Station. In fact, the row of houses was so precariously balanced on the railway embankment itself that it was only a matter of time before the whole lot of them slid down on to the track and caught the 7.42 to London. I just knew my mother would not have enough insurance cover. Me, I would have taken out a dozen policies and started tunnelling.

I also knew, even before I noticed there were no lights on, that she wasn't going to be in.

But it was not yet nine o'clock and not even dark, so I parked Armstrong outside her front door and decided to go for a walkabout and try and find a bite to eat. If she got back before me, she would remember Armstrong and know I was in the area. All I had to do was get back before she sold him.

There were quite a few civilians on the streets of the old town, all heading towards the Quay to look at the water (or mud) as the British always do on warm days. It must be genetic. Hey, it's a beautiful evening, let's go and stand by some stagnant water and get nibbled by mosquitoes and have wasps die in our beer, because we're British.

So I headed away from the waterfront and started to nose down the narrow side streets to see what there was to see.

From a distance, I saw the Railway Tavern and I decided to *keep* my distance, having a totally irrational distrust of any pub named after anything to do with railways, stations or locomotives. I also have similar prejudices against any pub with 'Silver' in its name and I've never had a happy experience in a pub called the Greyhound either.

Consequently, I realized I must be in hell when I turned the next corner to find myself staring at the frontage of a pub called the Silver Express, complete with a peeling inn sign depicting the particular Silver Express in question: a greyhound.

It was the sort of pub you wouldn't go in for a bet. The door to the Public Bar was accessible, just, if you fought your way through the casually stacked pile of empty casks and kegs which blocked the narrow pavement waiting for the brewery lorry to pick them up. From the dust on them, they looked as if they had been waiting some time and it's always a bad sign when not even the brewery lorry dares visit a pub. Perhaps they were hoping someone would pinch them and smelt them down for scrap aluminium.

The other door, nearest to me, was labelled 'Saloon' and judging by the fine sprinkling of broken glass on the step, it was maybe taking its western saloon bar brawl imagery too far.

The sash windows were open, allowing a mist of cigarette smoke and smells of stale beer and fried food to escape, along with the traditional sounds of a quiet night down the pub. In this case, that seemed to involve singing along to a cranked-up jukebox version of Meatloaf's 'Anything For Love', or at least by one slurred female voice.

And a slurred female voice I recognized.

It was her all right, but she didn't notice me, not even when I walked within two feet of the table she was sitting at to get to the bar.

It was not that she was too drunk; even though the slurred

66

Meatloaf lyrics were a bit of a giveaway, suggesting that while she certainly wasn't fit enough to drive, she might still be able to find her car. It wasn't that the pub was crowded – silver greyhound railways rarely are. And what if she hadn't seen me for a few years; hell, she was supposed to be my mother.

No, the problem was she had eyes for other things.

Or thing. And the thing in question was a tall streak of a bloke – a good six-footer even sitting down – with sandy hair which flopped carefully down over his left eye to give him a permanent schoolboy look. He was wearing a khaki linen shirt and almost-matching slacks in a colour Fenella would probably have called taupe. He wore no socks and blue canvas deck shoes. The linen shirt was unbuttoned to the navel and my mother's left hand was inside it, her fingers practising macramé on his chest hairs.

She was gazing deeply into his eyes as she crooned along with the song, oblivious to anyone or anything else in the pub, the town, the universe. Had she no idea what she looked like? What sort of an image she was presenting? And where had she got that dress? Did she not realize that everybody knew the trick by now, where if you're a size twelve you put on a size fourteen and everyone says, 'Darling, you've shed pounds.'?

And anyway, the bloke wasn't old enough to be my father.


'Good God, it's Fitzroy! And it's his round!'

It had taken her four and a half minutes. I had timed her on my Seastar.

I turned towards her and switched on the smile.

'Hello, Mom,' I said loudly. 'Can you put me up for the night?'

I was watching the tall guy for a reaction, but he was cool; simply straightening himself up in his seat, maybe checking his flies.

'Of course I can. Come here.'

She stood up and held out her arms as I approached. She was looking good in a loose orange low-cut dress which ended an inch above the knee. Her red hair casually swept up and back off her face giving the impression that there was more of it than there was. Minimum make-up, just a light orange lip gloss, and as we hugged I got a strong smell of tangerine-scented body oil. She'd always had a thing about citrus fruit.

As we unclinched, I said: 'Nice tan.'

'It's been a good summer,' she smiled, 'and I've been sunbathing instead of working.'

I doubted that. Redheads with a tan? Either the hair or the tan came out of a bottle.

She still held my arms as she looked at me, as if making sure it really was my face. Then I realized that her right foot was beginning to press down on the toe of my left trainer.

'Hey, come on,' she said, challenging, 'give your mother a proper hug.'

She came at me like she was docking into a space station and buried her face in the right side of my neck. I got a mouthful of hair and began to twist my head away as politely as I could when the pressure on my foot suddenly increased.

'If you let slip how old you are,' she was whispering in my ear, 'you'll never walk again.'

# Chapter Six

'Fitz, I want you to meet Philip Ryder. He's a friend of mine. Phil, this is my youngest son, Fitzroy.'

Ryder half raised himself out of his seat to offer his hand. Mother had to take her foot off mine to let me shake it. His grip was firm but he wasn't into pressure games.

'Pleased to meet you, Roy. I'm sorry, but I didn't know it was a family night. I hope I'm not in the way.' He looked at Mother. 'You only have to say, Bethany.'

The accent wasn't local, in fact it wasn't much of anything. But I wasn't thinking about that too much, I was wondering where 'Bethany' had come from.

'Don't be ridiculous, Phil. Fitzroy always turns up out of the blue, but he doesn't mean anything by it. It's just his way. Now get a round in, Fitzy, and come and join us.'

'No, I insist, let me,' said Ryder.

I indicated graceful defeat. I was good at that.

'Thanks, Phil. I'll have a bottle of Beck's, please, by the neck.'

I may have had to go into a pub named after a greyhound but that didn't mean I had to trust the beer there, or the glass-ware.

'Similar, Bethany?'

My mother examined her gin and tonic and ignored the fact that her glass was almost full.

'Yes, why not? Thank you, Phil, that's sweet of you.'

We had about two minutes while he got the drinks in.

'What are you doing here?'

'Just passing through. Why does he call you Bethany?'

'It's my name.'

'No, it isn't.'

'It's my *artistic* name. It's how I sign my paintings.'

'Bethany Angel? It sounds like an Irish hospice or a mission for distressed seamen in Liverpool.'

'Well, thank you for your support, darling,' she hissed. 'What are you doing here really?'

'I was just passing through. Thought I'd drag you out and buy you some dinner, say hello, see if you needed any little jobs doing around the house. You know, oil your zimmer frame or fix a fuse. The usual son-mother stuff.'

'Twaddle. What are you up to? And cut the ageist crap.'

'OK, OK. I popped in to see Finbar up at Windy Ridge but he seems to have gone walkabout. The place is shut up and there's no sign of him. I thought you might know where he was.'

'Tripple twaddle.'

'No, straight arrow, Mom. Nobody's seen him for weeks.'

'And you're worried about Finbar?' She seemed genuinely surprised. 'He must either owe you money or you've gone very girlie in the last few years. What's up, London making you soft?'

'Hey, come on, Mommy dearest, that's not fair,' I sulked.

'Fair? In your dictionary, fair is just a word between fart and fuck.'

'Then that's your fault for buying me a naff dictionary when I was a kid.'

'You're the one who ran off with Finbar's . . .' Her face broke into a huge smile aimed somewhere behind me. ' . . . Phil, how kind. Can you manage?'

Ryder carried our drinks in his two hands.

'There you go, didn't spill a drop,' he said jovially as he lowered them on to our table. 'Cheers.'

'Thank you, Phil,' said my mother, patting him on the knee just to annoy me.

Ryder waved his pint of bitter at me. 'Cheers, Roy.'

I returned his salute with my bottle and wondered who had told him to call me 'Roy'.

'If I'm interrupting a family reunion, just let me know,' he said to break the ice before it formed. 'I've got plenty of stuff I can be getting on with.'

'On your boat?' I probed.

'Why, yes, how did you know? Am I so obviously a weekend admiral? Isn't that what the locals call us?'

'Just a guess. If you lived here, I wouldn't have put this as the sort of pub you would use.'

'I use it,' said Mother.

'Yeah, well . . .' I rested my case on that one.

She glared at me.

'You're right, of course,' Ryder said smoothly. 'It's a bit of a busman's holiday for me, actually. I'm in marine insurance, which is basically messing about with big boats. So, to relax, I mess about in little boats.'

'You keep one here?'

'No way. Marine insurance doesn't pay that well. No, I hire one round at Mersea Island and nip in and out of the estuaries. The Colne, the Blackwater, sometimes up to the Orwell. Got a nifty little thirty-footer this year called *Direct Star*. Goes like the wind, when there is any.'

'But Phil has become becalmed in Romanhoe,' Mother chipped in, giving his leg a squeeze. He had the decency to blush.

'That's right, not a breath of wind for a week now. That's typical, isn't it? Hottest summer for twenty years and all we can do is complain.'

'Or sunbathe,' I said. 'Hasn't it got an engine, this boat?'

'Sure, but that would be cheating.'

'So Phil is temporarily marooned here and some of us are introducing him to the delights of village life,' Mother simpered in her best schoolgirl manner.

'Do you sail, Roy?'

'Oh, Fitzroy was never a sailor,' Mother answered for me. 'All he ever wanted to do was fly. Cost us a fortune on lessons when he was a teenager.'

'All those years ago,' I said, as if agreeing with her, and she gritted her teeth at me.

'Did you learn around here?'

'Just up the road in Suffolk,' I said vaguely.

Ryder nodded knowledgeably. 'There's been a boom in flying clubs lately, since the American airbases pulled out. It's very popular round here now the military traffic has declined. Hot-air ballooning's on the up, too, I hear.'

'Well, it would be, wouldn't it?' I said straight-faced. 'On the up, I mean. If it was going down, it'd be called crashing. Win a weekend hot-air crashing . . . it just doesn't have the same ring to it, does it?'

Ryder laughed nervously and muttered: 'Oh yes, very good.'

'Tell you what,' said Mother, slapping the table with both hands so the drinks rattled. 'Let's have another one here, then get some wine in and go back to my place and I'll rustle up some supper for us all.'

'Can't we get something here?' I pleaded.

'They don't do food in the evenings.'

'Fish and chips?' I tried.

'We had them for lunch.' She smiled at Ryder as if there were fond memories in battered cod.

'A takeaway? Chinese? Indian?' I was clutching at straws now.

'We don't have things like that in Romanhoe.' I knew; I'd checked on the way in. 'And I wouldn't hear of it, anyway. No, I'll be galley slave tonight.' She exchanged a look with Ryder. 'Or whatever it is you call your skivvies below decks. Now, get some more drinks in, Fitzroy, while I go to the loo.'

She smoothed down the front of her dress as she stood up, whacked back her gin and tonic and put the empty glass in front of me. Then she flounced across the bar, her heels clacking on the floorboards, to the door marked Ladies.

I watched Ryder to see if he was following the tick-tock of her hips. He started to, but averted his eyes as soon as he realized I was clocking him.

'Same again?' I asked cheerfully.

'Yes, thanks, Roy,' he said, glad to be distracted.

'Fancy some peanuts or crisps?'

'Yes, please, either.'

'I'll get a selection,' I said, taking pity on him.

He'd obviously tried Mother's cooking already.


'You came in a taxi?' Ryder asked me, pointing with a bottle of wine.

We were outside Mother's cottage and she was fumbling the key into the lock on the front door. The wine had been all the pub had had to offer, hadn't been chilled and was probably better for pointing with than drinking.

'It's mine,' I said. 'It's delicensed but it makes for a good runabout in London.'

'He calls it Armstrong and he's strangely fond of it,' Mother chipped in.

She got the door open and hit a light switch. The front door opened straight into the living room, though there wasn't much room in there for living. There was a battered two-seater sofa – the sort which springs out into a bed, usually when you least expect it to and never when you want it to – a television on a small square table and a painting easel and a bar stool. The floor was strewn with pages of newspaper shotgunned with blobs of paint. The easel had nothing on it, which meant that either Mother was very shy about her work-in-progress, or maybe there just wasn't any work in progress.

I shuffled into the room with Ryder following me. There was just about enough space for us to plant our feet on the floor, but if we all breathed out at the same time it could get intimate.

'I thought pottery was your thing, Mom, not painting.'

'Oh, it is. I've got my wheel set up in the bathroom. But the pots don't sell as well as the daubs just at the moment. Got to give the grockles what they want. No offence, Phil.'

Ryder looked puzzled and mouthed the word 'grockles' at me.

'Tourists,' I whispered and he raised his eyebrows.

'Control yourself, you beast!' Mother yelled suddenly, taking me by surprise.

Then I realized she was shouting towards the kitchen and the back door from whence came a rapid scratching, scraping noise, followed by a low growl.

'It's no good, I'll have to let him in,' she said, making for the kitchen.

'Who?' I asked as casually as I could.

'Elvis. He's a softy, really. Just wants to come and say hello, then he'll go back to sleep.'

The growling got louder and as she switched on the kitchen light I could see the back door and its bottom panel actually straining inwards as the scratching became more deliberate and more powerful.

I sensed Ryder moving behind me as Mother began to unbolt

the back door, saying: 'Down, Elvis. You know I can't unlock this damned door if you're leaning on it.'

Ryder was edging the sofa away from the wall and was positioning himself behind it. I decided to join him and he pushed the sofa out to give me space.

We were standing trying to look cool behind our barricade as Mother got the back door open and I was congratulating myself on my decision not to try and break in earlier and wait for her.

'Is he one of these overfriendly dogs, this Elvis?' I asked Ryder.

'What makes you think it's a dog?' he said grimly.

'It's a Vietnamese pot-bellied pig, actually.'

'It's still a pig, Mother. You are living with a pig.'

'I put up with your father for more years than I should have,' she retorted. 'Elvis is a lot less stressful.'

'Elvis, hey?' Ryder nudged me quietly, all boys together.

I looked at him deadpan. 'What's your point?'

I meant it. If you were going to call a Vietnamese pot-bellied pig anything, why not Elvis? Ryder looked at me in despair.

'Mother, Elvis is eating my trainers.'

'Nonsense, Fitzroy, he's just giving you a once-over sniff. Just saying hello.'

I wondered what he'd say to a snoutful of Nike, but then I remembered the two basic facts I knew about pigs. They are shaped like bullets, so never get in the way of one going at speed, and they also have plenty teeth.

'He's slobbering all over me,' I whined.

'Don't be such a baby. Here, get the wine open.' She tossed a corkscrew at Ryder. 'Just look at the two of you, hiding behind the sofa, for goodness sake. Come here, Elvis.'

She put an arm round his flank and tried to steer him back into the kitchen. He had a shoulder behind the sofa, though, and was levering it away from us, despite Ryder and me pulling it back for dear life.

'Oh, come *on*, Elvis. He thinks you want to play with him,' she accused us. 'I don't know what you're worried about. It's not like he's a puppy trying to shag your leg or anything.'

That particular image had not occurred to us and both Ryder and I doubled our effort to pull the sofa closer.

'I know what'll do it,' Mother said suddenly, dashing into the kitchen and grabbing a packet of cornflakes from a shelf.

She emptied a trail from the kitchen out of the back door and then casually threw the box into the garden.

'Come and get 'em, Elvis, it's your favourite.'

The pig raised its snout, gave me a rheumy, moist-eyed piggy killer look and began to crunch up the cornflake trail.

'They're very intelligent,' said Mother as Elvis shouldered her out of the way to get to the back door.

'Of course they are,' I said, limping out from behind the sofa. 'They suck shoes and eat cornflakes without milk. I know lots of Nobel Prize winners like that.'

'Why can't she keep a cat?' Ryder whispered as he helped me push the sofa back against the wall.

I began to feel sorry for him. Such innocence was rare these days.

'What do the neighbours think of Elvis?' I asked as I joined her in the kitchen, scoping the cupboards for glasses.

'I don't know and don't care,' she said primly, putting the unopened bottle of wine in the freezer.

'You mean they don't talk to you any more.'

There came a loud grunt from outside. Through the window by the sink I could see Elvis with his head stuck in the Corn Flakes box staggering around the handkerchief-sized garden, bumping into the fence on both sides, the dustbin and what looked to be several phallic gravestones but were probably Mother's sculptures.

He was like the first drunk at a party, pinballing off the furniture and I almost felt sorry for him. We've all been there; though maybe not on cornflakes.

'Don't worry about him. He sleeps in the shed. It's quite snug in there. Where's the wine?'

'Here's one,' chirped Ryder, popping the cork. 'It's not exactly chilled, I'm afraid.'

Mother produced three glasses like a conjurer. 'The other one's cooling off. Now, what does anyone fancy? I've got the makings for spaghetti if anyone knows how to defrost the ground beef in the microwave. I always end up roasting it.'

I wondered who had put my mother together with a freezer and a microwave. Indigestion was one thing, but now she was equipped to do food poisoning on a big scale.

'Why not let me do the cooking, Beth?' Ryder volunteered. 'I can drive a microwave and spaghetti is one of my specialities.'

'Why, Phil, you're a man of hidden talent,' she flirted. 'Why not?'

'OK with you, Roy?'

'Fine by me.'

'You hungry?'

'Yes. Suddenly I am.'


It seemed to take her an awfully long time to show Ryder where two pans and a chopping board were located. While she was doing that, I was tasked with putting some music on her midi hi-fi system, once I had found it under a pile of paint-daubed newspapers. I put on some Annie Lennox and sat on the sofa sipping white wine which was not so much not chilled as blood heat.

Eventually, Ryder threw her out of the kitchen amidst much giggling and gags about 'too many cooks' and 'whoops, I hope I heard that correctly'.

'So who is he?' I asked as she joined me on the sofa.

'He's a friend, that's all,' she said, sipping her wine. 'And don't spill on the sofa, you're sleeping on it.'

I thought that was rich, given what Elvis had probably done on it.

'Where's he sleeping?'

'On his boat, and I might join him if I feel like it. It's very romantic, doing it on a boat. Very soothing.'

'The tide's out. What's it like on mud?'

She reached out and nipped the lobe of my ear between the nails of her thumb and forefinger. It was something she used to do when I was a kid.

'Less of the lip, my lad. I brought you into this world and I reserve the right to take you out of it. Well, I should have. Is there a religion which says that? I'll sign up tomorrow. In the meantime, tell me what you're doing here.'

'I have,' I said, wincing as she increased the pressure on my ear.

'Are you checking up on me?'

'No, I told you, I thought I'd drop in on Finbar.'

'Did your father send you to check up on me?'

'No he did not. He sends his love, though.'

'You always were a lying little toad,' she said, patting my cheek. 'But at least you were an inventive liar. I could always see right through your father.'

'What about Finbar?' I asked, rubbing my ear and hoping Annie Lennox had drowned out my squeals.

'Oh, he couldn't lie for toffee. He was useless at it. In fact, it never . . .'

'No, Mother, I meant what's happened to Finbar?'

'Why should anything have happened to Finbar? He was perfectly all right the last time I saw him.'

'When was that?'

'Oh, I don't know. Two, no, three weeks ago. He's probably taken a holiday. In fact, he said he might. He's been popping over to France for the odd weekend all year. I suspect he's got a girl over there.'

'In France? Whereabouts?'

'I don't know. Look, when he was here once he said he had to go to the bank to change some money into francs because he was popping across the Channel for a few days. I'm sorry, but I never thought to give him the third degree about it. What's the problem?'

I sighed and wondered if I had an emergency packet of cigarettes stashed in Armstrong somewhere.

'Finbar hasn't been around Windy Ridge for ten or eleven days now and no one seems to know where he's gone. People are getting worried.'

'Such as?'

'Such as old man Ineson. He's worried about the farm.'

'Rubbish. He's nothing to do with it any more. Who else?' She made a pinching movement with her fingers, like she was pretending to be a crab. 'Come on, Fitzroy, tell Momma.'

'Well, Ineson rang Dad and he got a bit spooked and asked me to come up here.'

'I knew it,' she crowed. 'Trust your father not to want to get involved himself. But getting you to come here – bloody hell, I bet that took some doing. Is he paying you or does he have something on you?'

Ah, happy families.

'I just fancied a run in the country,' I said weakly.

'So he's paying you,' she said smugly. 'Well, I hope it's worth it, because if your father is parting with money, you can bet there's something fishy going on.'

I made one last attempt to defend my father, though I don't know why I bothered. His was the one case Perry Mason would phone in sick over.

'Father's worried about Finbar, that's all. It's not like him to suddenly up sticks and vanish.'

'Of course it isn't. The whole thing's ridiculous. Finbars don't just disappear.'

Great logic, Mother. Then I remembered me saying exactly the same thing.


'Spaghetti up in five minutes.'

Ryder was in the room with us, offering the wine bottle to top up our glasses.

'It smells delicious, Phil,' my mother beamed, but I had to admit she was right.

'I'm not interrupting anything, am I?' he said, and he sounded genuine. It's just that I couldn't help but overhear . . .'

'Family stuff, Phil. Fitzroy here is worried about his elder brother, but then he never thought Finbar could look after himself.'

'You're right, Mom,' I smiled. 'Why should I worry? After all, Fin must be thirty . . .'

'Well, old enough to fend for himself,' she said quickly, willing pain on me.

'Has something happened to him?' Ryder asked casually.

'Gone off for a dirty weekend probably.'

'With a young . . .' I watched my mother's face. '. . . With a Young Farmers' outing. They're always out and about doing whacky things.'

'So your brother's a farmer, is he? Mother an artist, one son a farmer, what do you do?'

78

'Me? I ran away to London to play trumpet in a jazz band.'
He grinned nervously.
'So you're the black sheep of the family, are you?'
I locked eyeballs with my mother.
'Oh, I wouldn't say that,' I said.

79

# Chapter Seven

Ryder did make a mean bolognese sauce, I had to give him that, which we ate with plates balanced on our knees. He even offered to do the washing-up but I told him to leave it, which somehow got misunderstood and they assumed I would do it.

Then Ryder said he really ought to go and Mother said as it was such a nice night, she'd walk him home to his boat. And Ryder said wasn't that the wrong way round, but Mother just laughed. So he and I stood shuffling our feet while she thundered upstairs to get her coat.

I thought that the bathroom was an odd place to keep a coat, but when she appeared in it and I noticed her make-up bag and a toothbrush stuffed carelessly into one of the side pockets, I thought it best not to comment. When she whispered that maybe I shouldn't wait up for her, I wasn't really surprised.

I joined them out on the street, muttering that I had to get my things out of Armstrong. Ryder said good night and what a good name for a jazz player's cab that was. And I said, 'What, Austin?' and he laughed and then I watched them walk down towards the Quay and the river and my mother had her arm through his by the end of the road.

I did, for a microsecond, consider snooping down to the river and finding where the *Direct Star* was moored. But then I thought what could I learn from watching a boat rock from side to side in the mud? Probably give me a complex.

So I settled for breaking open the emergency pack of Benson & Hedges in Armstrong's glove box and then searched for a light. I found a book of matches from Planet Hollywood, though I couldn't think of an alibi for not going there, in the back pocket of my jeans. But there was something else there. It was an envelope, unopened. It was a bill from Finbar's Visa card. I remembered picking it up and using it to write down anything interesting from the answerphone.

Back inside, I opened the other bottle of wine we had put in the freezer to cool off, took a hit on a cigarette and yelled at Elvis to stop howling pitifully at the back door. Then I opened Finbar's Visa bill for the previous month, working on the principle that other people's bills are always more interesting than your own.

So are their credit limits, and I was surprised to see that Finbar's was £5,000, though he didn't appear to come even close. He owed about £400, although he had paid off £200 the previous month. The itemized purchases were mostly small ones – an off-licence, various garages for petrol, a bookshop. Only two were over the £100 mark and both, about two weeks apart, paid to Alan Hedley Travel of Ipswich.

Maybe Mother was right. Finbar was taking short-break holidays to France, although the amounts seemed large for car ferry tickets even in the summer season.

I stuffed the bill back into my jeans and decided to give the travel agent's a ring in the morning. By the time I had knocked back the rest of the wine it was after midnight and I had reached my boredom level with my mother's CD collection. Elvis was still scratching at the back door and if there had been a moon he would have bayed at it. Maybe he was hungry.

I had a small sports bag with me containing a clean pair of underpants, socks, a T-shirt advertising a new Irish beer I hadn't tried yet, and a wash bag, which I carried upstairs to the bathroom. In between the potter's wheel, the toilet and various hose pipes, I found a wash basin and managed to brush my teeth. And while I was upstairs, I thought I might as well check out the bedrooms, if only to find out why I had been relegated to the sofa downstairs.

It became clear very quickly. The second, smaller bedroom was stacked floor to ceiling with paintings framed and unframed and pieces of pottery kilned, unkilned, glazed and recognizable. There wasn't room to swing a cat, let alone a Vietnamese pot-bellied pig.

There was only one other room upstairs, my mother's bedroom and I hesitated before I pushed the door open. The door wasn't even closed, there was no lock on it and I couldn't see a sign saying 'No Entry' or any warnings about high-voltage trip wires or laser alarms. So that was OK then.

I don't know what I had expected, but it was just a bedroom. She had a double bed with a strawberry-coloured duvet and matching pillows, a bedside table with a lamp and three or four paperback novels, a wardrobe stuffed with clothes to the point that only a wrestler or a woman could close it first time. On the wall was a framed photograph which I recognized. It had been taken about ten years ago on the big farm in Suffolk. There was Mother being thrown over a five-bar gate by her children while Father crouched as if to catch her on the other side. Everyone was laughing. Happy families, all five of us. I forgot who took it but I recalled it was taken on a Christmas-morning walk. There was frost still on the fields in the background and we all had rosy glows on our cheeks. We were probably all drunk. Christmases used to be like that.

I straightened the picture, even though it didn't need it, before turning off the light and closing the door on the memories and the lingering scent of tangerine and lemon body oils.

Downstairs, I finally beat the sofa-bed into submission and it twanged out into a bed. There was a quilt thing and a pillow squashed into it already. I arranged them, stripped down to my boxers, hit the light and only fell over about three things before I found the bed. I didn't remember drinking that much, but then that's the good thing about cheap white wine; you don't.

Elvis woke me just after five a.m. It was light, birds were chirping, a train rattled by and Elvis was trying to tunnel under the back door. I was looking forward to getting back to quiet, sleepy old London.

'Sod off!' I yelled at him, but the scratching got more frantic and he started grunting like – well, like a pig, really.

Maybe he really was hungry. I didn't remember anyone feeding him properly last night. What did they eat? If they were anything like British pigs, anything.

I stumbled into the kitchen and the snorting and grunting went up several watts per channel.

'All right, all right, give me a break. I'm getting there.'

On the floor under the sink was a battered metal bowl and a bag of something called Puppy Chow which looked like cubes of wet cork, but probably tasted scrummy to a pig. It looked the only logical thing unless Elvis was mainlining washing-up liquid or bleach.

I heard a slap at the window and looked up suddenly to find myself eyeballing Elvis. He had his front hooves on the window ledge and his head cocked on one side. His snout made contact with the window and twitched in small circular movements. It was like looking down the barrel of a hairy shotgun held by a nervous surrealist.

'This what you want, boy?' I asked, which was a ridiculous thing to do as I didn't even know if he spoke English.

He seemed to nod when I shook some Puppy Chow into the bowl and I said: 'Good choice, sir, one breakfast portion coming up. Do help yourself to fruit juice and cereal from the trolley.'

I was glad there was nobody around to hear me because I surely wasn't thinking straight. And what I did next convinced me of the old logic that some days you just shouldn't get out of bed.

I poured Elvis a bowlful of Chow and opened the back door to give it to him.

By the time I had got to my feet – slipping twice on the Puppy Chow, which seemed to be *everywhere* – Elvis was sprawled across the sofa bed, his snout rooting into the pillow where my own fair head should have been. The sad, dewy-eyed orphan face at the kitchen window had turned into a smooth-skinned Cruise missile as soon as he'd heard the back door lock turn.

'You . . . you . . . you're an animal!' I snarled at him.

He swivelled one eye at me and snuffled deeper into the pillow. I swear he wiggled his hips at me in body language which said: Go on, shift me then.

I didn't even try.

I brewed some coffee, a Mocha/Mysore blend (Mother and I always did share the same taste in coffee), shaved and washed and was dressed in time to give the milkman a fright and probably start another rumour in the village about the goings-on at five, Station Street.

I bought a pint of Gold Top from him for cash, which he didn't seem used to. But perhaps he was just surprised to sell Gold Top, as the health fascists have pretty much done for it because of its high fat content. It remains, however, one of the great stand-bys in the never-ending fight against a hangover.

As I drank the milk – deliberately not offering Elvis any – I unearthed a paint brush which still had some flex in it and a tube of red oil paint. I pinned a sheet of paper to the easel and painted: PLEASE DO NOT DISTURB, then positioned the easel next to the bed. Elvis snored softly.

Then I gathered my things together and let myself out. But before I closed the door, I said:

'Elvis, there's someone called Springsteen I'd like you to meet one day.'


By eight-thirty I was back at Windy Ridge, sitting in Finbar's office. No one had broken in via the back door I'd left unlocked, or if they had then Chuck Berry had probably killed them and dragged them into one of the outbuildings to eat later. As he wasn't around, it was odds on he was up to some sort of no good.

I used Finbar's phone to call Godfrey Ineson. He answered on the first ring and sounded disappointed when I said who I was.

'Still no sign of Barry, then?'

'No, there ain't. I don't know what the little bugger's playing at.'

'One thing, Godfrey. Did Barry ever mention going on holiday to France, maybe with Finbar? Or on business to France?'

'Don't be daft. Our Barry's never been abroad in his life. Never had a passport, though I did catch him applying for one just the other week.'

'Did he get it?'

'I don't know, I'm not privy to what's in his post these days. Why? Is it important?'

'Buggered if I know, Godfrey. Listen, I'll keep in touch.'

'You do that, young Fizzer. Do you want my mobile phone number in case I'm not here?'

I took it to keep him happy, scribbling it on the back of Finbar's Visa bill. Everyone had a mobile phone these days. Except me.

Phones, I thought after I had hung up. Phones and phone bills.

I found one eventually, stuck to the back of a copy of *Farmers Weekly* with what could have been raspberry jam. It covered a period up to two months before, but those very nice people from British Telecom had listed all the calls above the minimum number of units. There were two numbers which Finbar had rung twice and three times respectively. Both had the same code, obviously an international prefix, but not one I recognized instantly.

I knew Finbar couldn't keep numbers that long in his head, so there had to be a roladex or phone-numbers book somewhere. I found it in one of the desk drawers eventually, having missed it once thinking it was some form of accounts ledger.

It was an ancient, broken-spined thing rather like a school exercise book, and most of the alphabetical thumb index flaps had been torn off through too much thumbing. He must have had it for years, as some of the numbers went back to our schooldays.

I looked myself up and found a London number I hadn't used for five years. (Nobody had. That was the house that had sort of blown up.) What was even sadder was that he had drawn a line through my name and number and made no attempt to update it.

I put the address book to one side and concentrated on what I had actually come to find: some evidence of what Finbar had bought at the Alan Hedley Travel Centre.

There was nothing, or nothing I could see, so I resorted to Plan B, looked up Alan Hedley in the local phone book, dialled, and got someone called Wendy who wanted to know how she could help me.

'Hello, Wendy, my name is Angel and I'd just like to check on some tickets I bought through you last month on the' – I looked down the Visa bill – 'tenth and then again on the eighteenth.'

'One moment, please. Can you tell me how you paid?'

'Visa card,' I said honestly.

I heard the soft tapping of a keyboard.

'Ah yes, I have you now. What was the query?'

Good question, Wendy.

'Er . . . well, I was just wondering about the price . . . er . . . I'm doing some accounts, you see . . .'

'And you've noticed the surcharge on the flight you booked this month. Is that it, sir?'

'Yes, Wendy, that's exactly it,' I said, clutching at straws.

'Well, we did warn you that there's an August high-season tariff on virtually all flights, Mr Angel, and I'm afraid that applies to business-class flights to Brussels just as much as anywhere.'

Brussels.

I felt like clutching at Wendy.

'So that's why the ticket this month was more expensive. I see. Can you tell me the date? I don't have my diary in front of me.'

'August the eleventh, Stansted to Brussels.'

Twelve days ago.

'Many thanks, Wendy, you've been a great help.'

And I meant it. Praise where praise is due; we're far too quick to complain these days.

I picked up Finbar's address book and had one of the two international numbers pinned immediately. There was no trick to it. I knew Finbar had an old friend who lived in Brussels, or almost.

There he was, under 'B' and the number checked out.

B for Bumper.


Now it was me who needed an address book, and mine was back in Hackney.

I could have rung the number for Bumper there and then, but the one thing I knew for sure about Bumper was that it would not be him answering the phone. It might be a machine or a girlfriend, but it wouldn't be Bumper. His line of work involved him being out a lot.

So maybe it would be better just to drop in on him unexpected. See if Finbar was hanging out with him.

Of course, there was nothing to say that Finbar was still in Brussels, or that he had actually visited Bumper while he was over there, but it was worth a shot.

Especially if I wanted to stay out of Big Mac McCandy's way and especially if I knew someone who could get me there on the cheap, while stinging my father for the full fare.

That's where Sophie came in.

Sophie had been a real find. I had met her at a party down in Chelsea the week she was fired from British Airways and she was telling the story to a coven of girlfriends gathered around the kitchen table. I was floating around the kitchen trying to find some ice to go with the bottle of Rebel Yell bourbon I had brought as a peace offering to the woman who was throwing the party. (I couldn't actually remember who she was, so I had thought a peace offering might be needed.)

By doing so, I interrupted Sophie's story as she broke off to tell me to try the fridge, proving that she'd been to a party before. Then she turned back to her audience but didn't seem to mind me listening in.

She was, or had been, a stewardess working a long stint on domestic flights, mostly business-class traffic on the London–Newcastle or London–Edinburgh runs. These were frequent flyers – bored ones, that is. They wanted to get on, read the free newspapers, steal as many free drinks from the trolley as they could, and get off. Don't waste time on a smile or a thank you to the cabin crew; time was money, they were just robots.

For a sensitive soul like Sophie, this could only end in tears and it happened on the fifth or sixth consecutive day of her having to do the life jacket pantomime.

There she stood, at the front of the aircraft, pretending to inflate a life jacket using the mouthpiece to add extra buoyancy – 'why they don't just call it a blow job I'll never know' – in front of a totally disinterested audience. There was also the indignity of having to mime to someone else doing the voice about the exits being here, here and here, and waving her arms about like a parrot with Parkinson's disease. And all the time she was staring at a sea of open newspapers. They weren't even trying to look up her skirt or make nudge-nudge comments about the life jacket (which never does actually inflate during the cabin demonstrations).

And so one day, faced with this inhuman nonrecognition of her very existence, and aided by a slight hangover following a row with a now ex-boyfriend, she had snapped. In the middle of the safety procedures demonstration.

Grabbing an intercom handset from the wall of the cabin she overrode the tannoy system and yelled: 'Look, there may be fifty ways to leave your lover, but there are only six ways out of this fucking aircraft, so PAY ATTENTION!'

She left the company the next day.

I warmed to her immediately and we hit it off and saw quite a lot of each other.

Lately, though, we had drifted because of her new job, as a stewardess on the Eurostar train which ran through the Channel tunnel to Paris and, less frequently, Brussels. If anyone could get me a cheap ticket, Sophie could. If anyone fancied a dirty weekend in Brussels, Sophie would.

As I drove back down the A12 towards London, I had it all planned out in my head.

I just didn't move fast enough.

# Chapter Eight

Number nine, Stuart Street was under siege, though you couldn't tell from the outside, and I walked right into it.

There isn't that much room normally in the entrance hall where the communal phone is, but there was even less now there were two men in overalls lying on camp beds there. And there were two more men in overalls on the stairs, one sitting on a stair guarding the access to Doogie and Miranda's flat, and one standing outside the door to my flat holding a cordless drill as if he was about to operate on the lock.

I took all this in as if watching a film where the soundtrack had suddenly broken. I had one lightning flash of common sense: they were more surprised to see me than I was to see them.

But before I could act on this, we were all distracted by the commotion at the door of Flat Two and I was to find that flashes of common sense don't strike twice in the same morning.

The distraction was provided by Lisabeth and Fenella bursting out of their flat simultaneously, something I would have thought physically impossible without permanent damage to the door frame. Faces flushed, hair flying, they were shouting in stereo.

'Angel, get in here!' yelled Lisabeth.

'Angel, get out of here!' screamed Fenella.

One of the men in overalls in front of me was rising from his camp bed and saying: 'You Angel?'

The man in overalls sitting on the stairs was gaping at the girls. The one holding the cordless drill started swearing.

I didn't stop to check on the fourth one. I turned on my heel and left them to it, pulling the front door closed.

I hardly made it to the pavement, let alone ten yards down the road where I had parked Armstrong.

'Well, this didn't take as long as we'd thought,' said Domestos.

He was holding three cartons of milk against his chest with his left arm. On him, they looked like offensive weapons. His right arm hung loose. That looked dangerous too. He was wearing the same sort of overalls as the men inside the house. Somehow that didn't surprise me.

I heard the front door open behind me and a voice say: 'Is that 'im?'

I resisted the temptation to turn around, concentrating instead on how much space there was between Domestos and the cars parked at the kerb. Not enough. And anyway, Domestos was reading what was left of my mind.

'Don't make me 'ave to chase you,' he growled.

'Oh, was it me you were waiting for?' I asked innocently, but it was mostly nerves.

'Yeah, it was,' he nodded, not rising to the bait. 'We were getting ourselves settled in. Didn't know when to expect you back. Still, Mr McCandy'll be pleased. He was looking forward to an early chat. What say we pop inside and ring him?'

I felt the guys from the camp beds closing up behind me. From inside the house, I could hear Lisabeth and Fenella arguing.

'What a good idea,' I said cheerfully. 'After you?'

He just exhaled slowly.


'They've been here since last night,' gushed Fenella.

'Prisoners in our own home. It's outrageous!' snorted Lisabeth.

They were still at the door of their flat and were making no effort to come down the stairs. At the end of the hall, the door to Mr Goodson's flat opened an inch but no further.

Upstairs, the one with the cordless drill turned back to have a go at the door of my flat.

'That's not necessary,' I told Domestos. 'I've got a key.'

'He's not breaking *in*,' said Domestos reasonably. 'He's repairing your lock from last night. We 'ad to 'ave a toilet, didn't we? While we were waiting.'

He put his right hand on my shoulder to make sure I didn't dematerialize or anything. Then he handed over the milk cartons to the nearest one of his crew.

'Get packed up, Tommy, we're out of here.'

'Is that it, Dom?' asked the nearest pair of overalls. 'I was hoping for two or three days' work.'

'I'll let you know if anything comes up, Tommy.'

'I reckon I qualify for the Activity Bonus, though, Dom, don't you?'

He rolled up his right sleeve to show his forearm and a lint pad at least six inches long held in place with strips of surgical tape. Springsteen, taking after his dad.

'I'll ask for you, Tommy, I'll ask.'

Domestos took the communal wall phone off the hook and pressed buttons with a knuckle. I wondered if I should tell him about the book dangling from a string under the phone where we were supposed to log all our calls. Perhaps later.

'Mr M., please, Karen,' he said into the mouthpiece and then waited. 'Boss? Hackney crew checking in. Yes. Yeah, no problems. Yeah, I know it. See you there.'

He put the phone down and turned to me.

'Come on, it's drivetime. You've got a meet with Mr McCandy.'

'Can I drop my bag upstairs?' I asked and when he seemed to go along with that: 'And say sorry to my neighbours?'

He reached inside his overalls and I flinched but his hand came out with three plain white envelopes.

'I can help you there,' he said, handing them over. 'One each.'

I held one to the light. It was a £50 note.

'A drink for the civilians,' Domestos said. 'To cover the inconvenience.'

I took the first one to Mr Goodson's flat, pushing by one of the overalls who was struggling to roll up the canvas bed. The door opened wider as I approached. There was Mr Goodson, dressed ready for work right down to holding a briefcase.

'Can I go to work now?' he whispered.

'I think so, we'll be out of here in a few minutes. Take this.' I pushed an envelope at him. 'It might help you think up a good excuse for being late.'

Lisabeth and Fenella were easier to deal with. They were still in the doorway of their flat glaring at the henchman whom Domestos had obviously told to keep them there.

'We've not been allowed to go out, you know,' Lisabeth started on me. 'Not allowed to use the phone, bullied and pushed around in our own house . . .'

'Have this as a peace offering.' She snatched it from my hand in a blur. 'They're very sorry to have put you out. It was my fault, really.'

'Oh, we know that,' she said, pulling Fenella back into the flat along with the envelope. Fenella managed a weak smile as the door closed.

The guy on guard took his time standing aside so I could pass him to get to the stairs up to Flat four and Doogie and Miranda.

'So this is what we've been waiting for?' he sneered.

'You shouldn't have waited up.' I smiled at him. 'You could have phoned.'

He tensed, not sure what to do. Domestos, on the stairs just behind me, muttered, 'Get on with it,' and so I did.

Doogie yanked his door open even before I had raised my fist to knock. But it hadn't been *my* fists which had worried me.

'Are ye all right, Angel?' he muttered, his eyes roving over my shoulders to check out the guys in overalls. His accent was pure Glasgow. It went that way when he had violent thoughts.

'Yeah, Doogie, I'm fine. And thanks for asking,' I said, and I meant it.

'I'd have had a pop at them four, ye know, but yon big bugger is another matter.'

'That's OK, Doogie. I wouldn't have wanted aggro on my account. It wouldn't have been worth it.'

I was relieved. Doogie was a Scot, and he had a temper, and he was violent. But he wasn't suicidal.

'There's this – it's sort of compensation for your trouble.'

'Don't touch it, Doogie, it's blood money.' Miranda was suddenly behind him, hissing in his ear. 'I can check these goons out as soon as I get to the office. We can get the police in.'

Doogie looked at me as if to say the ball was in my court, but he didn't let go of the envelope.

'Don't even think it,' I told him quietly. Miranda was a journo on a local paper over in Islington and in reality I knew she had trouble checking out the office tea money. 'I'm just going to have a chat with these guys, that's all. No hassle. This is just a bit of a misunderstanding.'

'A bit –' she started, but Doogie cut in.

'Whisht, woman. You sure you'll be all right with these gawks, Angel?'

'Yeah. They don't mean me any harm,' I said confidently.

If they did, I wouldn't have been able to climb the stairs this far, would I?


'Help yourself,' said Big Mac McCandy, pushing the plate of oysters towards me. 'They're from Colchester. Best in the country. No debate about it. End of.'

I took one with a squirt of lemon, despite the passing thought that my mother and Phil Ryder had probably been having it away half a mile upriver from where they had come from. The damn things had probably passed me on the road to London earlier that morning.

We were in Bill Bentley's, the one in the City near the Lloyd's Bank tower. Mr McCandy often had a light lunch there, with Domestos picking him up about two-ish. Which was why Domestos had driven me there in Big Mac's diesel Mercedes, which I, of course, hadn't noticed on Stuart Street because I had been keeping one eye open for Domestos's Volvo. He hadn't used the Volvo because I'd obviously clocked it, which I took as a kind of professional compliment. For Domestos, that was quite a conversation.

I suppose I could have legged it outside the oyster bar, as Domestos made no effort to get out of the car, just told me to go in and I would find Big Mac waiting for me. I decided it was a kind of test. A test to see if I had medical insurance which covered plastic surgery.

'You've been difficult to get hold of,' said Big Mac.

*You start by buying me a large gin*, I thought – but now was not the time.

'I had to do something for my father,' I muttered. 'Kind of urgent.'

McCandy slurped an oyster. He'd put so much Tabasco sauce on it, it looked like it had been shot.

'Work for your father, do you?'

'No. This was a family problem; needed sorting.'

'That's good. Families are important, sons helping fathers, that sort of thing. Get it sorted?'

'Nowhere near, Mr McCandy. It'll take a couple of weeks and I may have to go abroad for a few days.'

'That's interesting. Anywhere nice?'

'Just across the Channel,' I said carefully. 'Spend a few francs, bring back the old duty-frees.'

I left it that way so he could make the same assumption my mother had, and I had, when she told me about Finbar having to change sterling into francs. Both of us had assumed *French* francs, not Belgian francs.

'Sounds very pleasant, very pleasant indeed. You don't have to go straight away, though, do you?'

'I was thinking of tomorrow, actually,' I offered.

He shook his head slowly.

'A Friday? In August? Oh, I doubt if you'd get on a ferry or even a plane at this notice. Monday or Tuesday would be your better bet.' He looked up at me, an oyster shell in his hand, and he had the look of someone who had just had a great idea. 'And that would mean you could do a little job for me which would give you a nice wad of holiday money, so you could really enjoy yourself abroad.'

'Play in one of your pubs, eh? I see. Trouble is I . . .'

He dropped an oyster shell on to the plate where it bounced among the others, put a napkin to his mouth and then waved it at the bar.

'Let's go another dozen, shall we?'

'Like I was saying, Mr . . .'

'Now don't spoil it, Roy – or whatever it is you call yourself this week. Oh yeah, I've been asking around. You use names like you use a stolen credit card. You said you weren't stupid enough to steal from me, and I liked that. It showed intelligence. Do me a favour, show some more.'

I moved swiftly into the second formal stage of negotiation. It's called giving in.

'What is it you think I can do for you, Mr McCandy?'

A second plate of oysters arrived, this time along with a bottle of Australian Semillion Chardonnay in one of those plastic cooler sleeves which never seem to work properly, and two glasses. McCandy poured out the wine.

'Dig in.' He waved a hand over the table as if blessing the feast.

'I want you to drive for me,' he said after trying the wine.

'You want me to drive a petrol tanker,' I said, hoping it didn't sound as if I was correcting him.

'On Sunday. Way I've got it figured is this. You're clean, well, unknown in this business, anyway. Nobody's got you tagged to my crew or as a driver. We put the word out I'm taking another delivery of diesel and doing it on Sunday, thinking nobody'll be expecting that. You pick up a tanker at Harwich, take an easy drive, with a couple of pit stops and give the thieving bastards a chance to move in.'

'And you'll have Domestos and some of his playmates ready and waiting to jump out and rescue me before I get duffed up. Is that it?'

'Not exactly.'

No, I didn't think it would be.

'We let them get the keys off you and they're off on their toes. My boys watch from a distance and then follow the buggers, see where the fuel ends up. Use three or four cars, do a real professional tail like the Job do. On a Sunday, it'll be a piece of piss.'

I wondered who in 'the Job' – the police – was acting as his technical adviser. Probably somebody he ran into at a Lodge meeting.

I sucked on an oyster to buy myself thinking time.

'It won't work, Mr McCandy. Be a waste of your money.'

'The tanker'll be empty,' he said defensively.

'I didn't mean that. How long was there between the first hijack' – he winced at that – 'and the tanker Taffy Duck lost?'

'Two and a half, nearly three months.'

'And you've not come across any reports of any other diesel getting nicked?'

'None at all, and I've had the word out.'

'So what does that tell you?'

'You tell me.'

His expression simply confirmed that I really did need a cigarette.

'It means someone is nicking only *your* diesel.'

'I guessed that.'

'But you've had other deliveries between that first lot and Taffy's, which got through OK?'

'Sure.'

'So someone is nicking it from you, but only when *they* need it.'

'What for?'

'I don't know. Maybe it's a question of storage. Like I said, where do you stash that amount of fuel?'

'In a garage – but God knows, I've put the word out strong enough on that network. You reckoned a farm, didn't you?'

'Passing thought only. Look, what I'm getting at is that you had three months between tankerload one and tankerload two going walkabout. What makes you think whoever's doing this actually *wants* to nick another load? Taffy lost his – what – less than a week ago? They're still burning that lot; they're well stocked.'

'You're saying it's too soon, is that it?'

'That's exactly it, Mr McCandy.'

McCandy took this in with a long drink of wine. I still hadn't touched mine.

'Mmm. Good point, Roy.' He put his glass down. 'Good thinking. Now think of another way you can help me. You're not drinking, Roy.'

I was now.


'You want me to meet you *where*?'

'It's called the Centre Pocket. It's in Hackney. Get a minicab there. Six o'clock?'

'An' it's a snooker club, right?'

'Yes, it is.'

'But you don't play snooker, Angel.'

'You do, Sophie.'

'I still don't get it.'

'That's not what I hear.'

'Oh, plug it, Angel. Not a word for over six months then you come out of the blue with the offer of a fun night in a tatty snooker club in Hackney at two hours' notice. What's going on?'

'Trust me, Sophie.'

'Not with my virginity.'

There was no answer to that.

'So you'll be there?' I pleaded.

'Do you think I've nothing better to do with my spare time?'

'I hope not.'

'Well, you're lucky because tonight I haven't. That makes me a really sad person, doesn't it?'

'What does it make me, Sophie?'

'A lucky bastard, but then you always were.'


I had needed every sliver and scratching of my weekly luck allowance when I talked myself down to McCandy that afternoon in Bill Bentley's. Eventually we had agreed on a way I could help him and though it sort of came out as my idea, I think McCandy had been ahead of me all the way.

It went something like this.

We didn't know the who and we didn't know the why, so what about the how? Not how they actually hijacked the tankers, which we knew, but how did they know when the tankers were on the move? And where they were coming from. Harwich was an obvious choice if you were importing goods off a ferry, but you wouldn't automatically think of the oil storage tanks there unless you were in the petrol or diesel business.

And within McCandy's empire, only he was really into buying diesel. Sure, he had managers running the garages he owned, but they were more interested in the service and repair and used-car dealing side of things. That was where the real profit was, after all.

So McCandy ordered the stuff himself. One of his accountants would know about it at some point, but only to check the lines of credit and tick off the invoices.

That left just McCandy and the drivers who would know the date and time of each pick-up, and the drivers were hired on a day-to-day basis. Sometimes they would be driving scrap metal to Leeds, other times they could be delivering cars, sometimes they could be running around McCandy's chain of leasehold pubs. None of them would know if they actually had work or not, let alone where and when, before the weekly meeting, that was. And anyway, the two who had lost their loads, Ferdy Kyle and Taffy, had both been seriously questioned by professionals –

once the police had finished with them. The odds on them being in on the scam were long.

Hang on a minute, what weekly meeting?

The one McCandy held every Monday down at the Centre Pocket where temporary labour was hired, drivers given jobs and so on. More or less where McCandy held court and dispensed largesse, in fact.

But surely all those kids practising snooker . . .

No way. Hadn't I been listening? Monday afternoon, when the club was shut. Nobody there except members of the McCandy crew.

Nobody?

No. Apart from the barman.

'That little fucker Julian,' McCandy had said.

'Justin,' I had corrected him.

Sophie went for a long pot on the brown into the top pocket. She had other colours closer but the brown offered her the straightest line. She made it, the cue ball coming back off two cushions to give her a nice cut on the remaining red into a centre pocket. From there she had a clear shot of the blue. The kid she was playing, who was maybe fourteen, kept tugging at the tails of his red silk waistcoat. He looked close to tears. He had only scored four and Sophie had been well ahead before she started her current break. As the blue went down, he used the tip of his cue to wipe his four points off the score line, nodded to her and reached for his jacket. I wanted to tell him it was only a game but I knew he took it seriously. He hadn't once tried to look up Sophie's skirt as she had bent over the table.

'We should have had a bet on,' she said as she joined me at the bar.

'I don't think he gets enough pocket money,' I said quietly, handing her a white wine spritzer. 'Thanks for coming down.'

'Hey, you know me, the original Good Time Sophie. First day off in three weeks and what do I choose to do? I get in a minicab at my own expense and come halfway across town to end up playing snooker with kids not up to speed on *Sesame Street* yet. And why? Because some person, who just happens to have given me the best shag I've had in recent years, calls me up after six months' radio silence. What does that make me? I don't know. Either my brains or my fucking hormones want testing.'

'Tone it down, Sophie,' I hushed her. 'Not in front of the children.'

Two other teenage hopefuls were giving her the eye and wiping the sweat from their cues with towels their mums had bought for them. Perhaps they were waiting for her to get drunk before they challenged her to a frame. They may be young but they couldn't wait that long.

'Only if you tell me you still fancy me,' she smiled, reaching out and squeezing my right thigh so hard and so quick that my bar stool scraped sideways a good six inches.

'Of course I do, especially when you play hard to get.'

She moved in closer, pushing my legs apart with her knees until she was standing inside my thighs. She put her left hand on my shoulder and leaned in towards me. She still held the snooker cue in her right hand, its base on the floor, like a soldier on sentry duty. Her skirt ended five and a half inches above her knees. I'm good on distances. I remembered why I hadn't seen her for six months. I'd needed a rest.

'Have you ever,' she said quietly, leaning even closer, 'done it on a snooker table?'

'Not where I've been a member. Now calm down. Play another frame. I've got somebody to see and then we're out of here.'

'Why are we in here in the first place?' she pouted, half turning so she could sit on my knee.

'Because I've just been made a member,' I said, scuffing my bar stool around some more, trying not to get too comfortable.

'Is that it?'

At least that bit was true.

'And I've got to see somebody, just briefly, give him a message. Be here in a minute, then we can go wherever you want.'

'Anywhere?'

'You name it.'

'To the Max,' she whispered and I knew what she meant.

'OK,' I said.

And it had already been a long day.

'That's my boy,' she said, with a hungry sort of smile. Then she patted my cheek, stood up and waved her cue at the two trainee snooker champions. 'Come on, then. Who wants their balls smashed all over the table?'

Sophie actually took on two of them together on separate tables. By the time Taffy Duck showed up, one of them needed snookers and the other was ten points behind and sweating profusely, even though he wasn't old enough for all his pores to have opened yet.

Taffy looked as flustered as the kid needing snookers, but as he threaded his way through the tables towards me, he took time out to give Sophie more of a once-over than the average garage mechanic would give a car in for its first service.

'Who's the blonde?' he asked, licking his lips as he spoke, although that was due to the fact that he was in front of a bar.

'A total stranger as far as you're concerned. I take it you got Mr McCandy's message?' I said loudly and just to make sure that Justin the barman took notice, I waved a £10 note over my empty glass.

Taffy rubbed the back of his neck as if easing the pain from a recent, unexpected blow.

'Yeah, I got the message. Said you wanted to see me. Large brandy, Julian.'

Justin didn't bother to correct him. He jabbed a glass up against the optic of a bottle on the back fitting, but only jabbed it a second time when I nodded permission. He wafted the £10 note out of my fingers.

'I wanted to tell you myself,' I said while Justin was in earshot. 'Mr McCandy wants me to do some driving for him, you know, join the firm, so to speak.'

'So I'm out, is that it?' Taffy paused between gulps.

'Nah, mate, no such thing. I just thought I'd tell you we'd be working together.'

I made to punch him lightly on the shoulder but he winced so much I hadn't the heart.

'Oh well, that's all right then,' he said, relieved. 'Could you see your way to giving me a sub?'

I sighed and reached into the back pocket of my jeans. I had told McCandy this would happen and he'd given me £100 expenses. I peeled off two tens and offered them up for sacrifice.

'Thanks, Angel. I thought I was in trouble when they said I had to see you. I usually am, these days. With everybody.'

I watched Justin move away down the bar and thought that for once, Taffy had done exactly what was required of him. I lowered my voice.

'When you do driving jobs for Big Mac, long distance ones, I mean, do you and the others talk about the best routes?'

'What do you mean?' he whispered.

'You know, quickest roads, where the cops have speed traps and weight checks, that sort of thing. I don't want to show myself up, you see. It's a while since I did this sort of work.'

'Oh, right, get you. Sure, I'll help out, you can call on me any time.' He was proud to be asked. 'One thing to watch out for these days, 'specially if you're coming in from one of the ferry ports, is the old Customs men. They reckon anything coming across the Channel is stuffed with cheap beer these days.'

'I thought it was tobacco which mostly came into Harwich,' I said, and watched him squirm.

'Yeah, so they say . . .'

'You know the other drivers Mr M. uses regularly?'

''Course. There's Eddie Aidrian, Big John Jarman, Slasher Carmichael . . .'

'You talk to them about best roads, where to get a good fry-up, stuff like that?'

'Yeah, with them. What else've drivers got to talk about? But on my life, only with the boys in the crew. Never anybody outside.'

'In here?' I asked, keeping one eye open for Justin.

'Usually. We have a drink and play a frame or so on Mondays.'

'OK, Taffy, now take your sub and go and drink somewhere else until Monday. Got it?'

I didn't want to push it too far, but life had leaned too hard on Taffy for him to challenge either my orders or why I was giving them.

'That it, then? That the message?'

'Yes. No, one other thing. What time does this place shut?'

'Midnight. Thinking of making a night of it?'

I looked over to where Sophie stood, her right leg on the edge of the snooker table as she lined up a corner pocket shot on the pink.

'Yes,' I said, concentrating on Sophie. 'But not here.'

# Chapter Nine

'You've got to do what?' Sophie screamed.

'Just pop out for an hour or so, about midnight.'

I had told her as soon as we had got back to my flat with a takeaway Chinese banquet for two. I got the feeling she was less than impressed with the news.

'Christ, but you know how to treat a girl, Angel. Get yourself a minicab, hang about a grotty snooker club, have dinner out of tinfoil but don't hang about because you might miss the last bus home. You been sleeping alone a lot lately? It wouldn't surprise me. You're turning into pond-life, Angel. *Lower* than pond-life.'

'Calm down, Sophie. I've got problems and I needed a favour from you. I admit this hasn't been a very impressive bit of chatting up so far.'

'You can say that again,' she said, hands on hips.

'But we've got three hours before I have to go, so for three hours, you name it.'

She didn't take long thinking about it.

'You got a microwave?'

'Yes,' I said slowly, trying not to show fear.

'Then let's leave that lot for now.'

I followed her gaze to the plastic bags of Chinese food I had put down, one on each of my CD speakers. By the time I looked back, she was kicking her shoes off and moving towards me.

'Don't ask the favour until afterwards,' she warned, raising an admonishing finger as she advanced.

'Until after we've been to bed?' I said stupidly.

'What makes you think you're going to make it to the bed?'


I sat in Armstrong watching the front door of the Centre Pocket, grateful for the indigestion reheated Chinese food produces as it was the only thing helping me to keep my eyes open.

I was waiting for Justin the barman to close the club and then I was going to follow him. It had been McCandy's idea and who

103

was I to say other than that it was a good one? He had convinced himself, with reason, that a delicensed black cab was the best vehicle in which to follow somebody in London. He wanted Justin followed, so I was volunteered.

As I had crept downstairs at Stuart Street, Fenella had whipped open the door of her flat, almost giving me a heart attack.

'Are you all right, Angel?' she had asked urgently.

'Yes,' I said, puzzled. 'I'm fine. Why?'

'It's just we heard all these strange noises . . .'

'Oh, I see. Sorry. I'll explain later.'

Later in the next century.

Apart from Fenella, I had hardly seen a soul or a car on the drive round to the club. I presumed the last players or drinkers had gone as the front lights were turned off on the stroke of midnight. I didn't think Justin would take long polishing the glassware or dusting the green baize tables.

He certainly hadn't planned to, as a minicab turned up at two minutes past twelve, parking outside the front door but leaving the engine running. Almost immediately the lights went off inside, Justin came out, waved at the driver, locked up, climbed in and the minicab, a battered Citroën, pulled away.

McCandy had been dead right about how easy it is to follow someone in London if you are in an anonymous black cab. Only I and a few purists would know that it was highly unlikely that a real black cab would stand for being behind a minicab for long. But then, there were few other purists around at that time of night. And let's face it, minicab drivers never look behind them unless they're reversing.

The Citroën wasn't in a hurry and appeared to know where it was going. That wasn't suspicious, as cabs were often used on a regular basis to take bar staff home. Justin's cab headed straight down through Bethnal Green and into Stepney, eventually doubling back on the Commercial Road and pulling up outside a pub called the Jubilee. It was shut, as most pubs were by now unless you were down the King's Road, but Justin wasn't going for a drink.

He piled out of the cab, shut the door and hit the roof with the flat of his hand and the Citroën drove off. Then he slipped down the side of the pub and out of sight.

I parked on the opposite side of the road just in time to see him being let into the pub through a side door. Somebody said something to him and he stepped out again, silhouetted by the light from the doorway. From inside, a pair of hands passed him a metal beer keg, obviously empty from the way he hefted it one-handed and placed it with half a dozen others stacked against the side wall of the pub. Then he said something to whoever was in the pub, went in and the door closed. Half a minute later, lights came on in two upstairs rooms and a minute after that I heard faint strains of music from a radio.

I gave it fifteen minutes, so I could look McCandy in the eye and say I had earned my consultancy fee. Nothing happened. Justin wasn't going anywhere tonight, even though Thursday was probably pay day. It was for a lot of people on a weekly wage. You could tell that from the number of beggars out on Oxford Street on Thursdays (where secretaries who had just been paid were regarded as the best soft touches).

Let Justin get a good night's sleep. One of us might as well.


The one plus point to the whole escapade was my detour down Brick Lane on the way home to visit an all-night bakery and delicatessen. There I loaded up with a poppy-seed loaf and some croissants. Sophie always did have a healthy appetite in the mornings.

The trouble was the morning came rather sooner than I had expected. At 5.31 a.m. to be precise. I knew because I had been sleeping on my left arm and my watch was about two inches from my eye. What had disturbed my well-earned slumber was a gentle scratching of nails down my spine.

'Not again, Sophie,' I sighed and edged my body away.

The nails stiffened, pinning me to the bed, threatening severe pain and possible blood loss if I moved.

'Oh, sorry, Springsteen. Where is she?'

'She's been making coffee,' said Sophie.

I rolled over – carefully – to see her standing at the foot of the bed looking at us. Springsteen had his head on the pillow and had stretched himself out, as only cats can, long enough to fill her place.

'I wish I had a camera,' she said. 'That cat is not of this planet.'

'None of them are. What's going on? Why are you up this early? Where are your clothes?'

She did the air stewardess safety routine, arms out: 'Here, here, here and . . . somewhere in there. Now put that cat down and get up. I have to go home, get changed and get to work by eight. And you're driving me.'

That's the trouble with owning a taxi, even a delicensed one. Everybody takes advantage.

'Where is it today, then?' I asked, trying to untangle myself from the single sheet that remained on the bed. Springsteen wasn't helping by lying on half of it.

Sophie made a swooping motion with her right arm. A downward movement like a swan dipping its neck, then horizontal, then a swoop upwards. Down, along, then up and out, going through the Channel tunnel. Doing the Chunnel.

It was a very sexy movement the way she did it, but then, she was naked.

'I'll be in Paris for lunch, which is just as well as there's sod all to eat on the train.'

Which reminded me why I had invited her over in the first place. I raised the subject over hot croissants, which we had to eat with thick-cut traditional English marmalade because I had forgotten to get in the more authentic apricot conserve.

'Do you ever do the Brussels run through the Chunnel, Sophe?' I dropped into the crumb-sprayed conversation.

'Uh-huh,' she said, mouth full. 'Doing it on Monday, 'matter of fact. I drew the short straw again.'

'You don't like Brussels?'

'Borrr-ing!' she shouted, as if she hoped the Belgians could hear her. 'They've got good white chocolate, though. And some great beers. Seafood's good over there, too.'

'But apart from that . . .?'

'Apart from that, it's the dark side of the moon, man, dark side of the moon. It's just got no atmosphere.'

'I've got to go over there – flying visit – any chance you could get me a ticket?'

'Get you a dozen as long as there's not a football match on.

They can't give 'em away at the moment. Nobody goes to Brussels in August. When do you want to go?'

'Monday?' I said too quickly, without thinking it through.

'Great. I've got a lay-over. If you know what I mean, sugar plum . . .'

'I can guess. What's it going to cost?'

'A night of passion in downtown Brussels. We must be able to liven up sprout city somehow.'

'No, I meant how much money?'

'Nothing – nada – zilch – zip – *rien*. Whenever the train is late they give out credit vouchers towards the next journey but most people don't bother with them. Most of the first-class punters swear that they'll never use us again and they give us the vouchers. I've got loads of them and I'll just trade a few in and get you a ticket.'

'First class?'

'Of course, including free champagne. Just get to Waterloo and jump aboard. The girls on the check-in desk usually pack up about fifteen minutes before departure so you may not even be asked to show a passport.'

'That's not a problem,' I said. I had two passports and would be happy to show either.

'It's worth remembering, though. I've seen it done many times and there's no baggage check or . . .'

Downstairs the communal phone rang five times before someone answered it. As Mr Goodson would have gone to work by now, it had to be either Lisabeth or Fenella.

'. . . anything. Could be a real smugglers' conduit if you could think of anything worth smuggling out of Brussels.'

'What about the white chocolate?' I began to slice the poppy-seed loaf.

'It's good, but you can buy Belgian chocolate at my local 7–11 now. Belgian beer, too, that stuff with peaches and raspberries in. Absolutely hideous. Vomit city, if you ask me.'

'You mean the *kriek* beers,' I said. 'You're right. You can get them all over London. In fact, you can probably get them just about everywhere except Belgium. I think the Belgians are glad to get rid of it. I've never seen a Belgian drinking one.'

Sophie held up a finger and cocked an ear towards the door. Sure enough, there came the thump-thump of Fenella running up the stairs. It had to be Fenella because Lisabeth wouldn't have taken a message for me and certainly would not have run anywhere.

'The phone,' I said, folding a slice of bread to make a marmalade sandwich to take with me.

'Why haven't you got a mobile? I have. They're cheap enough these days and I get mine from a guy at Waterloo. You can make as many calls as you like and you don't get charged.'

I shook my head.

'Would this be a man who just sort of appears on the station? I mean, it's not like he has an office or anything?'

'So?'

'And the free calls stop after two months – ten weeks? And then he gives you a new phone with a different number?'

'Well, yes. What's your point?'

'You've been cloned, Sophie.'

'What?'

There was a rapid knocking at the door.

'It's a clone phone. Somebody has cloned somebody else's number into your phone. Your calls go on their bills but you get rumbled after two or three months when the quarterly airtime charges come in. That's why you have to give the phone in and get another one, right? You're probably operating on someone else's carphone number.'

'So it's illegal?'

'Sort of. You should get a Fenella instead,' I said, opening the door.

'Your father's on the phone, Angel,' Fenella gasped, hopping from one foot to the other, trying to get a look at Sophie over my shoulder. 'Which one is she?' she whispered.

'Fenella, really!'

'Sorry, that's what Lisabeth asked me to find out.'

'Fenella, this is Sophie; Sophie, Fenella. Back in a tick.'

'Did you just say it was Angel's father on the phone?' I heard Sophie ask her.

'Yes, isn't that funny? I didn't know he had one, either, not until . . .'

I left them to it and took the stairs at a leisurely pace, knowing how much it irritated my father to be kept waiting on the phone.

'Good morning, Father,' I said cheerfully. 'Two contacts in one week. My, my, I'm beginning to feel less dysfunctional already.'

'Sorry for dragging you out of your pit,' he said drily. 'I hear you had a late night.'

'Jealous?' I asked, making a mental note to buy a muzzle for Fenella.

'Not in this lifetime, though that is rapidly slipping away.' I had forgotten that he swapped insults for a living. 'So listen. I've had Godfrey Ineson on the phone this morning. I thought you were sorting things out.'

'Sorting what out? I said I would go and see Mother. You know, jolly woman, likes to think she's an artist, drinks a lot, wears primary colours. Come on, you must remember her.'

'How is she?' he asked wearily. There were some times when even he knew when to give in.

'She's fine. Seems to have a new boyfriend.'

'Who?' A bit quick, there, Dad.

'Nobody you know. Guy called Phil.'

'Phil who?'

'I don't know,' I lied to wind him up. 'Anyway, she's cool and has no idea where Finbar is and isn't going to panic about it. She reckons he's having a holiday.'

'Where?'

'She thinks France, but I think he's in Brussels.'

'You think or you know?'

'I'm pretty sure. He's been in contact with an old mate of his called Bumper.'

'Bumper? What sort of name is that?'

Now *that*, I thought, was pretty rich considering what he'd called his children.

'It's a nickname, to do with his job. Best if you don't ask.'

'You know this chap?'

'Met him once or twice in the past. Do you think I should go over and check it out? I could go Monday.'

'Go today,' he said firmly.

'Can't. Got to do something this weekend. I can get on the Eurostar first thing Monday. I'll need some cash.'

'I was waiting for this. How much?'

'Another five hundred, two-fifty in Belgian francs. What's the exchange rate?'

'About forty-five to the pound. Not good and getting worse.'

Trust him to know that off the top of his head.

'So you can get it over to me, can you? Like, today? Are you going away for the weekend?'

He cleared his throat quietly. That meant he was working out how not to tell a direct lie.

'Yes, I am, actually. I'll get some cash biked round later this afternoon. What's the address?'

Oh no, Dad, not that easily. You tell me yours and I'll tell you mine . . .

'Send it care of the Centre Pocket,' I said, and gave him the address. 'It's a snooker club,' I said before he asked.

'I'll do what I can,' he said, businesslike. 'As long as you sort old Godfrey out.'

'Sort him out how?' In the thrill of the chase after Father's open wallet, I had quite forgotten Godfrey.

'Didn't I say? He rang me at some ungodly hour to tell me that Windy Ridge was broken in to last night. God knows what he expects me to do about it. Go and calm him down, will you?'

'And what am I supposed to do about it? Hang on.' I looked at my watch: 6.35 a.m. 'It's *still* an ungodly hour, or are they working in a different time zone in Suffolk?'

'Look, it's the circle of life. Godfrey disturbs me, I disturb you. You go and calm him down before he does anything stupid.'

He hung up.

It was shaping up to be a busy day.


On the drive over to Sophie's flat in West Hampstead, I gave her a rough outline of why I was going to Brussels, keeping it vague. Elder brother, bit of a twit, gone off on dirty weekend and had such a good time, forgot to come back on time, family business not able to function properly without him.

Sophie seemed to believe most of it except the possibility that someone could have a good time in Belgium.

'Why don't you just ring him?' she asked sensibly enough.

110

'We don't actually know where he's staying, but I know he's been in touch with an old mate who works out there.'

'Whereabouts?'

'Out at Zaventem,' I said, forgetting she'd been an air hostess before her demotion to railway hostess.

'The airport? What's his name? Is he a pilot? I might know him.'

'He's called Bumper and you definitely wouldn't know him. He has, or he had, a real space cadet of a girlfriend lived in a flat near the Grand Place when I met him.'

'Why don't you call her?'

'For a start, I don't think I'd get much sense out of her. I'd rather talk to Bumper. I'll ring him tomorrow. He doesn't work at weekends.'

'What does this Bumper do?'

'He makes a very nice living being bumped.'


Sophie had to shower and change and pack a bag once we got to her flat. I was the perfect gentleman and said no problem, we had plenty of time and once I heard the shower running, I grabbed her phone and started to press buttons.

Godfrey Ineson first, on his mobile, hoping I would catch him at as inconvenient a moment as possible. He answered on the third chirp.

'Hello?' Cautious, like he wasn't used to the equipment.

'Godfrey? It's Fitzroy.'

'I knew you'd call. What time can you get here?'

'Listen, Godfrey, I'm not sure I can do anything useful if . . .'

'Your father said you'd come straight away.' Oh, did he? 'Before I did anything stupid, he said.'

'Godfrey, *have* you done anything stupid?'

What a question. Sophie wasn't going to be in the shower that long.

'No, I haven't called the police, if that's what you mean.'

It hadn't been because I hadn't thought about it, but it was interesting if that's what had worried my father.

'Anyway, I couldn't,' Godfrey went on. 'But I didn't tell your father that bit.'

'What bit?'

'The bit about Barry. He was there.'

'Barry? He's turned up?' Then the penny dropped. 'He was the one who broke into Windy Ridge?'

'No. Yes. Well, he was there. They left him there as a sort of warning. For Finbar. You'd better get here.'

'I think I better had. I'll see you around lunchtime at Windy Ridge.'

'We'll be here,' he said with almost a gulping sound, then he broke the connection.

'Sophie!' I shouted towards the bathroom. 'Get a move on. My meter's running.'

I should have phoned McCandy. I knew I should have and I kept telling myself all the way down to Waterloo. I told myself that it was probably too early still, but then what did I know about the hours worked by the gangster of today? The traffic was building up to its morning crush and that gave me plenty to concentrate on, but then Sophie, doing her make-up, asked if I had ever done it in the back of a cab, and my blood ran cold. So much so, I almost creamed a cyclist messenger. But still I worried because part of our deal – my 'consultancy', as he'd called it – was to report in first thing. The fact that I had nothing dramatic to tell him didn't make me feel any easier.

Sophie was supposed to clock on at nine and we made it by the skin of our teeth. She suggested I come to the Eurostar platform so that she could nip into central control or whatever it was and just check that she could get me a seat on Monday. As I wouldn't see her again until then, this seemed a logical move. Maybe I could phone McCandy from the platform.

She was gone about fifteen minutes, during which I wandered aimlessly around the bookshops and newspaper stands, my eyes repeatedly coming back to the banks of public telephones dotted over the station forecourt. I must have read the warning notice about 'unlicensed taxi cabs operating from this station' five times when Sophie came up the escalator from the Eurostar platforms. She was waving a blue and white envelope which I could see, as she got nearer, carried the gold and white Eurostar logo. The plain company uniform didn't do her justice and the untailored knee-length skirt offered the least view of her legs I had ever seen.

'No problem,' she said as I palmed the ticket into my jacket.

'Thanks, kiddo. I owe you one.' I put my hands on her hips to pull her towards me.

'At least one,' she said. 'Not the lips. They're not dry yet.'

I gave her a brace of chaste kisses on the cheeks.

'So I'll see you Monday.'

'The train is ten twenty-three. If you get here just after ten you'll get straight through. You probably won't even have to show a passport and if you don't look too suspicious, you won't even get security checked. They just watch you on video cameras.'

'Sophie, I'm just going to Brussels, I'm not doing anything suspicious. What makes you think I might be?'

'I know you,' she said, straight-faced.


I gave her a last wave as she sank down the escalator, and made a firm decision to ring McCandy. Get it over with, then the rest of the day would be my own. Just do it. End of. I was already starting to think like him.

I bought a double espresso and a phonecard at a coffee stand and took up residence in a nearby bank of telephones.

McCandy had given me three numbers to call in rotation when checking in: an office, as he called it, his carphone and Domestos's mobile. I don't know why he thought I would want the last one. If I ever needed it, I would probably need the local Samaritans number as well.

I took a gulp of coffee and balanced the polystyrene cup on the phone, ripped the phonecard out of its plastic envelope with my teeth, stuffed it in the slot and pressed the digits for McCandy's office.

I was still spitting shards of plastic when a woman answered to tell me I had rung a garage in Chadwell Heath.

'Mr McCandy, please.' I took a deep breath.

'I'm sorry, Mr McCandy's not in the garage this morning. Who's calling?'

I exhaled with blissful relief.

'Oh dear,' I said, reaching for my coffee. 'Any chance I could leave a message for him?'

''Course you can, Roy,' said McCandy from about six inches behind me.

'Tell you the truth, Domestos there lost you over in Camden,' McCandy said as we walked the platform.

'He was tailing me?' I croaked.

'Yeah, well, I like to keep an eye on new employees. Nothing personal, you understand. But I think you threw him a bit when you were up and out at sparrowfart. Having seen the blonde bit, I know what he meant. Can't blame you there, Roy. Lucky man. Anyway, the big fella phones in saying he lost you. By the way, I'd get that shirt under some cold water soon if I were you. That's a bad stain. Coffee can be a bugger to get out.'

'Thanks. I'm sorry you were disturbed, Mr McCandy.'

'Disturbed? No, I was up and about and I'd told Domestos to ring in any time – same thing I told you, come to think of it. And it was just as well it was early, otherwise your little housemate would have gone to work by the time I phoned.'

Fenella. I had wondered what she was doing being up and dressed at that time of the morning. I had forgotten that she had to go to work. Maybe she had to get up at that time every day. Poor thing. I felt a twinge of sympathy for her, but no forgiveness.

'She told me all about Sophie and what an interesting job she had on the Chunnel train and how she was doing the Paris run today.'

Well, she would have done. I had left them together for nearly three minutes.

'So I thought I'd just pop down here myself,' McCandy said, not looking at me but following the flight path of a pigeon zipping through the station.

'And make sure I didn't do a runner through the tunnel?'

'Something like that.'

We had reached the end of the forecourt near the exit which would take me to Armstrong. I didn't even think about it. I had seen Domestos lurking under the archway twenty yards back.

114

McCandy turned on his heels and we began to walk back towards the ticket office.

'So what did Justin get up to, then?' he prompted.

'Nothing, really, Mr McCandy. I did like you said. I made myself obvious –'

'So did the blonde, I hear,' he said out of the corner of his mouth.

'– and I made it look like Taffy Duck was reporting to me now, and then I followed him when he closed up. But all he did was shut up shop and get a minicab down to the Commercial Road and a pub called the Jubilee.'

'It's one of mine,' he said casually. 'It's got bedrooms to spare so we let them to bar staff. My boy Nigel's idea. He manages all my boozers for me.'

Someone would have to. With his record, McCandy wouldn't get a licence.

'But that's it, Mr McCandy. Nothing else happened, he just went home.'

'Early days, Roy, early days. Just do the same tonight.'

'Er . . . Mr McCandy . . .?'

'Yes, Roy?'

'Are you sure this is going to work? I mean this trying to spook Justin into doing something . . . anything. I mean, it might unsettle him but is it going to scare him into admitting anything? Even if he knows anything.'

'It's a management technique I've practised for many years, Roy. I've always got results sooner or later.'

# Chapter Ten

By the time I had called in at Stuart Street to pick up a clean T-shirt (one of a dozen advertising the California Angels, which everyone thinks make really original birthday presents) and then stopped to put fifty litres of diesel in Armstrong's tank, I was much later leaving London than I had planned. There was also much more holiday traffic on the A12 than I had bargained for, heading both for Harwich and the ferries to the continent, and up into the Norfolk Broads.

It was one o'clock when I spotted a Cessna 150 and a Piper Cherokee circling the flying club at Shelton Green and I had a brief pang of regret that I hadn't kept up my flying hours. The only problem you have up there is getting down. People tend not to worry you at heights over three hundred feet. Not even family.

There were no roadblocks or armed police support units in Earl Shelton, so I assumed old Godfrey had still not reported the break-in. I didn't know if there was still a local constable in the village. There had been when Finbar and I had been kids, but he'd disappeared one day and the adults had muttered darkly about 'mental strain' and 'too much for him'. He'd probably opted for a quiet life as a mercenary in Angola or somewhere.

Windy Ridge was similarly unguarded except for a beat-up old Land Rover parked near the Dutch barn. That, I knew, was Godfrey's. He had been driving it for twenty years to my knowledge and it was second-hand when he bought it.

He came out of the front door as I parked behind his Land Rover. He had a broken shotgun over one arm and was easing out two bright orange cartridges. He hadn't shaved that morning either, another sure sign he was worried about something.

'You took your time,' he greeted me.

'Give me a break, Godfrey. It's been a day and a half already and even with the blunderbuss, you don't scare me.'

That was true. McCandy scared me; Domestos scared me. Sophie terrified me sometimes, but not Godfrey.

'Something's scared the shit out of our Barry, that's for sure. But he's not talking about it. I can't get a word out of him, except no police. That's what your father said, you know.'

So it worried him too.

'OK, what happened? And where's Barry?'

'He's out in the back yard, trying to be sick.'

'That seems reasonable.' I nodded wisely before turning on him. 'What the fuck are you talking about, Godfrey?'

'You'd better come in,' he said, leading the way into Finbar's office.

If there had been a break-in it had been a neat one. The mess of papers in the office was certainly no worse than I had left it. Through the kitchen I could see the back door was open and from the yard came the faint sound of somebody retching.

I pointed a thumb at the sound.

'Barry?'

Godfrey nodded and took a deep breath after leaning the shotgun up against Finbar's desk.

'I wasn't straight with your father, young Fitzroy,' he began.

'That's fine with me, Godfrey. I forgive you.'

'I didn't tell him exactly what happened this morning.'

'You left out the bit about Barry. Fine, I guessed that.' My stomach began to rumble and I hoped he would take it as a hint to get a move on.

'I saw old Ben Whiteley this morning. You remember Ben? He still does the milking for Stoney Brook farm and he lives –'

'Across the road, yeah, I know.'

Old Ben, who made Godfrey look juvenile, had a small cottage near the turn-off to Windy Ridge and was Finbar's nearest neighbour on two legs.

'Ben heard a car about one o'clock this morning, coming up the track here. Thought it might be Finbar, so he looked out. Saw some headlights stop here at the front door then drive off two minutes later. He put it down to joyriders or kids looking for a place for a bit of nooky and was going back to bed when he saw the light in here. Like a torch, he said, waving about. Swears he did.'

'But after the car had gone?'

'That's right.'

'And did he get a good look at the car?'

'No, he couldn't make it out. But the torch thing was *after*, like somebody had been here all the time.'

'Then what happened?'

'Torch went out but no lights came on, Ben went back to bed. Told me about it this morning when I went to help bring the cows in to milking – he can't manage it by himself at his age – and I came straight up here. Found Barry.'

His voice dropped.

'What was Barry doing here?'

He eased his buttocks away from where he had rested them against Finbar's desk and motioned for me to follow him.

In the kitchen, on the table, were a dozen or so lengths of fine wire. Some were curled and would have been circles had they not been cut at one point, some were straight pieces about a foot long. At least four of the longer pieces had been twisted together at the end in a knot which could only have been tied with pliers, not fingers. Almost all the pieces had streaks of blood on them.

I was suddenly glad I hadn't had lunch.

'And that,' said Godfrey, pointing.

On the draining board of the sink was a white, soggy mess. It took me a minute to work out that it was the remains of a bar of white soap; scented white soap, I discovered as I put my nose within range. And the soap had what appeared to be teethmarks in it and had been stuck to three or four pieces of wide insulating tape. Slightly chewed insulating tape.

'They tied him up with wire and gagged him with that,' said Godfrey quietly. 'Bastards. They left him on the floor, trussed up so he couldn't move. Must have been there five hours or more.'

'Why?'

'I don't bloody know why. He hasn't said a word to me since I found him. I had to get wire cutters . . .' He was getting angry, and angry at me, which was understandable. He couldn't get angry with Barry.

'Let me try,' I said.

Barry was sitting on the stump of a tree which had been used as a chopping block for firewood, in the corner of the courtyard. I could smell him from five yards.

He was wearing a filthy white roll-neck, stained on the front

118

and the sleeves with vomit, and black jeans stained with God knew what. He had trainers on his feet. I noticed them because his right hand was massaging his right ankle and when he moved it I could see that his socks were stained with blood. In his left hand he held a bottle of Talisker, one of Finbar's favourite whiskies. I wondered, briefly, where he had found it.

'Long time no see, Barry,' I said, keeping a good yard away from him and trying to work out which way was upwind.

He turned his face to look at me and there was recognition in his eyes, but no interest. There were flecks of dried soap on his chin and a blue-black bruise on his left cheekbone. He raised the half-empty bottle to his lips and I wondered where the top had gone.

'Hey, Barry, I know your old man can be a bit of an old woman, but it's too hot and too early to hit the hard stuff like that,' I tried.

Barry took an extra large swig on the bottle, like a child trying to prove it could get a whole quarter-pounder in its mouth at one go. But he wasn't drinking it. He swilled around his mouth and cheeks in a passable imitation of a chipmunk, then he spat the lot out over a pile of halved logs.

'They'll burn well this winter,' I observed, but he wasn't listening.

His head dropped and he began to retch on to a spot he seemed to have carefully selected between his feet. Then he transferred the bottle to his right hand and began to massage his left ankle.

'Bugger to get rid of, isn't it? The taste of soap, I mean.'

I didn't know, of course, never having eaten any myself, but I had once used the same trick of a soap gag to keep a psychotic Dutch gangster called Gronweghe quiet. Looking at Barry, I could understand why Gronweghe had been severely pissed at me.

Barry stopped retching long enough to look up and say: 'Fuck off.'

'Not the breakthrough I had planned, Barry, but it's a start. That's probably the punchline to a very obscene joke, but I just can't think of it at the moment. I can never think straight when I'm hungry, can you?'

Barry put the bottle to his lips again.

'Would you rather talk to the cops?'

Barry snorted and swallowed the Scotch this time.

'You won't fetch the police,' he mumbled. 'Your lot'll stick together. Your family.'

This was going nowhere. Barry was beaten as well as beaten up. He had been frightened by someone who scared him more than his father. My problem was that he wasn't scared of me. At least not yet.

'Tell you what, I'll get your dad to go and buy us something to eat. How about that?'

Barry retched some more.

'I'll take that for a yes.'

Godfrey had been watching from behind the kitchen door. I had a ten-pound note in my hand by the time I got inside.

'Nip down the pub and bring back some grub, would you?' Then I whispered: 'He's been like this all morning?'

Godfrey nodded sadly.

'He spent two hours trying to wash his mouth under the tap, then he found the whisky.'

'Where was it?' I asked automatically. 'Just out of interest.'

'Under the sink with the washing powder, where it always is.'

Of course. Silly me.

'Try and get some orange juice as well. And take your time. I'll have another go at him.'

'Does he need a doctor?'

'Maybe later,' I said, but Godfrey didn't notice anything.

He thought about going out through the back yard where Barry was, then thought the better of it and headed for the front door.

'Was the door open this morning?' I asked him as he got there.

'Barry had a spare key to the place. Finbar gave it to him ages ago. It was in the lock.'

'Just wondered,' I said.

It made about as much sense as everything else did. I had run my hand over the edge of the kitchen door while talking to Godfrey and had not detected any sign of it being forced. Who-ever had come and gone here in the night had used the front door.

When I heard Godfrey's Land Rover pull away I nipped out to Armstrong, took my jacket off and left it on the driver's seat. From the glove compartment I took a pair of aviator sunglasses and then from the boot, a pair of distressed leather gloves which I had ruined when changing a wheel in a torrential downpour.

I looked around as I put them on. It was a beautiful summer's day. Grasshoppers clicked in the grass, birds swooped against a cloudless blue backdrop and in the distance I could hear the hum of a combine harvester.

I could see Godfrey's Land Rover turning on to the road to the village. Apart from that, not a human soul in sight. Excellent. No witnesses.

Back in Finbar's office, I picked up Godfrey's shotgun and checked just to make sure it was empty. Holding it, hopefully as if it looked like I meant business, I strode out into the back yard.

Barry was where I had left him, head bowed, staring at his trainers over which he had finally managed to be sick. The bottle of Talisker dangled from his right hand. This was going to be nastier than I had thought.

I swung the shotgun like a scythe, holding the butt with both hands. The end of the barrels sent the bottle flying from his grasp but amazingly it didn't break until it hit the wall of the old dairy.

'Wake up, Barry!' I shouted as loud as I could. 'Time to stop feeling sorry for yourself.'

His reaction was to sit bolt upright and when he saw the shotgun barrel coming back at him on its return arc, he threw his arms around his head. I altered my swing and whacked him around the ankles.

He pitched forward off the tree stump and rolled over as he hit the cobbles, so that I had to dance out of the way, until he came to rest in a foetal position. He was still screaming when I used the shotgun to roll him on to his back, though he kept his knees pulled up to his chest.

I held the shotgun like I meant to use it, the barrels no more than two inches from his face. I don't care what anyone says, looking down the barrel of a gun – even if you know it's not loaded, even if it's a toy one painted pink – is an unnerving experience. Anyone who doesn't think that is destined to spend time in a padded police cell wearing a paper suit.

'Start talking, Barry!' I yelled, at the top of my voice. 'Where's Finbar?'

'I don't know,' he sobbed. 'I don't know any fucking thing.'

'Come *on*, Barry. This is my brother we're talking about and I'm worried 'cos he's disappeared. So did you. But now you're back. Who else am I gonna ask?'

'Don't know, don't know . . .'

He clutched his knees and rocked from side to side.

I was glad I had put the sunglasses on so he couldn't see my eyes, because I shut them as I swung at his ankles again.

He didn't scream this time, because the pain was such he couldn't catch his breath. He rolled over again, this time on to his knees and he scuttled around so he was facing me. He gagged and retched but there was nothing left to throw up.

As he blinked at me through his tears, I jabbed the end of the shotgun into his forehead just hard enough to produce a red twin circle imprint.

'What's going on, Barry?' I was screaming now. 'Tell me where Finbar is.'

'I told you, I don't know,' he almost sighed and seemed to shrink. 'They didn't believe me either.'

'Who are *they*, Barry?'

'Fucking Finbar's fucking partners.'

'Partners in what, Barry?'

'In a scam, a fucking scam and he's got me involved and now he's fucked off and his partners are looking for him.'

Keep going, Barry, look on it as therapy.

'What sort of scam?'

'An EEC scam.'

'The Common Market? Scamming the European Commission? How?'

'Set-aside subsidies. Get paid for growing stuff nobody'll buy, so you claim for twice as much as you've planted. You get more if it's an experimental crop which'll probably never bloody grow anyway.'

'And somebody did this to you for the sake of a farming grant? Come on, Barry, everybody takes the Eurocrats to the cleaners when they can, but this is a bit extreme.'

'There's a lot of acres involved. Two hundred.'

'Finbar hasn't got two hundred acres.'

'That was the scam,' we both said in unison.

I took a step away from him to give him space and pointed the shotgun at the ground.

'Finbar couldn't think that one up himself,' I said, eyeing him suspiciously.

Barry shook his head. He was still kneeling as if awaiting execution.

'He didn't, it was one of his so-called partners, a psycho Dutch bloke called Gronweghe.'

'Let's go inside. You need to get cleaned up,' I said.

And I needed to look under the sink to see if there was anything else to drink. Quickly.


I had seen Paul Gronweghe maybe five times in my life and spoken to him only once. That conversation had centred on the whereabouts and ownership of round about a quarter of a million tabs of E and had been conducted in the back of a truck carrying concert gear for a very loud heavy metal band called Astral Reich. It had also been conducted with him tied up and me holding a gun (his gun, actually) on him and that had ended with me gagging him with the bar of soap and the roll of insulating tape.

As it turned out, he really did own the Ecstasy tablets but I had needed them for a noble cause, to rescue an old friend from a rival, and pretty amateur, French gang. In the end the drugs had gone up in smoke and we'd left Gronweghe and his Dutch heavies engaged in a gunfight with the French mob.

I tried desperately to remember if he had ever known my name. I certainly never expected him to send a Christmas card and it had been four years since I had even thought about him.

Astral Reich, incidentally, had done reasonably well for themselves and were shortly to release their fifth album.


Barry had taken (and I had smashed) the only thing really worth drinking under the sink, unless you were into industrial-strength bleach, that is. It was probably just as well. I had plenty more driving to do, Barry to sort out and Godfrey to calm. And then I had to go back to work for Big Mac McCandy. The chances of me slipping in the twelve hours' sleep I needed to recover from Sophie seemed remote.

I told Barry to go upstairs and have a shower in Finbar's bathroom. I didn't say anything about using soap, but I promised to find him something to wear. He was smaller than Finbar but I didn't think he would worry about the Fashion Police today. And no, I didn't think Finbar would mind. As if I gave a tinker's toss about what Finbar thought at the moment.

I heard the shower run and thought about listening to Sophie's shower that morning and wished I could start the day over. Then the water stopped and Barry yelled out: 'Jesus, it's freezing!'

Well, it would be. There had been no one in the house for ten days.

I fished out a pair of towels from the airing cupboard at the top of the stairs and left them at the bathroom door, shouting to Barry that they were there and I was getting him some clothes.

In Finbar's bedroom, I raided a chest of drawers for socks and a pair of clean boxer shorts and then the wardrobe for a denim shirt and a pair of grey trousers. I noticed that Finbar had a pair of white Levi 501s but I thought Barry had suffered enough.

Godfrey returned as Barry was getting dressed. I headed him off in the kitchen.

'What have you done with Barry?' he asked, dumping an armful of French bread sandwiches on the table, then producing a carton of orange juice from the poacher's pocket of his jacket.

'He's getting cleaned up, upstairs,' I said.

Godfrey's eyes flicked to the shotgun which I had abandoned near the sink, not where he had left it.

'Barry's coming round,' I said to distract him. 'I think, though, he might want to tell me some things he wouldn't tell you.'

''Bout Finbar?'

'Yes. Things I need to know.'

He looked down at the table.

'There's cheese, cheese and tomato and cheese and ham,' he

said, picking one out for himself. 'I'll go and put that in the car.'

He indicated towards the shotgun then shouted up the stairs:

'I'm in the car, Barry. I'll take you home when you're ready.'

I heard the stairs creak. I suspected that Barry had been creeping down to hear what was being said.

'OK, Da. Shan't be long.'

Godfrey nodded to himself at that, almost smiled. Then he carried his sandwich and his shotgun outside.

I found two mugs and ripped the corner off the orange juice then tore at the cellophane wrapping on one of the sandwiches. As I poured a mugful of juice for Barry, I told him:

'Get this down you. You can never have too much Vitamin C.'

He took a gulp.

'It still tastes of soap,' he said, unwrapping the last sandwich.

'So does this,' I said, waving mine at him. 'So tell me.'

'Tell you what?'

Oh dear, I hoped he wasn't getting his confidence back.

'How did Finbar get involved in this scam?'

'He met this foreigner at some do put on by the Farmers' Union. He was like a visiting dignitary on a fact-finding mission round the local farms. Last year, this was.'

'Gronweghe posing as a Commission . . .?'

'No, not *him*. This was a guy called de Bondt, Jan de Bondt. He's a Belgian. We called him James de Bond. He was here for a week or so and Finbar showed him round. They cooked it up between them then.'

'What does this de Bondt do?'

If it was anything to do with European cheese regulations, then I had a complaint for him.

'He's something in the agriculture department over in Brussels. I don't know exactly. He told Finbar how to do it – how to pick fields that weren't together, and ones that were backed up to somebody else's with a similar crop, so they couldn't be spotted by the spy in the sky.'

I had heard farmers talk of 'the spy in the sky' before. They were convinced that they were being watched by the European

Commission's personal spy satellite which could identify fields of less than half an acre. I had never been convinced they were that efficient. Everyone knew that Sicily claimed a subsidy for about four times as many dairy cows as could actually fit on the island and that the entire population of Greece grew at least an acre of tobacco, if you believed their applications for grants. But then, you have to be slightly paranoid to be a farmer.

'It was de Bondt who told him what to grow. New varieties of stuff, experimental strains of things, and always claiming for double or treble the amount of land used.'

'And you took a cut?'

'I had to help out at planting. Finbar couldn't do it all himself. But since the last sowing in May, I haven't seen a penny.'

'So how did Gronweghe get involved?'

'He turned up out of the blue about a month ago and I had the bad luck to meet him. He came here to Windy Ridge.' I shuddered at that but Barry didn't notice. 'Finbar said he worked for de Bondt and was making arrangements for the harvest. They were worried about some sort of spot check and getting their stories straight.'

'Like explaining why the acreage planted didn't tally with the crop yield?'

'Yeah, that's it. Anyway, once they started on that, Finbar clams up and gets all nervous, losing his bottle, acting strange. Then he ups and goes – and, honest, I don't know where – and a couple of days later I get this mad Dutch fucker and his bouncers coming round giving me a hard time.'

'Bouncers?'

'Two brothers from Ipswich, Willy and Dave Miller. They're locals; don't know how they are involved.'

'Local muscle,' I said knowledgeably. In London, bodyguard or extortion work like that was called 'temping', as in getting in a temp secretary. Unless he had mellowed, I couldn't think why Gronweghe needed it. 'Did they do this to you?'

'They leaned on me a couple of times last week, wanting to know where Finbar was, what arrangements had been made for the harvest. They were just a bit heavy at first. Then they started saying they would come out here and do things.'

'To Finbar?'

'And me, and Dad, and the farm.'

Hence the message on Finbar's machine.

'How did they get you?'

'They rang me the other night and told me to come and meet them or they would call round and see Dad. I told him I was going out with some mates for a drink. The Miller boys stuck me in a van and took me to this barn somewhere.'

'Where?'

'I don't know. Couldn't see anything going and wasn't in a fit state on the way back. I reckon it was half an hour away. And it was a new barn, a metal prefabricated job.'

'And Gronweghe was there?'

'He turned up in the morning. Told the Millers that his ferry had been delayed or something. He wanted to know where Finbar was hiding.'

'He said that, did he? He said "hiding"?'

Barry's eyes flashed with nerves.

'Yeah, he said that. It was all the fucker did say, all day.'

Barry fumbled at the buttons of Finbar's denim shirt. His ribs and stomach had been worked over with a knuckleduster. If you had ever seen the marks, you would know.

'You should get that seen to,' I said weakly.

'The bollocks I will. They know where I live.'

He had a point.

'In the end, even the Dutch nutter gave up. The Millers wired me up and he told them to dump me at Windy Ridge as a warning to Finbar if he came back. He did the soap thing himself. He'd bought a new bar of soap specially. Bastard.'

I didn't like to say he'd had a good teacher.

'You had a key?'

'Yeah. I told them that. I told them to look for themselves but I think they already had. They knew more than they were letting on. They just drove here and dumped me in the hall, trussed like a battery chicken.'

'They didn't look around, these Millers?'

'No, not interested. And no sooner had they pissed off than the other bloke turned up.'

'What other bloke?'

'The bloke with the torch. I thought it was Finbar at first. Scared the hell out of me.'

'Who was he?'

127

'No idea. I couldn't see a fucking thing with that torch in my eyes. All I saw was his shoes. They were like plimsolls and they had pig shit on them. I could smell it.'

'Barry, what did he do?'

'Nothing, bloody nothing. The sod just stood there shining that bloody torch in my face. Then he pissed off and left me.'

'Didn't he say anything?'

'He just said: "You're not Finbar," and then he was off.'

'And what did you say?'

And that was a really stupid question.

'Nothing. How could I? I had a bar of fucking soap in my mouth!' Barry shouted.

# Chapter Eleven

Back down the A12 to London just in time to get snarled up in the rush hour and taking no comfort from the radio traffic news which told me that the average speed in London was 10.3 miles per hour. That was the good news. Two years ago it was around eight miles an hour, roughly the same speed Sherlock Holmes would have been reaching in a horse-drawn cab.

I headed straight for the Centre Pocket, resisting the temptation to head straight for my bed.

McCandy had told me he would be there between six and seven. I had thought: fine, but why should I be? But I didn't exactly press the point. It was all part of the McCandy psychological offensive against Justin, working on the theory that if I was seen as some sort of new whizz kid in his crew, giving orders to the likes of Taffy Duck, then eventually Justin would blab about it. If he blabbed – or sold – information on McCandy's empire, then McCandy would, somehow, get to hear of it.

All I had to do was play the part of the latest juicy morsel of gossip and then follow him when he knocked off work. It wouldn't even matter if he spotted me; in fact, McCandy might actually count that a plus if it helped to spook him.

Personally I thought it all too elaborate and a waste of (my) time. Why didn't they just take him into a back room and beat the crap out of him?

Despite not reporting in on time that morning, forcing him to come down to Waterloo and terrify me, it turned out that I was McCandy's blue-eyed boy.

'Roy!' he boomed from his seat at the bar as I entered. 'Just the very man I wanted to see.'

I wondered if overacting had ever appeared on his Police National Computer record.

The practising snooker players got the message and parted to let me through like a bus queue dealing with a drunk. Just to make sure Justin did, McCandy snapped his fingers twice and then knocked on the bar with his knuckles.

'A drink for my new associate, Julian. What'll you have, Roy?'

Justin had appeared at the bar behind him but McCandy stared at me, ignoring him.

'It's Justin,' I heard him say, 'not Julian.'

'Yeah, yeah,' McCandy said under his breath.

'I'll take a bottle of Beck's, Mr McCandy.'

The index finger of McCandy's hand moved about an inch, pointing first to the fridge behind the bar and then downwards to the bar counter. Justin waited two seconds, glaring at the back of McCandy's head, then he moved to get my beer. When he put it down, he allowed himself a brief smile, then he moved away to find a paying customer.

'Let's sit over there, Roy. You look knackered.'

McCandy picked up his drink, which looked suspiciously like a mineral water, and we sat at a small round table near one of the unoccupied snooker tables.

'Seriously, Roy, you look shagged out.'

'It's been a long day, Mr McCandy.'

'And it's not over for you, is it?' he asked with a fake smile.

'Don't worry, I'll follow him again tonight, but I don't . . .'

'You don't have to worry about anything, Roy. Just do what I told you. Put yourself about a bit down here and leave the rest to me. Stir the pot enough and the scum will come to the surface. And I'll tell you now, it was a stroke of genius to have that package biked over here this afternoon. That raised a few eyebrows. I'll bet young Julian was itching to take a peek inside.'

'Justin,' I said automatically. 'What package?'

He pulled an oblong brown envelope from the wallet pocket of his jacket. I had forgotten all about it.

'It's some cash, actually, Mr McCandy.'

He handed it to me, watching my face closely but not saying anything.

'Foreign currency. I told you I had to go abroad for a few days next week, didn't I?'

I ripped open the envelope, hoping that my father had done what I had asked for once. He had, but only partly. There was a wodge of colourful paper money in there, but not the extra sterling I had tried to con him for. There was no note.

'See, they're francs – a bit of spending money. I didn't think I'd have time to get to a bank today so I got a mate to get them for me.' He was still watching me, half amused. 'And he sent them round here.'

'You've got some important friends, Roy,' he said quietly.

'What do you mean?'

'Look at the envelope.'

I should have known Father was too mean to buy his own envelopes. The one the money had come in had a Houses of Parliament portcullis logo in the corner and the handwritten instructions to the messenger service: 'To be collected from Central Lobby'.

'Oh, this?' I turned on the innocence. 'I have a mate who works there. In the catering section. He's a barman.'

'Oh, I see,' McCandy said, giving the impression that he did anything but. 'Going away for long?'

'Just a few days. I told you, it's a sort of errand for my dad.'

McCandy nodded wisely.

'I can't argue with that, Roy. If you can't help your family who can you help?'

The poor, the homeless, the huddled masses, the ladies who hang around Shepherd Market late at night, the humpback whale, the last square yard of rain forest . . . I could think of lots of alternatives.

'Still,' McCandy went on, 'that gives us a couple of days to stir things up. Don't forget, the club shuts at one a.m. Fridays and Saturdays.'

'If you say so, Mr M.,' I sighed.

He reached out and patted me on my right knee. I didn't flinch but I was relieved to see the knee was still there when he took his hand away.

'You're showing good attitude, Roy, and that's always a reflection of considerate management. Bad management leads to bad attitude. Do what I've asked and I won't forget it.'

What he didn't say was that if I didn't do what he wanted, he wouldn't forget that, either.

'You're the boss,' I said.

'You don't look convinced, Roy.'

'Oh, nothing surer in my mind on that score. The only thing is, I don't think I'm helping solve your problem.'

'Let me worry about that, Roy. You help me and maybe someday I'll be able to help you.'

'Perhaps you can, Mr McCandy,' I chanced. 'Have you ever come across a couple of brothers called Miller?'

'Anything to do with Mechanic Miller down in Tulse Hill? Does he have a brother?'

'Doubt it. These two are from Ipswich.'

He thought about it, then shook his head.

'No, but that's off my turf. Do they deal in diesel?'

'Not that I know of. Never mind, it was just a thought.'

He patted my knee again.

'Leave it with me, Roy, leave it with me.'

After McCandy had gone – 'some bloody dinner party with the wife' – I hung around the club for twenty minutes or so. Justin and I made eye contact twice but he wasn't doing anything suspicious, or if he was he was good at it or I was too tired to notice.

Back at Stuart Street I had to park some way down from the house because of the number of cars around. Every other house seemed to be having a party or something that night. I wondered where they got their energy. Drugs probably. Then I wondered if they had any to spare.

I opened the front door of number nine as quietly as I could and smothered it closed behind me. Automatically I glanced at the communal wall phone for messages. There was a single sheet of lined paper, folded, with 'Angel' in green ink, drawing-pinned to the wall mount. I took it down and began to creep up the stairs, determined to avoid contact with all known life forms.

I had successfully negotiated my way beyond Lisabeth's door when I started reading it.

'Angel has a daddy and now a mummy too.
    We're looking after your visitor.
                            Love, Fenella.'

132

I almost twisted my ankle doing an about-turn on the stairs.

'Fenella, have you got my mother in there?' I shouted, rapping on the door and skinning my knuckles in the process. When the latch clicked off, I pushed my way in even as she was saying: 'Not exactly, Angel, just a friend . . .'

Sitting on a scatter cushion in the middle of their floor, with Lisabeth perched on a chair within easy reach of the cutlery drawer, was a sheepish-looking Philip Ryder.

'You're sure you won't have a drink?' he asked as the waitress at the Red Lantern hovered politely at the end of our table.

'No, mustn't. Got to keep awake. Make it a pot of green tea.'

'And I'm driving later but after an hour with those two . . . Large gin, small tonic, please.'

He had desperately needed rescuing but my initial reaction had been to let him suffer. After all, I hadn't invited him. But then, why had he invited himself? He said he was in town briefly, called back on business, and had promised my mother he would buy me a drink. I agreed, knowing that it would take an Emergency General Meeting of the Lesbian Avengers to get Lisabeth out on the mean streets of Hackney on a Friday night. And that meant Fenella couldn't go either. Once outside, though, my stomach suggested a race memory that hot food was occasionally a good idea, so I decided to sting him for dinner. The Red Lantern was the newest Chinese restaurant in the area and though the food was four star, it was cheap enough to be unfashionable so we managed to get a table for two easily enough.

When the waitress returned with our drinks I ordered bean curd with chilli beef sauce, Mongolian lamb, crab claws, spicy prawns, chicken in black bean sauce, Singapore noodles and lotus-leaf rice. Then I asked him what he wanted.

'I thought you were ordering for the two of us,' he said, genuinely surprised. 'Can I just share a taste here and there?'

'That depends on how fast you are with chopsticks,' I said, pouring myself a thimble of scalding tea.

'Your neighbours certainly are something,' he opened the sparring.

'Yes, but we're not sure what,' I agreed, digging in to the prawn crackers.

'They seemed very keen to know all about Bethany.'

I must have blanked him.

'Bethany. Your mother,' he prompted.

'Oh yes, of course. Sorry, not with it this evening. What did Thelma and Louise want to know?'

It was his turn to blink twice.

'Thelma and . . . Oh yes. Well, the attractive one – Fenella – kept saying she hadn't even known you had a father until this week and it had come as a surprise to her that you now had a mother. Lisabeth asked if there was some sort of family gathering in the offing, especially when I mentioned you had a brother. She was, shall we say, a bit forward about it, really.'

'Forward? How?'

'She asked if there was a will being read somewhere and then she asked if you'd been cut out of it.'

So she hadn't forgotten that forty quid I'd borrowed.

The waitress started to slide dishes on to our table and I began to shovel food into my bowl without waiting for Ryder to unwrap his chopsticks. I had warned him.

'I hope you told her no such luck,' I said, concentrating on a crab claw. 'Did my mother give you my address?'

'No, just your phone number. She told me to give you a ring. It was Fenella who gave me the address, when I rang this evening.'

Bloody woman. There are several ways of getting an address if all you have is the phone number, but asking Fenella is certainly the quickest.

'So how is Mother?'

'She's fine, but she seems to have something on her mind.' He fumbled a prawn into his bowl. It seemed to be the last one left. 'I hope you don't mind me mentioning this, Roy. Do you?'

'You haven't said anything to upset me yet. Pass the rice, would you? Thanks.'

Ryder licked his lips before speaking, but he wasn't savouring the food.

'Is there something going on with your brother?' he said, and I just stared at him without answering. 'Your mother seems very worried about him.'

'Can't think why,' I said. 'She seemed very cool about him the other night. She reckons he's taken a few days' holiday, that's all, without telling anybody where he is. For Finbar, that's not unusual. Why? What has she been saying?'

'Nothing specific, and it was only after you'd gone the other morning that she started to worry and she rang round all Finbar's friends to see if they had heard from him.'

'She doesn't have a phone, does she?' I said, maybe too quickly.

'I let her use mine. I have a mobile on the boat.'

Bad move, Mother. Never use someone else's mobile if you want to keep things private, they can get a print-out of all the numbers you've called or tried to call, even when you don't get through.

'But no luck?'

'No.'

'I wouldn't worry about it. Finbar's nipped off for a dirty weekend and it's just got out of hand. He's probably shacked up with some horsey blonde from the Pony Club in a small *auberge* in Normandy somewhere. Won't have been out of bed for a week.'

Ryder surveyed what was left on the table and scraped some black bean sauce over the teaspoon of rice in his bowl.

'So you think that's all it is?'

'Uh-huh,' I said, mouth full.

'And you think he's in France?'

'That's what Mother thinks and I believe it. Did she ask you to talk to me about this?'

'No, she just gave me your number when I told her I had to come back to London for the day when the office called. Said I should look you up and buy you a drink – or a meal,' he added quickly.

'So the office can't manage without you, is that it?' I asked, to change the subject.

'Something like that,' he grinned.

'Marine insurance, you said, didn't you?'

'Yes, and a very tricky case about reinsuring a Liberian-registered tanker which has been accused of delivering cannabis to Ireland. Have you any idea of the sort of trade that goes on over there?'

It was thought serious enough to have been raised at the new Europol Drugs Unit and there had been talk in the newspapers of forming some sort of European Union coastguard system. The problem was that Ireland has 2,000 miles of shoreline but less people than there were Irish-Americans in New York, and as most of the resident Irish would sensibly be out of the rain in a pub of a moonlit night, it was dead easy to float bales of the old Mary Jane on to a deserted shore from a passing ship. There had been some spectacular seizures: £10 million worth off Ballyconneely, £20 million worth off Loop Head, £7 million worth south of Skibbereen, another £7 million worth off the Old Head of Kinsale. Even allowing for the Garda exaggerating the value of their seizures, as all police forces do, if they were finding this much, how much was getting through?

'Drug trade – in Ireland?' I said innocently. 'That's a new one on me.'

'It's a big business,' said Ryder. 'Ireland is seen as the gateway in to Europe now that the Customs over here have tightened up. We had a ship last year at Felixstowe where they found ten tons of cannabis in a consignment of Christmas candles.'

'Gives a whole new meaning to singing "I Saw Three Ships Come Sailing In", doesn't it?'

About the same time, over 200 pounds of heroin had been lifted at Sheerness in Kent, packed in the doors of a truck carrying a load of Mars Bars. I decided not to volunteer this, though.

Ryder thought about the Christmas carol joke and laughed, but only politely.

'The east coast used to be the main route in to this country. You know, up where your mother lives. All those estuaries up near Romanhoe.'

'Is that why you go sailing up there?' I asked, wondering where all this was going.

'Only because I've read so many insurance claims from there that I feel I know the waters like the back of my hand. But that trade has dried up. Customs have made it too difficult.'

'I wasn't suggesting you were moonlighting,' I grinned, waving at the waitress for more tea before Ryder had to get his credit card out.

'It's not a sideline I had ever considered. Have you?'

'No way,' I said indignantly. My mother might be sleeping with him but I didn't know him from Adam.

'But there's dope everywhere in London, isn't there? Come to think of it, I've seen people smoking it in Romanhoe. Most people don't regard it as a crime, do they? Though they'd treat hard drugs differently.'

I scoped the table to see if I had missed anything worth eating and tried to sound casually disinterested.

'Maybe it should be decriminalized. I've read somewhere that the medics want to use it to treat multiple sclerosis. It seems a bit daft that doctors can give prescriptions for derivatives of heroin but can't recommend a whiff of weed that you could buy in a pub in Holland quite legally.'

'Fair point, Roy.' He called for the bill, then lowered his voice. 'Would you be shocked to hear that your mother smoked dope?'

Was that it?'

'No, to be honest, I wouldn't be surprised. She's from Generation X-minus-one. It's her age. These days you'll find the mums and dads more into dope than their kids.'

Of course they were, the kids were into Ecstasy or the new (legal) cocktails of herbal stimulants, or injecting temazepam 'jellies'.

'So you don't see it as a problem?'

'No, I don't. I take the Church of England line on soft drugs.'

'What's that?' He was reaching for his wallet.

'I don't know if it's policy or not, but there was this vicar in – oh, I don't know, the Home Counties somewhere. One of his flock had written in to the parish magazine convinced that the next-door neighbours were growing something odd in their garden and what should they do about it. The vicar writes back with his advice, telling them to pick some that night, roll it and smoke it. If they were still worried the next day, it wasn't cannabis.'

He laughed and only stopped when he saw the bill was written in Chinese script.

'Service is extra,' I lied. 'I would add on fifteen per cent if I were you.'

As we were leaving, the waitress winked at me. She'd see me all right on my next visit.

Ryder had parked a hired Ford Escort on Stuart Street. I asked if he was driving back to Romanhoe and he said he was.

'Give my love to Mother, won't you?'

He turned at that, his hand on the door handle of the car.

'About that, Roy, are you happy with the situation? I mean, me and her.'

'Are you picking out fabric samples together?'

'No.'

'Are you worried about me having to call you daddy?'

'No, no,' he spluttered. 'Nothing like that.'

'Then have a nice life.'

'You too.'

I will, I thought to myself, just as soon as people left me alone to get on with it.

I watched Ryder's car disappear before going back into number nine, reflecting that the Chinese blow-out may not have been such a good idea. It had just made me more sleepy.

Too tired to try and work out what Ryder was really after. It certainly had not been my blessing on his new role as my mother's toy boy. And I couldn't believe that a man of his age would be remotely shocked by someone white, middle-aged and middle-class smoking dope. Where had he been for the last two decades? What sort of a sad life had he had?

To hell with him. Finder of brothers I might be, adviser to gangsters I might have to be, but agony aunt I was not.

I put cat food down for Springsteen and he materialized in the kitchen as if he'd just beamed down. He sniffed the air several times as if looking for Sophie. He had taken to her immediately. I knew that because Sophie had treated him with total indifference and he had not once attempted to flay her. He definitely preferred strong and domineering women who treated him tough. He was a weird and sick animal.

I allowed myself twenty minutes under the shower and then made a pot of coffee, which I drank black with enough brown sugar to chew on in a vain attempt to get some form of energy rush, as the bathroom cupboard was bare when it came to benzedrine.

By half past midnight, I was parked opposite the Centre Pocket, waiting for something – anything – to happen.

I made myself as uncomfortable as possible, which was not difficult in the front of Armstrong, so that I could stay awake. The punters were actually starting to leave as I got into position, but a hard core stayed on until the bar closed and they were shown the door at around one fifteen a.m.

Another ten minutes or so and the Citroën minicab turned up again, obviously a regular booking. And five minutes after that, Justin opened the door.

He didn't go to the cab, though, he wedged the door open and stepped back inside. I sat up and tried to take an interest.

But all he was doing was carrying empty beer kegs out on to the pavement. He stacked six in three piles of two and then closed and locked the door, nodding to the minicab driver, who started his engine and I took the opportunity to crank up Armstrong.

Justin climbed in the back of the Citroën and the cab pulled away, with me following on sidelights about a hundred yards behind.

I need not have worried about being spotted; in fact, I could have overtaken and got there ahead of them because it quickly became obvious that they were following exactly the same route as the night before.

Outside the Jubilee pub the cab pulled up and Justin got out, said good night and went down the alley at the side. The cab drove off and a light came on in the downstairs bar. The front door of the pub opened and Justin humped two more empty kegs out on to the pavement, where a half-dozen or more were already stacked.

Then I heard the bolts on the door go home and the downstairs light went off and an upstairs light came on.

The chances of him doing anything other than getting a well-earned, warm, comfortable, soothing, full night's sleep, were remote, but I thought it better to stick to my arrangement with Big Mac, just in case he was watching me watching Justin. I would hang about for twenty minutes to see if Justin decided to walk in his sleep.

Twenty minutes, absolute tops. Maybe fifteen, that should be enough.


The next thing I knew, I had been shot in the neck.

I knew I had. I heard the crack of the shot and there was an excruciating pain in my neck and I couldn't move. My spine was gone. I was paralysed.

But I could use my hands and I began to feel frantically for the wound in my neck. And my eyes seemed to be OK because they were picking up bright light and sending an explanation to my brain: it was morning and I had fallen asleep in Armstrong.

I was stiff and sore and went through agony trying to get my neck to turn so I could see my watch. It was six twenty-five a.m. and I had been asleep in an unlocked vehicle outside a pub on the Commercial Road for over four hours without being either mugged or arrested. So much for the local Neighbourhood Watch. I bet they hadn't heard the shot either.

Because, of course, it hadn't been a shot. There was a white Ford box van parked outside the Jubilee and two draymen were loading empty beer kegs from the pavement. As they slung them in the back of the van, the metal kegs clashed together and anyone starved of proper sleep and with a lot on his mind could easily mistake the sound for a gunshot.

I examined the stubble on my chin in the mirror and the fur lining to my tongue. I hadn't felt this bad without alcohol for a long time. Still, I said to myself, it could have been worse. I could have been in one of those select areas of London where the brewery drays come drawn by pairs of shire horses. I could have been woken up by a huge horsey snout snuffling in through the window and that was the stuff of nightmares.

And then I was wide awake.

Breweries didn't deliver beer to pubs on Saturdays, or come round to collect the empties.

# Chapter Twelve

I followed the box van to another pub down towards the old docklands in Shadwell. Then another off the West India Dock Road going into Poplar; then two within sight of Canning Town Station; then one in East Ham.

At each one, the van stopped and the driver and his mate got out and loaded empty kegs from the pavement outside into the back. In most cases, it was six or seven kegs, but at one of the pubs in Canning Town, at least thirty. This gave me enough time to prise myself out of Armstrong and nip into a newsagent's where I bought three cartons of orange juice and some chocolate to keep me going, and a copy of the *Daily Mirror* in case I needed a newspaper to hide behind.

Not that the two 'draymen' had given Armstrong a second glance, even though black cabs in this area at that time on a Saturday were pretty rare creatures.

I was able to get a good view inside the back of the van at virtually every stop. It was stacked floor to roof with aluminium beer kegs. Well, it would be. That's what they were loading, so why shouldn't they leave the sliding curtain door up? They had nothing to hide and in fact were probably doing a public service by clearing the pavements outside all those pubs. Otherwise they would clutter up the highways and byways until the local council got round to picking them up.

By the time they got to the pub in East Ham, the back of the van was full to the point of bending the sides. It headed towards Barking and then turned left as if going north to Ilford, but quickly turned left again down a residential street on the edge of Little Ilford. (There are people in Ilford who don't know there *is* a Little Ilford.)

I was getting worried now as it was still not eight o'clock and there was virtually no other traffic about. The van driver must surely look in his mirror sometime and wonder what a taxi was doing cruising this area. And then things got worse when the street of houses gave way to an unmarked road, the sort which

141

led you on to an industrial estate. I guessed it had to be something like that as there was a river – the Roding – somewhere around here and so any road would be a dead end.

An industrial estate was exactly what it was, or rather, had been. On the left-hand side of the road was a ten-foot-high fence of wooden planking, with about every eighth plank missing, and it was a close call whether there was more paint on the fence in the form of graffiti or on the signs every few feet saying 'Industrial Units To Let'.

I had allowed the box van to get well ahead of me, out of sight, in fact, as I was sure the road would be a cul-de-sac.

I was proved right. The end was a barbed-wire fence overgrown with vegetation; and the van had disappeared.

I did a rapid turn, just like a real cabbie who had spotted a tourist, and pulled up to the fence, now on my right, and killed the engine.

I scrambled out of Armstrong and climbed on to his bonnet, leaning forward and grasping the top of the fence with both hands. It swayed unnervingly but was secure enough. Peering over, I could see the box van about two hundred feet away, bouncing over rough ground towards a collection of semi-derelict brick buildings. It disappeared out of my line of vision behind one of them and then its engine cut out.

'How the fuck did they get in there?' I said aloud, but Armstrong wasn't in a mood to help.

I jumped down, wincing at the shock in my stiff legs, and started him up again, driving slowly, cruising the fence. When I got to what I estimated was the spot they must have gone through, I left his engine running and climbed out on to the bonnet again.

Looking over the fence I could see the tyre tracks of the van starting from the inside of the next panel. I jumped down and felt along the panel with the palms of my hands. Near the left fence post, the panel gave easily for about four inches, just enough to put a hand in and undo the iron hook which held it fast from the inside.

I had no intention of going in, so I pulled the panel back to its original position and then stood away to look at the graffiti so that I would remember the right panel.

Among the spray-painted haikus eulogizing West Ham Football Club, the obligatory stencil painting advertising *Socialist Worker* and numerous signatures of graffiti artists who had nothing else to communicate, was a simple message in blue paint saying 'Reality sucks'.

I liked that and I said it aloud to myself to make sure I would remember it: 'Reality sucks.'

'Bloody hooligan!' yelled an old man walking his dog on the other side of the road, almost scaring me to death.

I jumped into Armstrong and floored the accelerator.

In my mirror, I saw him waving his walking stick at me and cursing. It wasn't the first time that had happened and it probably wouldn't be the last.


'You're looking a damn sight more chipper than you did yesterday,' McCandy said when I met him that evening.

So I should. I'd had nine hours' sleep and only made the meet because I had the foresight to set my alarm clock. When I had rung him on my return to Stuart Street that morning, I'd had problems stopping myself yawning.

'And you said you had some news for me,' he prompted, leaning back in the leather seat of his Mercedes.

Meeting in his car outside the Centre Pocket rather than inside had been my idea as I was far from sure how well he would control his temper.

I had also not counted on Domestos being in the driving seat, but he was hardly likely to leave on my say-so. I only hoped that McCandy's advanced theories of business management didn't include shooting the messenger when the news was bad.

I told it like it had happened. How I had picked up Justin and followed him home to the Jubilee and how I had noticed him putting the empty kegs out on the street. Naturally, I had clocked this as being suspicious, given that it was a Saturday, and so I had selflessly, above and way beyond the call of duty, spent the night staking out the pub. My perseverance had paid off and a blend of expert driving and natural cunning had enabled me to follow the box van – the box van full of Mr McCandy's beer kegs – out to Little Ilford.

So I put it on with a trowel, but I didn't care. This was the

143

equivalent of my retirement party speech on leaving the McCandy crew and I was going to enjoy it.

Not surprisingly, McCandy didn't appear overamused. In fact, he seemed more puzzled than anything.

'Did you get the number of the van?' was his first question.

'Er . . . not exactly. I think it was E7 something, something, G something P.'

'That's interesting,' he said, but I couldn't judge whether he was being sarcastic or not. 'But it doesn't get us much further.'

'I'm sorry.' I said. 'I thought you'd be pleased.'

'What for? To be told some little toe-rag is nicking empty beer barrels from me?' He snorted a laugh. 'It's not as if I even own them. I buy the beer inside them. Once they're empty I couldn't give a shit what happens to them. Who loves a beer barrel when it's empty, eh?'

He thumped Domestos playfully on the shoulder at this and Domestos laughed politely.

'Er . . . Mr McCandy, I don't think you understand,' I said nervously.

'Understand what? What is there to understand?'

He fixed me with a glare and I had a pretty good idea of what a seal felt like when it saw the fin of a Great White between it and the shore.

'Your beer kegs. They can be smelted down for the scrap aluminium. I don't know what the price is per ton these days, but it's fairly easy to do and there must be a good profit in it if your raw materials don't cost anything.'

'Yeah, yeah, I know that racket, it's been around for twenty years. You could get up to twelve hundred notes a ton at one time, but scrap aluminium is about seven hundred now. Still, I take your point, Roy, somebody is on a nice little earner at my expense and I don't like that.'

I took a deep breath.

'There's another aspect to that, Mr McCandy.'

'What?'

'To smelt down the kegs, you need an oven or a furnace.'

'So?' He looked vague, genuinely puzzled.

'What sort of fuel does a furnace need?'

It took about three seconds for it to click into place.

'Diesel,' he said. 'The *little fuckers.*'

I watched McCandy in the wing mirror of the Merc as he paced up and down the street, coming close to the car as if to get back in, then turning on his heel and walking off again. He kept his hands in his trouser pockets and his head down, as if searching the pavement for a dropped coin.

'He does this when he has a nasty decision to make,' Domestos said, unprompted.

'And then what does he do?' I asked from the back of the car.

Domestos didn't answer.

After about twenty minutes of pacing, McCandy rejoined us.

'One last little job, Roy. You take me to see this smelter tomorrow morning and I reckon you'll have earned your pay.' He didn't look at me as he spoke, he stared at the door of the club.

'But . . . er . . . I have to . . .'

McCandy tapped the headrest of the front passenger seat and clicked his fingers. Domestos held up a brown envelope and waved it at me. Gingerly, I took it from him and I didn't have to open it to know what it contained.

'About ten o'clock should be right,' McCandy went on. 'Meet me at the Jubilee.'

'Er . . . right for what?'

'To catch them at it. They'll be smelting about that time.'

'We'll need different wheels. Arms – My cab would be out of place and this thing might be recognized.'

'Good thinking, Roy. You're worth your consultancy fee. I'll pick something up off the lot in the morning. You look worried, Roy. What's the matter?'

I gripped my envelope tighter to give me courage.

'You're just going to have a look, Mr McCandy? You're not planning on doing anything else, are you?'

'Just a look, Roy, just a look. Survey the scene so I can assess the overall situation and then make a considered decision. That's sound management technique. This is a problem which could produce a number of different solution scenarios. They all have to be considered carefully, with all the pros and cons weighed up. A hasty decision, based on the hunch not the head, is usually a bad one.'

I was impressed. I wasn't sure I was any wiser, but I was impressed.

'OK, Mr McCandy, whatever you say.' Then I decided to push my luck. 'But how do you know they'll be smelting tomorrow?'

'Just a hunch,' he said, straight-faced.


McCandy picked me up in a small, dirty white Vauxhall van and he drove over to Little Ilford, not talking much except when he had to ask directions.

On the dead-end road down the side of the old industrial estate, I pointed out the fence panel which acted as an unofficial back door and he stopped the van so I could get out and then pulled it up as close to the fence as he could. I climbed on to the bonnet and then the roof and McCandy followed suit, the roof of the van bending and flexing under our combined weight.

I was looking to make sure the van roof would hold us but McCandy must have thought I was checking his fashion sense. He was wearing badly scuffed brown suede shoes and balding cord trousers and a pullover which was frayed at the cuffs and going at the elbows.

'Sunday is gardening,' he said. 'The wife thinks I'm down the garden centre buying compost.'

'Oh,' was all I could think of to say. The idea of a domestic McCandy was far too much for me to get my head round any morning.

'Over there, to the left,' I said, grabbing hold of the top of the fence.

I unzipped my jacket and took out the small pair of binoculars I had slung around my neck. They were no bigger than opera glasses, but twenty times more powerful. I had once taken them from someone who had been annoying a friend of mine. He was a birdwatcher, but not in the conventional sense.

They had built their smelter oven inside a disused single-storey brick building with a sliding metal door at the rear. You probably couldn't see anything at all from the front, and from the back you could only see something if you were three hundred yards away standing on a van and peeping over a ten-foot fence. Even then, a chance passer-by would be unlikely to turn a hair as, after all, what was there to steal? And even if a civilian noticed what was actually going on, eight out of ten would not realize it was a crime and the other two would probably think it was an initiative by the local council to clean up the environment.

'Try these,' I said, offering the glasses to McCandy. 'Look at the chimney.'

You don't actually need much hardware for a smeltdown set-up. A basic oven can be just a firebox with a couple of gas pokers or heating elements from a central-heating boiler. The one thing you do need, though, and the one thing which usually gives them away, is a chimney. They had taken a bit of trouble with this one, keeping its height down to ten or twelve feet of wide-bore metal tube, with a cowl on top and – nice touch – two small fans, probably battery powered, to disperse the smoke further.

'That the van you saw collecting?' McCandy said. He had my binoculars clamped to his eyes but they had disappeared inside his hands.

The box van was parked side on to the metal doors.

'Looks like it.'

'Yeah, it would be,' he said, but didn't explain. Then he handed the glasses back. 'Have you clocked the tank at the side?'

I aimed the binoculars to where he was pointing. There was a large black oil tank on a brick plinth to the side of the building with pipes running both into the building and, from the back of the tank, into a concrete block on the ground.

'That's just a feeder tank,' said McCandy. 'It couldn't hold a tanker's worth of diesel. They're using an underground tank from the place next door.'

I swung the glasses to the right, but there was only a pile of building rubble.

'It used to be a garage,' McCandy said. 'I checked out the old planning applications last night. It closed down three years ago.'

Planning applications from over three years ago, checked out on a Saturday night? I was impressed at his contacts. Most people had trouble checking out current ones that were putting a super highway through their back gardens, even during office hours.

'We've got to get closer,' he said, levering himself on to the unsteady fence. Just before he swung his legs over the other side, he looked at me. 'Come on, son. I may be getting too old for this but you've got no excuses.'

Oh yes, I had, but none he would listen to.

I dropped down on to the rough ground next to him and we set off in a flanking jog to the right of the smelter, putting the demolished shell of the next-door garage between us and the smelter. Before we got there, though, we halted behind the wreck of a burned-out caravan and McCandy held out an arm to prevent me rushing on ahead. As if I would.

There was nothing wrong with his hearing. We were still two hundred feet from the smelter and he had heard the first squeak of the metal doors sliding open.

I ducked behind the wheelarch of the caravan while McCandy flattened himself against what was left of the end frame and the towing bar. From the smelter, across the piles of rubble and the thigh-high weeds, you would need infrared to pick us out against the jagged outlines of the caravan. Or a hunting dog.

They had a dog.

It came out first, followed by a young guy I didn't recognize, wiping his hands on some oily rag.

'Go on, get out of it,' he said superfluously, as the dog had already taken off, nose to the ground, bounding along in a series of widening circles.

'Shit,' I said helpfully, looking back over the open ground to the fence.

The guy who had let the dog out was busy opening the back of the box van, ignoring the dog which by now was picking its way over the rubble of the old garage.

'Let's get out of here,' I hissed, but McCandy didn't move, just held out his arm again. Then he flapped his hand twice in a 'stay down' signal.

The dog was sniffing at a pile of bricks. It couldn't be our scent as we hadn't been there. Were we upwind or downwind? There wasn't any wind. Did dogs have good eyesight?

This one did. Mind you, a myopic mole could have spotted us

now that McCandy had stood up and put himself in plain view.

The dog was a big, sleek, brown Doberman and it was coming for us at Mach 2, ears back. I looked around frantically for a weapon among the bricks and bits of wood, but I couldn't decide on anything likely to stop, or even distract, the dog. And all McCandy was doing was standing there, arms at his side. I did the sensible thing and edged away to give him more room to get on with it.

The dog was ten feet from him when he went into a crouch and slapped the front of his thighs with both hands.

'Here, Sheba, that's a good girl,' he said quietly.

The dog skidded to a halt and rolled over, exposing her stomach and extending her tongue to wrap around Big Mac's hand.

McCandy rubbed the dog's face, then her chest and stomach. I stood up and stretched my legs, which had stiffened with fear. The Doberman put her head around McCandy's ankles and looked at me, upside down.

'How long have you had this strange power over dogs?' I asked.

'Ever since she was a puppy and we bought her for my son Nigel,' he said, without looking up.


'Sheba – stay.'

The bitch stayed, and we moved closer to the smelt, climbing over the rubble of the garage.

They had left the metal door half open and we could see right inside. There were five men in there, all youngish and all either stripped to the waist or in T-shirts and shorts. One had what looked like a homemade wrench which undid the pressurized seal on top of the kegs. That way the steel spear, which fed carbon dioxide into the beer, could be removed. It had to be unsealed in that way or the keg would have blown up once they slung it in the furnace. One of them had the job of collecting the seals and spears and lopping off the steel tubes with a power saw. I'd heard that many a smelt had been discovered when hundreds of steel tubes were found on rubbish tips or dumped in the local canal. They hadn't found a way of making money out of them. Yet.

We could see the furnace itself, nothing more than a crude, three-sided oven made of fire bricks. Two of the lads, wearing gauntlets, took it in turns to roll a keg up some sort of ramp and push it into a curtain of flame. Each time, it was as if a giant invisible hand was crushing them. One minute they were there, shaped and framed against the flames; the next, they had folded in on themselves, turning to liquid metal which ran down a brick channel at the side of the oven.

The liquid ran into moulds which were themselves made of beer kegs cut in half lengthwise. Two of the smelters were on mould duty, pulling them away from the oven to cool, then turning over the set ones and tapping out the blocks of resolidified aluminium. Each block looked like a plastercast of half a beer keg. It seemed to me to be a bit of a giveaway as to where the scrap had come from, but that was their business and they seemed to know it well enough.

One of the smelters strolled out of the door carrying a bottle of Perrier water and a plastic dish. McCandy ducked down behind the bricks and I did likewise.

'Sheba!'

McCandy turned and signalled the dog, which had remained sitting on its haunches by the caravan. He made a circle with his forefinger and then a dismissive wave. The dog took off to its right, running in a semi-circle back to the smelt, giving us a wide berth. I was glad McCandy had been strict with her when she was a puppy.

'Come on, girl, drinkies,' came the voice.

'Nigel?' I whispered.

McCandy nodded and raised his head to look. When he kept it there, I did the same.

Nigel was pouring Perrier into the plastic bowl and Sheba was lapping it up. He drank what was left in the bottle himself and turned back inside. He said something we couldn't hear to one of the others coming out holding an ingot of smelted aluminium to his chest.

'Julian,' said McCandy.

'Justin,' I said automatically.

Justin loaded the ingot into the box van and stayed in the back as another guy came out carrying a second ingot to hand to him.

'That's Terry,' said McCandy, 'and the other two are Gary and Mark.'

'Friends of Nigel?'

'Yes, all mates of his from university, all working in my pubs.'

'Which Nigel runs for you.'

'Most of 'em. I thought it was a nice gesture on his part, you know, giving a bit of work to his mates when he came into the family business. They all play football Sunday mornings.'

'That's how you knew there would be a smelt on this morning, wasn't it?'

'A fair guess. The van's mine as well. I knew as soon as you told me about it.'

I could almost feel sorry for him. His son and his employees using his van to rip off beer kegs from his pubs, and using his diesel to fire the ovens.

'Come on,' he said, 'let's get out of here. I've seen enough and they'll be going once they've loaded up the scrap.'

'Do you want to follow them? See where they're selling the stuff?' I don't know what possessed me to offer that. As far as I was concerned, my consultancy was terminated. End of.

McCandy stayed in a crouch until we reached the wreck of the caravan, then he straightened and patted brick dust from his trousers.

'No need to follow them, Roy. They'll be going down to Griffin Scrap Dealers in Plumstead and they'll get paid in cash.'

'Would that be one of your . . . er . . . businesses, Mr McCandy?'

I stood back, just in case.

'Yep,' he said grimly. 'You got it in one.'


He was silent, driving on autopilot, all the way back to Hackney until we neared the Centre Pocket. Then he cleared his throat with a growl and I thought I was going to get another lecture on business management strategies, or alternatively the Riot Act according to Big Mac.

'About them Miller boys,' he said, surprising me. 'The ones you asked me to check out.'

For a moment I thought he had said 'take out', but I tried not to appear too startled.

'You shouldn't have gone to –'

'No trouble, not much to tell, really. They're a couple of lowlifes from bumpkin land.'

I presumed bumpkin land was anywhere north of Tottenham or south of Catford where there were trees.

'They're trying to establish a crew of their own up in Ipswich based around stuff coming in from the continent. Booze, fags, rolling tobacco, perfume. A fair bit ends up down here but there's no London end to their operation as yet. If they've any sense they'll look at their marketing carefully before trying to set up a distribution network.'

Before they infringe on McCandy turf, that is.

'Any drugs?'

'Not that I've heard, but it would seem to be a likely way to grow their business.'

'You don't have any . . . er . . . business interface with them yourself?' I asked, hoping it didn't sound as if I was being chopsy.

'Oh no, Roy, the Millers aren't in my league. And they never will be. It's not in my long-term plan to deal with the likes of them. That would be very negative, downward trading for me. Are they giving you grief?'

'Not yet,' I said carefully.

'Well, I can always send Domestos to give them a slap if they do.'

'Thanks, Mr McCandy.'

Now there was a man you could do business with.

# Chapter Thirteen

'We're not actually supposed to serve drinks so early,' said Sophie, leaning over me in her Eurostar uniform. 'Normally we wait until the train has actually started.'

'I won't tell if you won't,' I whispered.

I opened my first-class complimentary copy of the *Daily Telegraph* so that it covered my first-class free quarter-bottle of champagne (and plastic cup), then leaned back in my first-class seat and rested my head on the first-class headrest.

'I think I'm going to enjoy this,' I hissed out of the corner of my mouth as Sophie began to move to the only other passenger in the compartment; a business suit who was already opening his laptop computer.

'Me too,' Sophie hissed back.

I had left Armstrong back at Stuart Street, commuting to Waterloo by bus and then tube, on the fast City Line from the Bank, clutching a Nike sports bag of clean clothes and a copy of Norman Mailer's *Oswald's Tale*. Even as a paperback, the book would have counted as excess baggage on an aeroplane but it could always come in handy as a weapon. With Sophie around, I suspected I would have little time for reading.

I had followed Sophie's advice and waited until fifteen minutes before departure time before hurrying through the entrance hall. No one asked to see a passport or even a ticket and no one asked to see inside my bag or tried to x-ray it. I just followed the signs for the Brussels train, found the right platform and walked until I found Coach 12 where my ticket told me I had a window seat, and Sophie was waiting on board to greet me. It was that easy and I was really disappointed I had not brought anything to smuggle.

The train was still creeping through the south London suburbs when Sophie served me breakfast – an individual brioche with a biscuit and a cup of coffee – and managed to slip me another 25-cl bottle of champagne as well.

'You'd better eat,' she said, standing over me and still

managing to ooze sensuality despite the drab uniform. 'It's all you get unless you want to go to the buffet and pay. We serve free drinks from eleven o'clock but there's no lunch and you need to keep your strength up.'

'For tonight?' I leered.

'Maybe sooner than you think,' she said with a worryingly sweet smile.

She served the other passenger and then, as she went by on her way back to the steward's cabin, she leaned over me and pretended to rearrange my cup and plate.

'I've told the Chief Steward you've said you're a claustrophobic so you might need your hand held.'

'What?'

'In the tunnel, dork-brain. Once we start going through, give me a call. The others will be too busy with the sweepstake.'

'Others? Sweepstake?'

'They have a sweepstake on the driver. See how long it takes him to get up to three hundred kilometres per hour to the nearest minute after going down the drain. Sorry, through the tunnel. We're not supposed to say down the drain. It's bad for passenger confidence.'

I was now totally bemused and wishing the champagne came in larger bottles.

'What's going on? Why should I call you?'

'You've heard of the six-mile-high club?'

'Yeah, sure.'

The great folk myth of the travelling business classes; having sex in an aeroplane at over 32,000 feet, thereby qualifying for some sort of exclusive club. Like all good myths, it had more than a grain of truth in it, but the club couldn't be that exclusive if it had me as a member.

Sophie smiled again.

'Fancy joining the one-mile-down club?'


Perhaps it was the phallic imagery of the train shooting into that long dark tunnel under the Channel which turned her on. Perhaps she had a side bet with one of the other stewardesses.

The driver (pilot?) had announced over the tannoy that we were leaving Kent and going underground for twenty-five minutes and that we might at last reach our maximum speed. He didn't actually say how deep we would be going, or how many billion tons of water there were over our heads.

The tinny echoes of his voice had barely died away when Sophie appeared at my table.

'Come on,' she ordered, 'and try and look pale and wan.'

'Try and look what?'

'Look as if you're going to throw up. Now come on, and leave your jacket.'

'But it's got all my money . . .'

'Leave it. There isn't room.'

'Room where?'

'In the toilet. It'll be a squeeze as it is. Come on, you're supposed to be travel sick and I'm supposed to be helping you to the loo.'

There are times, I decided, when it is far less complicated just to stand up and think of England. I shrugged out of my leather jacket and Sophie took me by the arm.

'This way, sir. You'll feel better in a minute,' she said for the benefit of the other passenger who was staring out of the window hypnotized by the blackness rushing by.

'Much better,' she said softly in my ear.

'I know your sort,' I whispered back. 'A couple of freebie nips of the old bubbly and you think you can have your way with me.'

'Hey, Angel, I'm offering to float your boat for you deep below the English Channel and going at about a hundred and fifty miles an hour. Not a bad offer, thinks I, considering you didn't even pay for your ticket.'

'Fair enough,' I conceded. There's no such thing as a free Chunnel express any more. Hey, whoa!'

We were almost at the end of the compartment and just beyond the luggage racks was a glass door into a second-class compartment. A *full* second-class compartment.

'You didn't say anything about an audience,' I snapped at her.

'Shut up. In here and make it look as if I'm helping you.'

I had walked by the toilet without noticing it. Unlike domestic trains, the Eurostar loos – maybe they were Euroloos – had sliding doors.

They also had a lot of mirrors and possibly many other space-age features but I didn't get time to check them out as Sophie was pulling me inside, close up against her.

'Let's rock and roll, lover,' she breathed, kissing me so hard that I banged my head on the door. 'Lean forward.'

'Your wish is . . .'

'So I can close the door,' she hissed.

Her hands moved behind my back and I saw the door close and heard the lock click.

'Now, let's get busy,' she said, her hands moving to the belt of my jeans.

We were squashed so close together that we would have had sex whether we had wanted it or not. Just to make sure there was no doubt on that score, Sophie had already removed her underwear, as I discovered when I hitched her skirt up her thighs.

We kissed and then she licked and bit, we fumbled frantically. The train hammered along.

'Up, up,' she moaned.

'Yes, yes,' I said impatiently, 'I know roughly what to do.'

'Up on the sink,' she gasped in my ear.

There was a small wash basin mounted high on the wall behind her. I grabbed her thighs and helped her up until she was sitting on the edge and could grasp me between her legs.

'That's it, that's it,' she moaned. 'Watch your feet.'

'Mmmm?' I moaned back, wondering what perversion she was thinking of now.

'Your feet. Watch where you – aghhh!'

I hadn't realized that the hot and cold water to the basin were controlled by foot pedals and I had just stepped on the hot tap.

'God, I'm sorry,' I said, moving quickly.

'Don't move,' she ordered. Her eyes sparkled. 'That was quite pleasant. Surprising, but quite pleasant. But for Christ's sake be careful because one of those pedals down there is the hot air drier. Now where were we?'

'About here,' I murmured, concentrating.

'Oh yes,' she began to melt. 'Oh yes, right about . . . there . . .'

The tannoy clicked on and the driver announced that we

would approach maximum speed as we entered France, and we both giggled.

'So . . . this . . . is . . . what' – Sophie ground into me – 'three hundred . . . kilometres . . . an hour . . . feels like . . .'

Of course, she blamed me for what happened next although it really was her fault.

Sure, I was holding her left leg, my hand behind her knee, but she'd put it there. And she had told me not to move my feet in case I triggered off icy jets of water or superheated blasts of air. And it was very cramped in there. If we had been in the back seat of a car we would have misted all the windows by now.

But anyway, her foot (my fault, but her foot), scrabbling to get purchase on the door, somehow managed to dislodge the lock.

I had my face buried in her neck and her hair in my eyes and my mind was on other things, but I was still horrified to see, in the mirror, the door behind me slide slowly and unstoppably open.

And in the mirror I could see the glass door into the second-class compartment.

And all the second-class passengers who had suddenly lost interest in watching the tunnel walls fly by. Even at three hundred kilometres an hour.


I waited for Sophie for nearly an hour on the Eurostar platform at the Gare du Midi. All the passengers disembarked and walked by me, two female ones giving me a smile and a wink and saying things to each other which I understood even though my Flemish is limited to arguing about beer prices on bar bills.

I found a kiosk and bought a packet of Gitanes and smoked one leaning against an advertising hoarding for a French brand of sports bra.

The train staff disembarked, groups of stewardesses eyeing me suspiciously, some giggling, one mouthing silently that she would be on the return trip the next morning. I smiled at her and tried to look humble in an aw-shucks-it-was-nothing sort of way, but I took a good look at her face so I would remember it. You never knew.

Sophie emerged eventually, wearing jeans, a red vest top and one of those waterproof windcheaters which women scrunch up to fit in a handbag. She had a huge black leather sports bag, four times bigger than mine, over one shoulder and was walking like a yacht in a high wind.

She came up to me and took the cigarette from my mouth, drawing on it deeply.

'Well, so much for sneaking you into the Eurostar hostel tonight, Angel. It looks like we're dossing on the streets.' She spoke and exhaled smoke at the same time, something I could never do with French cigarettes.

'You got fired?'

'No, I got the fourth star on my Ronald McDonald merit badge. Of course I got fired. OK, suspended, actually, but then I had a disagreement with the supervisor. That's when I got fired.'

'Disagreement about what?' I took the cigarette back.

'About whether shagging passengers in the toilet was good for public relations or not,' she snapped.

'I'd say it was,' I said.

'So did I.' She laughed. 'But he said somebody in steerage had complained. I wonder which one it was.'

'I think they all did, Sophie. Still, don't worry.' I put an arm around her. 'I've come into a bit of cash since I saw you last week. Let's find a hotel and go have a blow out meal. The food here is good, you said so yourself, and I haven't seen a thin Belgian so far.'

'OK, squire, let's hit this town. And it's on you. Who needs a job, anyway?'

'My sentiments exactly.'

We squeezed each other.

'Now, where's the Grand Place? It's not far from the station from what I remember.'

'You mean the Gare Centrale. This is Gare du Midi. Didn't you look at your ticket?'

'Er . . . no, I didn't.' Why should I? I hadn't paid for it.

'Businessmen are always moaning about that. They don't twig until they get here that they're not in the centre of town. Still, not my problem any more.'

'Can we get the Metro?'

'Sure, but they're few and far between this time of the afternoon.'

I had lifted her bag off her shoulder, doing the gentlemanly thing. It weighed a ton.

'Then bugger it. Let's get a taxi.'

'Taxis are shit in this town,' she said knowingly as we headed for the exit. 'The cobblestones shoot their shock absorbers to pieces inside six months. Riding in the back is like screwing on a sack of coal.'

'Now there's one you are *not* going to talk me into.'

We had reached the street and I waved at a cream-coloured Mercedes waiting at the rank. The driver pulled up to us and leapt out, offering to open the boot for our bags, but Sophie said, in French, that we would keep them with us.

The driver shrugged and said: 'Where to?' in English, and I told him the Grand Place. He set off at whiplash speed and I saw immediately, or rather felt, what Sophie had meant about the shock absorbers.

I turned to her and whispered:

'Is it true you don't take a driving test in Belgium until you've had your first accident?'

'No, it just feels like it,' she muttered.

She had her giant shoulder bag across her knees and was unzipping it. Inside, I could see at least eight of the Eurostar's quarter-bottles of champagne.

'Redundancy payment,' she said, twisting the plastic cork out of one with ever such a slight 'pop'. 'Let's start as we mean to go on.'

She drank and then handed me the bottle.

'My kinda woman,' I toasted her.


I paid off the cab and we walked into the Grand Place, one of the great unspoilt squares of Europe and the centre of a web of small streets and alleys almost all named after something you could eat. In fact, they were named after the street markets which specialized in certain foods, but the idea of giving someone directions such as turn left at Butter Street, then on to Herb Street, down the Avenue of Chicken Stranglers and through Herring Way, made you think you needed a menu not a street map.

At least I knew roughly where I was, having hung around the

Grand Place with the best of them in my student days, hoping against hope that we could con our way into the headquarters of the Belgian Brewers Association for some free samples.

I led Sophie across the square, though she moaned about having to hump her champagne-stocked bag, and into a short street where I remembered a hotel which, with luck, wouldn't remember me.

The Amigo would have been an impressive building anywhere else, but it looked more like a doll's house than a chateau when compared to the surrounding architecture of the Grand Place. It was the sort of building you used to see in war films as the local Gestapo headquarters. It would usually be the building the heroic Mosquito pilots went after with a spot of pinpoint bombing. Not surprisingly, it had been the Brussels headquarters of the Gestapo and I had once been told that to be 'invited to breakfast at the Amigo' during the war was something the Belgian resistance fighters dreaded.

Certainly they had a double room the concierge told me, all I had to do was fill out a registration form for myself and my wife. I did a double-take at that, then realized that he had assumed, because Sophie was carrying the biggest and heaviest bag, that she must be my wife. Fair enough. I filled in the card as Roy Maclean, which was actually what it said on the passport I had brought, though he did not ask to see it.

An ageing porter who made old Godfrey Ineson an Olympic possibility in comparison, took Sophie's bag and showed us up to the third floor. I tipped him without thinking about the exchange rate and realized too late that I had given him almost £10. Still, he could put it towards a pacemaker.

'So what do we do, after I've had a shower and after you've taken me for a sow-out dinner, and after we've drunk too much and staggered back here for sex in a decent-sized bed?'

She bounced on the bed to illustrate her point.

'Sounds like a pretty full evening to me,' I admitted.

'Haven't you got a brother to find?'

'Oh yeah,' I said, taking my eyes off the way she was nuzzling into the duvet. 'I've got some calls to make. How good's your French?'

'Probably more obscene but less fluent than yours,' she said, interlocking her fingers and stretching her arms above her head.

'Then I'll do the phoning while you go first in the shower.'

'Isn't there a phone in the shower?'

'It's not that good a hotel.'

'I always knew you were a cheapskate.'

She flounced towards the bathroom, shedding clothes as she went. I unzipped my sports bag, concentrating like mad.

I had copied the two Brussels numbers I had found in Finbar's office on to a scrap of paper. The first, I knew, was Bumper's home number (his work number was quite another matter) and I knew it wasn't far away from the Grand Place, above a restaurant in one of the warren-like side streets. But I couldn't remember the address or the name of the restaurant.

What was worse, I couldn't for the life of me remember the name of Bumper's space-cadet girlfriend, even assuming he had the same one. I did remember that although she rarely went out, she was very rarely 'in' as far as the rest of the planet went.

Still, it was worth a shot and I got an outside line and dialled.

A female voice answered with a vague, 'Uh-huh?'

'Good afternoon,' I said in French, 'is Bumper there?'

There was a pause while her brain clicked into gear and she decided which language she was speaking. It was something which happened a lot with Belgians, who usually speak excellent English from all the British television they pick up, as well as two languages of their own. They are just spoilt for choice.

'No, Bumper' – she pronounced it *Bumpaire* – 'is at work.'

'Out at the airport,' I said, proving I knew him, I hoped.

'Yes, that's right. Who is calling?'

'A friend from England. When will he be back?'

'About twenty-one hundred hours,' she switched into English.

'I'll call later,' I stayed in French. 'You must be his friend.'

'No, I am his wife.'

She wasn't giving anything away and she didn't seem to be joking.

'And do you still live in the same place?'

'Yes,' she said carefully. 'Have you been here?'

'No,' I said truthfully, and then had a brainwave, 'but I have eaten in the restaurant downstairs. Does it still sell lobster?'

'Of course, this is Brussels.'

'I must go there again when I visit. Do you know the telephone number?'

'Sure,' she said now she thought I was out of town, and she rattled off a number as if reading it from a sign.

'Thank you,' I said cheerfully. 'I'll call again later tonight.'

'Can I say . . .?' she started, but I hung up.

I had written down the number on the hotel's notepad. There was just time to ring them, if they were like the other restaurants in the city, before they closed for a couple of hours to recover for the evening trade.

Whoever it was who answered had a worse French accent than mine, though that didn't mean much. Brussels had actively encouraged a cosmopolitan image since it became the hub of the European Union and in recent years had been one of the few places to actually welcome refugees from the civil war in the former Yugoslavia.

'Hello? This is the Westend.'

'The Westend restaurant?'

'Yes.'

'Thank you. Goodbye.'

That was enough. One of the porters would know it, that's what they were paid for. And even if they weren't, after a £10 tip they could bloody well go out and find it for me.

'Shower's free,' said Sophie, struggling to stay in a hotel bathrobe. 'How's it going?'

'So far so good. Fancy eating lobster tonight?'

'Yeah, good call. I'll have two.' She thought about it. 'Three if they're small.'

She must have spotted the expression on my face.

'And before you say anything, that's not a rule I apply to men. We going down the Fishmarket?'

The Fishmarket had all the best seafood restaurants, usually the ones the locals used, off the main tourist trail.

'No, nearer. Round here somewhere but not far. I'll have to ask.'

'Any brothers turned up?' She started to towel her hair dry.

'Not yet, but I know where to find Bumper later on.'

'What exactly does this Bumper character do?' she asked,

crossing her legs as she sat on the edge of the bed, her damp thighs making a soft kissing noise as they met.

'I'm sorry, what did you just say?'

'Bumper,' she said wearily. 'Why is he called Bumper? You said it was something to do with his job.'

'He bumps people. Well, *he* doesn't, the airlines do.'

'I don't follow.'

'Look, it's simple.' I sat down on the bed and took the towel from her and began massaging her scalp with it. 'There are always loads of businessmen trying to catch an early flight out of Zaventem in the evening. They've finished their business early, or they're drunk or their mistresses have thrown them out, whatever. They just get the urge to leave, and there are never enough seats. So the airlines offer cash to anyone willing to be bumped on to a later flight. Maybe £75 or £100 a go. Sometimes they'll pay more than the ticket is worth to keep a regular flyer happy.

'So what Bumper does is turn up every morning and buy a few tickets, to, say, London or Dublin or Bonn, on whichever flights look like they'll be full. Then from about four thirty in the afternoon he allows himself to be bumped off various flights, eventually selling his tickets as the last flight approaches. Along the way, he picks up a cash wad from the airline to recompense him for the inconvenience *and* he gets access to the club class lounges so he can eat canapés and drink himself silly all for free. Hardly ever has to buy food.'

'And he does this for a living?' She leaned back and pressed into me. 'Don't do that, I want to get my hair dry.'

'Sorry. Yes, he seems to do all right, and he used to pick up the odd courier job along the way.'

'Very odd, I'll bet. OK, that's enough, I'll do the rest or we'll never get out on the town.'

'Spoilsport,' I said, pretending to sulk. 'One more call.'

I moved back to the bedside phone and punched in the second number from Finbar's office.

A man answered on the second ring.

'Deegee sees, der bunt.'

Or at least that was what it sounded like.

I covered the phone and repeated it for Sophie.

'Hello? I'm sorry. Hello?' I floundered in English.

'DG Six, de Bondt,' he said. 'Can I help?'

De Bondt, as mentioned by a very wary Barry Ineson.

'Mr de Bondt, my name is Maclean. I am ringing you concerning a Mr Angel.'

There was a definite intake of breath there.

'Yes?' Cautious.

'A Mr Finbar Angel. I believe he has had dealings with your . . . office?' I made it a question.

'I could consult my files . . . What was the subject matter?'

The language may have been stilted but the guy was keeping his cool.

'I would rather speak to you in person if that is possible.'

'Are you in Brussels?' he said quickly. Too quickly.

'No, but I could be there tomorrow morning. I could ring you then.'

'And you . . . represent . . . Mr Angel?'

'In a manner of speaking.' Well, that was sort of true.

'Very well, if I can be of some assistance . . .' He let it hang.

'I think we might be able to help each other,' I said, just to prove I could be as enigmatic as he could.

'Then you will call me?'

'Yes, as soon as I get to Brussels.'

'Good. And your name was . . .?'

'Maclean.' As if you hadn't written it down.

'Until tomorrow, then, Mr Maclean.'

'I look forward to it.'

I hung up again. Sophie was looking at me.

'What was all that about?'

'I'm not sure. It was a guy called de Bondt. I've heard the name before and in bad company. Sounded like some sort of civil servant or official from the way he spoke.'

'Well, he would, wouldn't he? Is there a hairdryer in the place?'

'Why?'

'I want to dry my hair, pea-brain.'

'Ha-ha. What did you mean about he *would* sound like an official?'

'Because he works in the Commission.' She took pity on me. 'In DG Six. The "six" is in Latin, VI. It's one of the main Directorates.'

'How do you know this?'

'We used to grade the businessmen on the planes. The ones who were visiting DG Six were bottom-pinchers. DG Three attracted the drunks. DG Four . . .'

'I get the picture. What exactly does DG Six do?'

'That's Agriculture. Yeah, I'm sure it's Agricultural Policy. All those bottom-pinching farmers . . . My arse was black and blue by the time we landed.'

Farmers. Agriculture. Finbar.

It all made sense.

Somehow.

# Chapter Fourteen

Sophie got her lobsters, both of them, and she deserved them. I hadn't been able to understand a word the old porter at the Amigo had said, but she had translated his directions to the Westend, which turned out to be in a small alley off the Cheese Market.

The alley was wide enough for a car, as long as it wasn't an American one. Or at least it probably was during the couple of hours when the restaurants were shut. By the time we got there, the tables and cold cabinets and tubs of ice showing off the seafood had all invaded the cobbled street and there was just room for two pedestrians holding hands to run the gauntlet of the greeters. Every brightly lit restaurant seemed to have a meeter/greeter. Their job was to chat up the would-be eaters by yelling the menu at them as they walked by and if that failed, to try physical force. Their first captives would be given sidewalk tables and extra-large portions. That way they were a sitting, munching advert for the restaurant, but the greeter's main task was to get people inside and, usually, upstairs into a boring, badly decorated room with no view where the portions were small and the service rare, as the waiters all hated climbing the stairs.

On this occasion I didn't mind that at all. In fact, I would have insisted on it and the meeter/greeter at the Westend looked faintly disappointed when I gave in so easily. He almost forgot to push in front of me so he could follow Sophie, who was wearing a very short flower-print frock, up the narrow staircase.

I didn't mind that either. While he was trying to peek up the back of Sophie's dress to check the colour of her pants – pink – I was checking the staircase up to the floor above. Next to a door marked 'Toilet' was another marked 'Private' and on the door frame to the right was a piece of card, suspiciously like the back from a book of matches, on which was written 'Cork'.

Now I remembered. Bumper's real name was Thomas Cork

and the girlfriend, now wife, if it was the same one, was Helga.

There was no point in beating on the door. She wouldn't tell me anything, so I decided to wait for Bumper to come back from work. And there was the fact that Sophie would probably have had my leg off if I didn't feed her.

Picking a table with a view of the toilet further convinced the meeter/greeter that I was insane and unworthy of Sophie's favours, but he was not going to lose sleep over it. He had people to greet, diners to mug, tourists to con.

I ordered a couple of strong, dark Scotch ales which came in thistle-shaped glasses and Sophie put a foam moustache on her upper lip while scoping the menu for all of three seconds before deciding on lobster salad. I went along with her and ordered fish soup to start and a bottle of Muscadet because it was the only white wine I recognized on the list.

Sophie got stuck in to the bread and we chatted about what she would do now she was unemployed again. That lasted until the bread ran out and the soup arrived and then she asked me what I had in mind when Bumper showed.

'Ask him a few questions, I suppose. See if he's seen Finbar lately. They used to be really good mates,' I said.

'And this de Bondt guy?'

'Go see him, see if he'll tell me anything. I'm sure he knows something, he was totally anal-retentive over the phone.'

A different waiter removed our soup plates and yet another came up the stairs with our lobsters. They were taking it in turns to have a look at Sophie, but if she realized it she didn't care.

'And then we can get back to London?'

'Sure.'

The expression on her face rang warning bells.

'But maybe we won't go back on the Eurostar . . .'


Bumper turned up just before nine o'clock, walking through the restaurant and greeting the staff in a mixture of pidgin English and Flemish, several of them greeting him by name: 'M'sieur Bumpaire.'

Outside the door to his flat he paused to fumble for a key. He wore a charcoal-grey suit, red-striped shirt and red silk tie with white dots. He carried a slim brown briefcase and had three or four British newspapers tucked under his arm.

He was no more than six feet from our table but he had not looked in to the upstairs dining room and when I spoke, he jumped in surprise.

'Hello, Bumper; long time no see.'

'Bloody hell, Fitzroy,' he stammered nervously. 'What are you doing here? Where's Finbar?'

'Funnily enough, Bumper, that was what I was going to ask you.'


We invited ourselves in to Bumper's flat for coffee and brandy. The brandy was from the airport's Duty Free shop, so was the coffee. So was probably everything in the flat except Helga and whatever it was she was on.

Not that she was leaping about the room or anything, she was unnervingly quiet. She was thin enough for you to worry about her falling downstairs and her straggly black hair plastered the side of her face like running mascara. She made coffee for us with the maximum of clatter and clashing, saying nothing but sniffing loudly. I wondered if it was a hint to Bumper that her nasal passages were waiting for a refill.

Bumper poured drinks and the three of us sat around a small table covered with a small blanket with tassels at each corner. Helga sat in an armchair two feet away. She had taken great pains to position the chair there, as if the distance was significant. From above we must have looked like a seance with a reluctant medium.

'Your hands are shaking, Bumper,' I said. Sophie kicked me lightly under the table, though I had no idea why.

'Too much coffee, old boy,' he said, pouring himself a large brandy. 'One of the drawbacks of this town. That and a diet of peanuts.'

'What's this? Cutbacks in the club-class lounge?'

'Tell me about it. No more canapés, no cheeses, no hot snacky things on sticks.'

'Life's a bitch,' I agreed. 'So what happened to Finbar?'

Bumper put down his glass and concentrated his gaze on it. He looked as if he was waiting for it to spell out the answer.

'Look, I never asked what he was into. All we did was put him up when he was in town, gave him a bed, that's all. And then Helga nursed him after the accident.'

There was one of those pauses when all you can think of is where you had put your cigarettes.

'Please go on, Bumper,' I said gently. 'Don't make me pull your tongue out and nail it to the table. What fucking accident?'

Bumper said something guttural and Helga stood up and floated over to a small bookcase. She produced a newspaper, folded open to page five and she offered it to me.

'I don't read Flemish,' I said.

'I can,' said Sophie, taking it from her. 'This small bit? It says that a man, believed to be a tourist, was thought to have been hurt in a traffic accident near the cathedral – St Michael's. Man ran off, driver said he just ran into the street and bounced off the front of his car. That it?'

'How badly was he hurt?' I asked.

'Broke his forearm,' said Bumper, indicating his left arm. 'We got him a doctor here. He wouldn't go to a hospital. Didn't want to go out at all, actually.'

'He was probably shaken up,' said Sophie defensively. 'He'd just been in an accident, for Christ's sake.'

'Who was he running from?' I asked quietly.

'He wouldn't say, but he was scared of them.'

Bumper took a stiff drink.

'Anything to do with a guy called de Bondt?' I tried.

'That was the guy he was seeing here. He works in the EC, in the Agriculture section. That's all I know. Finbar must have seen the guy three or four times this year, but nothing like this has ever gone down before.'

'Did he mention a guy called Gronweghe at all?'

Bumper shook his head slowly.

'Not by name.'

'Dutchman?' said Helga, and we all turned on her. 'Is he a Dutchman?'

'Yes,' I said, 'and he is the sort of guy Finbar would be frightened of. And not just Finbar. Gronweghe should carry a health warning.'

'He spoke of a Dutchman when he was on drugs,' she said, matter-of-fact.

'On drugs? Finbar on drugs?'

'Helga gave him some . . . painkillers,' Bumper said sheepishly. 'He was in considerable discomfort. Couldn't sleep without them.'

'But he's OK now?'

'As long as he keeps his arm strapped up, it will heal. It's OK, Roy, honest.' Bumper looked as guilty as sin. 'They were just painkillers, straight up. OK, they were pretty strong but he didn't have enough to get a taste for them.'

'He'd better not have,' I said in a voice which was intended to imply that the jury was still out on that one. 'Didn't he give you any idea what he was up to?'

'No. He always said it was better if we didn't know, but he dropped a few hints that there was a lot of money involved. He called it his "cash crop" and it was going to set him up for the next few years. That's all we know, God's truth, Roy. You know me and him went back a long way. I pleaded with him to let me phone someone after the accident. I even suggested you, but he said no.'

'Did he say why?'

'He didn't want anyone else involved. He also wanted to get home under his own steam, which he did.'

'When?' I snapped.

'Saturday morning,' said Bumper cheerfully. 'We put him on the plane ourselves. You've only just missed him, really.'


'Are you going to talk to this de Bondt tomorrow?' Sophie asked as we walked back to the Amigo. The Grand Place had just about closed up for the night but in the side streets the cafés were doing good business and in one there was a half-decent rock band doing old Ramones numbers, though they had turned down the volume by fifty per cent.

'I don't know,' I answered truthfully. 'I'm going back to the room to make a few calls, see if Finbar has turned up. Do you want to go exploring?'

'No.' She shook her head. 'I'll come back with you. Might as well see it through now I've got no job to go to.'

170

'Er . . . yeah . . . Sorry about that.'

'No worries. It was my idea, after all.' She reached out and held my hand. 'One of my better ones, I think.'

'Oh, I'm sure you can do better,' I said. 'In fact, I know you can.'

In our room at the Amigo, Sophie busied herself opening the remaining champagne bottles she had lifted from the train while I lay face down on the bed with the phone beside me.

I tried Windy Ridge first and got Finbar's answerphone. I waited for the tone as instructed and then said, 'Come on, Fin, it's Fitzroy. Pick up the damned phone,' but no one did.

Then I tried Godfrey Ineson's home number, but again there was no answer and old Godfrey had forgotten to put his answerphone on. There was nothing for it but to phone home and check my answerphone for messages. If she was still awake, that was.

She was.

'Fenella, it's Angel.'

'Hi there. Do you know what time it is? Where are you? What's the weather like?'

If this was Fenella's new, confident, telephone-sales voice, then I hoped she wasn't on commission.

'I'm in Brussels and one of the servants is peeling me a grape' – I sucked in air as Sophie slapped me on the back of the thigh – 'so I can't talk for long.' It was always wise to say that to Fenella even if it wasn't true. 'Has anybody called me?'

'Oh, yes. Lisabeth says I should send you a bill for being your secretary. How much should I charge?'

'I'll pay you in white chocolate,' I said. 'They make good white chocolate here. Ask Lisabeth.'

'All right, but you'd better not forget. When are you coming home? Is Sophie with you? I liked her.'

'Yes, Sophie is with me and at this rate I'll be home before you've told me who called.'

'Oh yes, well, the first one was an elderly gentleman called God. No, that can't be right. I'm reading from my scribble on the pad here.'

'Godfrey. Godfrey Ineson.'

'That's right,' she said, as if genuinely surprised. 'Well, he said to tell you that Larry –'

'Barry.'

'Hey, you're right. I didn't know you did shorthand. Anyway, the message is that this Barry has gone again and you've got to ring him. Godfrey, that is, not the Barry person.'

'Fine, Fenella, got that one. Who else?'

'That man with the tall voice. He said his name was Mack or something. I think it's your father, Angel. Is it your father?'

'No, it isn't. When did he ring?'

'This evening; said he had some more information on somebody called Miller. Does that make sense?'

It probably did when McCandy said it.

'Yes. Did he say what?'

'Yes, he did, but it was so odd he made me write it down.'

Good old Big Mac.

'So what was it, Fenella?'

'It was a question. He said why would one of the Millers – that's what he said – why would one of the Millers need to hire a combine harvester? That's what he said. I wrote it down. It can't be right, can it?'

'Yes, it can, and it's a very good question.'


We had breakfast in the room. Just the light, continental version, Belgium-style, of pastries, croissants, toast, boiled eggs, rillette, salami, more toast, honey, grapefruit and coffee. The bed looked like an explosion in Selfridge's Food Hall.

'I'm going to ring de Bondt,' I told Sophie, who was glued to CNN on the room's TV. 'But not from here. I need a pay phone. Fancy a shopping trip?'

'Why not? At least it will be safe.'

'Excuse me?'

'I've no money and there's sod all to buy in this town.'

'Hey, come on, loosen up. If you're good, you can have lobster again, for lunch.'

'How can you talk about food after that lot?' She waved at the desolation of the breakfast trays on the bed. 'Still, the walk might give me an appetite.'

She took a lightweight white sweater out of her bag and shook it. I was learning that almost everything in Sophie's wardrobe was designed to be scrunched up to the size of a tennis ball. She used the sleeves to tie it around her waist, over her behind, then she found a pair of Armani sunglasses and put them on.

'Touristy enough for you?'

'Perfect,' I said, and I meant it.

She slung a small black purse on a long strap over her shoulder, then unzipped it and peered in.

'I wasn't kidding about the money, Angel. I really am pretty broke. I can get some pay-off cash when I get back to London.'

'Don't panic,' I said, peeling off some Belgian francs from the wad my father had supplied.

She stuffed them into the purse.

'Thanks, though there's nothing in this town I want to buy.'

'Yes, there is,' I remembered. 'Buy the biggest, most obscene block of white chocolate you can find. It's for Fenella, although Lisabeth will eat it, to pay her for feeding Springsteen while I'm not there.'

'And chocolate is enough – for that?'

'I did say a big bar.'

Down in the lobby I asked the concierge if he could phone the airport and check on the times of arrivals from London for me. *Pas de problème*, he had most of the airline timetables behind his desk and I found that there was an early flight from London City Airport which had already landed.

He also gave me some coins in change for a fifty-franc note and was generally very helpful and polite. Any day now they would have earned that tip I gave them.

Sophie and I walked hand-in-hand through the Grand Place where the tourists already had their cameras locked and loaded, the cafés were setting their outdoor tables and colourfully dressed black Africans were selling fake gold jewellery from trays around their necks, going for the conscience vote by saying it was from the Congo.

In a pedestrian precinct near the Place St Jean, I picked out a café with a sidewalk terrace called the Pelikan. There were at least three side streets nearby, any one of which would circle back to the Grand Place as just about every street did in the old city. And as I didn't have wheels, I didn't see why de Bondt should have, hence the pedestrian precinct. I somehow didn't think he would want to meet in his office.

I was right about that.

From a phone booth outside the huge King Albert library, I got through to him on the second ring.

'M'sieur de Bondt? My name is Maclean, we spoke yesterday.'

'Of course,' he said, then paused and I bet myself he was covering the mouthpiece to talk to someone else. 'It was about a Mr Angel, I believe.'

'That's right, and I think it is essential that I talk to you as soon as possible.'

I liked the 'essential' touch. Bureaucrats go for that sort of thing.

'I can consult my appointments diary, of course,' he stalled.

'It will have to be very soon, Mr de Bondt. I am here in Brussels already. I flew in this morning and I was hoping to see you at about, say, eleven o'clock.' I tried not to make it sound like a question. They like it when you're strict.

'Eleven? Oh, I do not think . . .'

'The reason for the speed, Mr de Bondt, is because the harvest season is almost upon us, or so I am told . . .'

I let it hang there to see how good his nerve was. (Rule of Life No. 81: Pretend you know more than you do and people will usually fill in the gaps.)

'Where are you?'

'On my way into central Brussels. There is a café I know called the Pelikan near –'

'I know it and I can be there at eleven. How will we meet?'

To say that I would be the one wearing jeans, aviator sunglasses and a black T-shirt advertising the Daytona Beach 1995 Bike Week Bar Tour, probably wouldn't inspire confidence, so I turned it around.

'Can you get hold of an English newspaper?'

'Yes, I read the *Daily Telegraph*.'

'That'll do nicely. Be reading it. I'll find you. And, Mr de Bondt?'

'Yes?'

'We are agreed that this is a private meeting, aren't we?'

There was a slight pause then he said: 'Yes, that would be best.'

As I hung up, Sophie said:

'So you want me to get lost for a couple of hours?'

'Certainly not. You're watching my back.'

He wasn't reading the newspaper, he had it rolled up as if ready to swat flies or waft the steam off his double espresso. And he was early, but I wasn't sure whether that was a good or a bad sign.

I walked by twice, letting him sweat and waiting for Sophie to take a table next to him so that they sat back-to-back. If it had been me, I would have been in the final stages of dehydration before being served, but Sophie had two waiters hovering before her jeans slid on to the chair.

On my third sweep, I moved swiftly up to the seat opposite de Bondt and slung my jacket over the back of the chair.

'Don't get up, Mr de Bondt,' I said, though he showed no intention of doing so.

'Mr Maclean?'

'Yes. Cappuccino, please.'

He bridled at that, but waved his paper for a waiter.

He was somewhere in his mid-forties, thinning black hair combed left to right across a bald patch, his eyes hidden by steel-framed glasses with green-tinted lenses. He had a briefcase on the ground by his chair and he stuffed the newspaper into it before levelling the green glasses back at me.

'I need to understand what you want from me, Mr Maclean, and what your exact relationship to Mr Angel is. Would you like to lead on this?'

Gosh, I bet he was good at taking meetings in the Commission. Still, I had to hook him before I could reel him in.

'I am very close to Mr Angel,' I said carefully. 'But I am very worried about his recent behaviour. I think he has got in over his head, but into what, I am not sure.'

'You are not sure, but you suspect?'

'I suspect he is claiming set-aside subsidies for crops which do not actually exist on his farm in Suffolk. It's called Windy Ridge. Do you know of it?'

He remained impassive; if anything he seemed to relax slightly.

'I can consult the files, but Mr Angel is one of thousands of farmers claiming subsidies throughout Europe. If he has problems, perhaps I could talk to him . . .'

There was something going wrong here. Maybe I hadn't offered enough.

'He's not very keen to talk to anyone at the moment. He is very concerned that other – shall we say – parties, are preparing to harvest some of his crops.'

Now I had his attention. He had tensed, but forced himself back in his seat as the waiter brought my coffee.

'Which crops are you referring to, Mr Maclean?'

'The ones which Mr Angel has been to see you about on numerous occasions this year.'

He shrugged and lifted his cup to his lips without a tremble.

'I would have to go back over my files,' he said confidently. This was not going well at all.

'I hope your files are in order, M'sieur de Bondt.'

'What do you mean by that? I have nothing to hide.' He was still cool, not half as niggled as I had hoped he would be.

'Not many of us can say that, certainly not Mr Angel. He's very keen to keep things hidden.' Notably himself.

'Do you know where Angel is?'

'In England,' I said confidently.

Over his shoulder I could see Sophie talking to a waiter and ordering *moules et frites*. She certainly had an appetite, that girl.

'Where in England?' asked de Bondt, his lips tight.

'*Not* back at his farm, that I can tell you.'

Then he did something totally unexpected, at least to me. He turned to his right, looked down and spoke, quite casually, in Flemish.

'I'm sorry,' he said quickly, 'I was thinking aloud. Thinking that you really know very little, Mr Maclean, and I see no profit in continuing this meeting. Unless, that is, you can tell me where Mr Angel is. I take it you really do know him?'

'Oh, I know him very well. Why should I pretend otherwise?'

He shrugged his shoulders and pushed his coffee cup away.

What had gone wrong? What had I said, or not said? He was far too confident.

'I am sure there are lots of reasons possible. Greed is the most likely, of course. You think there is money to be made out of this.'

'There usually is. Finbar called it his cash crop.' I wasn't sure where I had dredged that one up from but it appeared to claim his interest for a millisecond.

'It is an expression common in farming,' he countered.

'Especially if it's all cash and no crop,' I tried and that certainly got a reaction.

He smiled.

'Did you ask to see me thinking you could do some sort of trade deal, Mr Maclean? Because I do not think you have anything to exchange. I think you know nothing at all about Mr Angel.'

I didn't get a chance to answer.

A chair scraped up to the table and Paul Gronweghe sat down next to me.

# Chapter Fifteen

I suddenly knew what being a rabbit caught in headlights was like.

I couldn't speak even if I had wanted to, although my brain was into overdrive. I realized why de Bondt had been so cool. He had back-up, all I had was Sophie and she was engrossed in reading the label of a bottle of Trappist beer. I stared at de Bondt's briefcase and realized that there must be some sort of microphone or radio in there, which was why he had turned that way to 'think aloud' in Flemish, except it hadn't been Flemish, it had been Dutch. And Gronweghe had been around the corner or across the street with a receiver probably concealed in a Sony Walkman, listening to every word. And now he was here, sitting next to me, close enough for me to read the Hugo Boss label on the open jacket of his suit.

And he was talking at me.

'We no longer need Angel, you know. He is no longer necessary just as long as he does not get in the way. Does he understand that?'

I tried not to respond, to avoid eye contact, anything, nothing. De Bondt said something to him in Dutch and his attention switched long enough for me to see Sophie blissfully ignoring us and deep in conversation with a waiter who was offering her a huge bowl of steaming mussels.

'I do not agree with my partner de Bondt,' Gronweghe said, back at me although I saw de Bondt wince at 'partner'. 'I think you do know something about the Angel farm . . .'

He was staring at me intently and I could no longer keep my eyes out of range.

'You . . .?'

He screwed up his face in puzzlement. There was a scar on his forehead which hadn't been there four years ago.

'You . . . you are . . .'

Here it comes, I thought, and wondered if Sophie had the

sense to stay put and finish her lunch, then rendezvous back at the hotel if anything happened.

I was going backwards in my chair, I swear I was, when Gronweghe moved like a snake. His hands shot out and caught my left hand by the wrist, pinning it to the table. He gabbled something at de Bondt in Dutch.

'You know him?' yelped de Bondt, in English. 'He knows you?'

It was the first sign of worry he had let slip. Good, at least I had one of them on the run. Unfortunately, not the psychopathic, violent one.

'I know Paul,' I said, trying to divide them and not let my voice crack. 'We did some business together about four years ago. Some drugs business.'

That set de Bondt off in Dutch again, but Gronweghe cut him short, his grip on my wrist tightening into numbness.

I glanced around. The table on my right had been set for lunch and I thought I could just about reach the fork on the place setting. Sophie had turned in her seat and was still talking to her waiter, pointing to the bowl of *moules* as if asking him to name them individually.

'You are coming with me, Maclean. Is that your name?' I nodded. 'I always meant to find out who you were. I have a score to settle with you. And we can find out what you know for sure.'

'I don't think so, Paul.'

He tilted his head as if he was interested in my answer.

'And why not?'

'Because I'll cause such a riot they'll have to call the cops and while you may just beat the crap out of me, I don't think Mr de Bondt here wants to get involved in a very public brawl.'

I could tell I was on a winner on that one from the look of horror on de Bondt's face.

Unfortunately, Gronweghe didn't see it that way.

'I think I would enjoy it,' he said, and I didn't think he was kidding.

'I am leaving,' said de Bondt, bending over in his seat to pick up his briefcase.

'So am I,' I said.

Gronweghe tightened his grip even further. He was now

actually hurting me quite a lot, but I wasn't worried about breaking his grip. Or at least, not without help.

Behind de Bondt, Sophie twisted like an eel, scaring the hell out of the waiter standing there, and grabbing the bowl of mussels. With de Bondt leaning over, she had a clear shot at Gronweghe's head and Hugo Boss suit.

They were hot, that was for sure as they were still steaming, and no doubt the china bowl hurt as it bounced off his head, but his real howl of pain came when I swept the fork off the next table and jammed it into the back of his right hand.

As soon as he let go of my wrist, I started moving backwards, one eye on Gronweghe, the other on de Bondt, who had frozen while bending over, his face at table height and his gaze fixed on the fork sticking out of Gronweghe's hand.

It was just as well he stayed down because Sophie hadn't finished. She grabbed her hapless waiter by the lapels of his white coat, shouted, 'Now look what you've done!' and then tripped him in a basic judo throw and he cannoned on to Gronweghe's lap.

By the time they both crashed to the floor, I was two paces away, dragging my jacket from the back of my chair, tipping it over in the process, right in the path of another waiter who was either coming to help or aiming to detain me. It didn't matter which; the more chaos the better.

And then I was following Sophie who was already running down the street, lots of innocent tourists and shoppers giving us the odd glance, but none saying anything or trying to stop us.

I drew level with her and grabbed her arm, pulling her into another pedestrianized street to the right.

'Hurry, but don't run,' I wheezed.

'Fine by me,' she panted. 'Where now?'

'Let's get out of here. Back to the Amigo, pick up the passports and blow.'

'Won't they check the hotels?' she asked, glancing behind her.

'They might. I don't know what resources they have, but it'll take time. Down here.'

I pushed her into an alley which I knew would come out on Grasmarkt, from which we could circle the Grand Place.

'It's a small town,' she said.

'You're right. And I checked in as Maclean, so all they have to do is phone around.'

'You mean they could be waiting for us? Jesus Christ, whose side are you on?'

'Look, we'll be there in five minutes. In, grab the passports and out.'

I tried to sound reassuring and confident, hoping she wasn't going into shock. I might need her to get me out of trouble again.

'I've got mine.'

'What?'

'I've got my passport.' She held up her tiny shoulder purse. 'I always carry it when I'm abroad. You never know when you might have to make a quick exit.'

I reached into my jacket.

'And I've got mine, same reason. And I've got all the cash we need. Well, all the cash we have. What say we grab a cab out to the airport and catch the first plane out?'

'Have you got any tickets?'

'No. But Bumper will have.'


We flagged a taxi as it cruised the area outside the central station. The driver was delighted to get a fare out to Zaventem before lunch and maybe he would put it towards a new set of springs for his ageing Renault.

'I know what went wrong,' I said to Sophie as we sat in the back, holding hands. I wanted to keep her talking in order to stop her trembling. 'At least what went wrong with de Bondt. Nothing has to go wrong with Gronweghe, he's just a natural born psycho.'

'You didn't get anything out of him?'

'Didn't give an inch. He sussed me early. Realized I didn't know as much as I was pretending to know.'

'That's what he said when he spoke in Dutch.'

'What?'

'When he was talking into that radio thing in his briefcase. I spotted it straight away.'

'You saw he had a radio?'

'Yeah, didn't you?'

''Course. I knew he'd be bugged,' I blustered. 'Anyway, what did he say?'

'He said: "He knows nothing of any consequence." But the Dutch gangster didn't seem to agree, did he?'

'Like I said, he's just naturally paranoid. God knows why he should be, it seems to be Finbar everybody is after.'

She squeezed my hand.

'You're worried about your brother, aren't you? You're actually concerned.'

'Don't say it like that,' I sulked.

'Well, it is a side of your character we don't see very often. It could be rather cute if you worked on it.'

'Don't let it fool you, it's an act,' I snarled. 'When I find Finbar I'm going to break his other arm.'

'Do you know what he's up to?'

'I'm getting a good idea. It was something I said to de Bondt which didn't get the reaction I'd expected. In fact, didn't get any reaction at all. I said something about scamming the subsidies for crops which don't exist. That was when de Bondt was sure I didn't know as much as I thought I did. I had assumed that Finbar was claiming the grants for fields of stuff which didn't exist. But de Bondt didn't rise to that one. And if Gronweghe is involved with him, that means drugs.'

'Your brother is smuggling drugs in from Europe?' Sophie was genuinely shocked.

'No, I think he's growing them.'

'But that's outrageous!'

'It is if you're getting a farming subsidy for doing it.'


'There was no need to put my name out over the tannoy,' said Bumper. He was really quite cross at being dragged from the club-class lounge. 'And I don't suppose I really have won the lottery, have I?'

''Fraid not, Bumper, but we thought it would bring you running.'

'It's a bit of an emergency,' Sophie chipped in, flashing her eyes at him, which always works with me.

'Is it Helga?'

'No, no, nothing like that. We need to leave town. Like now.'

Bumper looked at his watch.

'There's a British Airways flight at one o'clock. You might just make that, otherwise there's a Sabena at fourteen thirty and then British Midland at sixteen hundred hours.'

He didn't once glance at the flight departure board. What a professional.

'Can you get us on the one o'clock?' Sophie pleaded.

'I might be able to do something. The flight's not full, that I do know. How do you want to pay?'

'Ah, there's the rub, Bumper,' I said. 'We want you to pay.'

'Me? Just like that? Buy you two tickets?'

'Haven't you got an account you could put them on?' I said, trying to make a constructive suggestion.

'Well, yes, but . . .'

'Please, please, please,' Sophie whined. 'It really is very important and there isn't much time if we're to get into the Duty Free.'

'Come on, Bumper, you'll get your money back.'

He gave me a cynical sideways look.

'Oh yeah, sure. You're forgetting I know your family.'


On the plane on seats either side of the aisle, Sophie said: 'Are you sure about your brother?'

'It's the only thing which makes sense. There are too many people worried about harvest time near Finbar's farm. They're either keen to get the combine harvester out or they've disappeared. And, funnily enough, someone mentioned drugs to me the other night.'

'But if you're growing that much, I mean, where? Wouldn't somebody see it?'

'Only from the air,' I said, more to myself than her.

The plane started to taxi out to the runway and near the cabin door, a pretty black-haired stewardess began to go through the safety drill, pulling on the fake life jacket and pantomiming the emergency-exit procedure.

In the seat in front of mine, a suited businessman was deep

into his free copy of the *Financial Times*. Sophie leaned forward, straining against her seat belt, and tapped him on the arm.

'Pay attention,' she said, pointing to the stewardess.

Thankfully he did.


Ironically, the plane came in over Essex, just down the coast from Romanhoe, before circling London to the north. I pointed out to Sophie that I would have to slog all the way across town back to Hackney to pick up Armstrong in order to drive up the road we were currently flying over.

'I'm looking forward to a few days in the country,' she said.

'Going somewhere nice?' I asked.

'With you,' she said calmly. 'Might as well see things through.'


From Heathrow, we trekked by underground and then bus out to Sophie's flat in West Hampstead. (I went along with her and called it West Hampstead like the estate agent had, but it had always been Kilburn when I'd played in the pubs and clubs there.)

At her place, she packed a haversack with handfuls of crumpled clothes and dug out a spare toothbrush and a few basic cosmetics. I like a woman who moves light and fast.

As an afterthought, she checked the answerphone and found three calls from girlfriends all wanting to know if the Eurostar story was true. She ignored them, but took her second phone, the mobile, from its charging unit and stuffed it in the haversack.

'I'm ready to roll,' she said.

'Let's get a minicab,' I suggested and phoned a company I knew based in St John's Wood.

While we were sitting out the obligatory twenty-minute wait, I called Godfrey Ineson.

'Finally got you, Godfrey,' I lied. 'I've been trying for ages.'

'Fitzroy? Where have you been? We've had some very strange happenings up here.'

'Had a few myself, Godfrey. I hear Barry's gone walkabout again.'

'I don't know about walking. He took my Land Rover and just

cleared off. Left me a note telling me to cancel all his harvest jobs and that he'd be back in about a month.'

'And that's not like him, is it?' I said vaguely.

''Course it's bloody not. Harvest is his busiest time of the year.'

'Who does the harvesting at Windy Ridge, Godfrey?'

'Well, I used to, but Barry took over from me to help Finbar. And that's the other thing.'

'The two of them could handle it?'

'Yeah, usually. But they're not here. Neither of 'em,'

'I'd worked that out, Godfrey. What other thing? You said there was another thing.'

'Yes, there is. If Finbar's still missing and Barry's not here, who hired the Claas they delivered this morning?'

'Hired the what?'

'The Claas. It's a combine harvester, a new one. It's parked at Windy Ridge.'

'I'm on my way, Godfrey.'


I had to direct the minicab driver across Islington and Stoke Newington to avoid the worst of the traffic and when we finally made Stuart Street, he looked distinctly nervous at pulling up behind a black cab. That was probably when he gave up all hope of a tip.

Inside number nine, I told Sophie to go and present Fenella with the two jumbo blocks of white chocolate we had bought at the airport. The labels, which for some reason were in Italian, warned that eating too much could have a laxative effect. I was pretty sure Fenella didn't read Italian.

'Tell her to keep on feeding Springsteen and taking messages, and you'd better give her the number of your mobile,' I said, then I knocked on Fenella's door and left Sophie to it.

There was no sign of Springsteen in Flat Three, which was just as well as I didn't need to think up excuses. I found an ancient leather shoulder bag under my bed. I couldn't remember how it had got there or how long it had been there. It rattled when I shook it and a pack of Gold Flake cigarettes fell out, so old and dry they scattered shreds of tobacco everywhere. I tried to remember the last time I had smoked Gold Flake, but couldn't.

There was also a pack of coloured 'fun-time' condoms in the bag, with two missing. That didn't ring any bells either.

It would have to do. I pushed in what clean underwear I could find, along with socks which were relatively fresh, a spare toothbrush (I always keep a supply) and a battery shaver which I have for the mornings with hangovers when a wet shave would be suicide.

Finally, I opened the small metal safe which was concealed behind the covers of Brogan's *History of the United States*. It allowed just enough space for my passports and whatever cash I had in reserve. I put in my Maclean passport and the few Belgian francs I had left and transferred most of the sterling notes to my wallet.

That was it. I had money, I had wheels, I was going to be on my home ground, literally. I couldn't think of anything else I might need.

That was the trouble.


'So this is where you were brought up? Nice country,' said Sophie.

'It was. It is. Sunset's a good time to see it. Do you want to grab a bite to eat?'

I had just realized it was twelve hours since we had eaten breakfast in Brussels and we had been on the go ever since.

'Is there a McDonald's around?' she said from the back of Armstrong, where she had her legs curled under her on the bench seat.

'Not likely, but there's a garage up ahead with an all-night shop. Sells most things and we could do to stock up on iron rations, as there is sod all in the larder at Windy Ridge. I could do with some fuel, too.'

'Fair enough,' she said. Then, serious: 'Have you thought any more about what we're going to do here?'

'Talk to old Godfrey and see what he knows about the farm. The answer's got to be there somewhere, it must be. All the people who should be there are staying away like the plague was in town, and people who shouldn't be around are taking a very unhealthy interest in the place. If Godfrey doesn't know anything, then we go over the place ourselves tomorrow.'

'And you know what we're looking for?'

'Not really, but it has to be big.'

'How big?'

'Big enough to need a combine harvester.'

She thought about this for a minute.

'Angel, that's *a field*. How do you hide a fucking field on a farm?'

'Where else would you hide one?'

The garage loomed up and I pulled in, giving Sophie some cash to hit the food shop with whilst I filled Armstrong to the brim with diesel.

'I got some cheese, bread, salami and some tins of soup, plus biscuits and some coffee. They'll have things like milk, won't they?' she said as we hit the road again.

'It's not that sort of farm, Sophie. Get your mobile out and I'll call ahead and talk to the local milkman.'

I fumbled in my pocket and pulled out the paper I had written Godfrey's phone numbers on. Sophie dialled for me, pressed 'send' and handed the phone through to me.

'Godfrey? It's Fitzroy. I'm about half an hour away, can you meet us at Windy Ridge?'

'I'm there already. Is Finbar with you?'

'No, I was just going to ask you that. I'm with a friend. What are you doing there?'

'There's been visitors, but no sign of Finbar.'

'You mean the combine?'

'No, this evening. Somebody's been snooping around. Almost caught them at it.'

'Is there anybody there now, Godfrey?'

'Just me.'

'Well, you watch yourself.'

'I'll be all right an' I'll be here to welcome you home.'

'Don't kill the fatted calf just yet, Godfrey, but what you can do is dig out a map or a plan of all the land Finbar and Barry farmed. Can you do that?'

'I should think so. What did you have in mind?'

'A bit of surveying.'

Godfrey took an immediate shine to Sophie, ignoring me and

telling her that he had got the boiler going for hot water in case she wanted a bath, and also warning her that if a big, mangy black cat came sniffing around, she was on no account to touch it.

I didn't mind about the hot water, that was just being polite. Warning her about Chuck Berry, though, was giving away a tactical advantage.

Sophie took him up on the offer of a bath while I volunteered to rustle up some food. Once she had gone upstairs, Godfrey did a little mime, without saying a word and holding a finger to his lips all the time, to indicate that he had his shotgun with him and had hidden it behind the door to Finbar's office. It was nice of him to be so considerate. He didn't know that it would take more than a shotgun to stop Sophie when she was in one of her moods.

I think Godfrey realized that when she reappeared wearing an extra-large T-shirt, longer than most of her skirts, bearing the legend: 'Just Because I Slept With You Doesn't Mean I Have To Drink With You', and because she was just out of the bath, it was damp and steaming slightly in all the right places. Sixty-odd years of Suffolk protestantism flashed across his face, but by then I had poured soup into mugs and he had a large scale Ordnance Survey map of the area spread out over the kitchen table.

'So we're looking for a haystack in a hayfield, are we?' Sophie asked.

'Something like that,' I said, waiting for Godfrey to stop looking at her and start concentrating on the map. 'Er . . . Godfrey?'

'What? Oh, yes, well there's nearly a hundred acres left of the old land which is around the house.' He stabbed a gnarled finger at the map, where the farmhouse was marked but not named, then described a small circle around it. 'Most of it is this side of the road, but there are a couple of fields across there that had barley this year. That was all harvested in July. Bit early this year due to the weather.'

'And this side of the road, these fields here round the house itself?'

I indicated with my mug, leaving a semi-circle stain of tomato soup on the map.

'About eighty acres over seven fields. Three are down to maize for cattle food this year, a couple set-aside and the others wheat.'

'Nothing unusual? Anything like oilseed rape?' Sophie's eyebrows shot up. 'It's a plant,' I said. 'A pretty yellow one.'

'I know that,' she said defensively.

'Rape ain't very popular any more. So many farmers grew it for the subsidy a few years back that there's a bit of a glut now,' said Godfrey sheepishly. 'Not that anybody knew what to do with it anyway. It all ended up as pig food. There don't seem to be much sense in farming these days.'

'Is that it, then?' I stared at the map but it didn't give me any clues. 'There must be something else somewhere.'

'Such as?'

'I don't know,' I snapped. 'Hothouses or something like that. Didn't Finbar try any market gardening? Greenhouses or anything? Something away from the road, you know, tucked away out of sight.'

'You mean like the hemp?' Godfrey said.

Sophie spluttered into her soup and as she took the mug from her lips, she had a red moustache of tomato.

'Hemp? As in *cannabis sativa*?' I said, showing off.

'That's probably the one. You've got to grow it off-road where people can't see it. It's one of the rules when you get a licence to plant it.'

'Are we talking about the same thing here?' asked Sophie.

When I nodded she said: 'What do they do with it?'

I took her left hand and placed it on my right thigh.

'They used to make Levi's out of cannabis fibre,' I said as she squeezed the material, 'and rope. Nowadays it goes for paper – cigarette papers, believe it or not – and tea bags, stuff like that. And you can find the seeds in bird food if you look closely, but it's also being seriously reconsidered as a medicine, which it was used for originally. It's supposed to be very good for treating multiple sclerosis sufferers.'

'You mean you can get a joint on a doctor's prescription?'

'Not yet. And you can let go of my leg now.'

'There's a lot of stuff and nonsense talked about that stuff,' snorted Godfrey. 'The hemp that's grown in this country you could smoke all winter and not feel anything.' He saw us looking at him. 'Or so they say.'

189

'I'm afraid he's right,' I said. 'The stuff grown under licence here has less than half a per cent THC, that's tetrahydrocannabinol, the stuff that gets you high. You need five or six per cent THC to get a bang out of it.'

'But it's all controlled anyway,' Godfrey argued. 'It all goes to a storage place over near Bishop's Stortford. You don't get paid otherwise.'

'Hang on.' Sophie held up a hand to both of us. 'How do you two know so much about this business?'

'I read about it in *Farmers Weekly*,' said Godfrey.

'I read about it in *Time Out*,' I said.

'Fine,' she said. 'Carry on.'

'Did Finbar have one of these licences?'

'Not that I know of, but I could try and find out tomorrow.'

'There may not be time. If he was growing hemp without a licence, where would it be?'

'Not round here. All the fields on the old farm can be seen from one road or the other.' He paused. 'But I suppose it could be one of the fields down the river margins.'

Godfrey and I unfolded the map another section as Sophie asked what the river margins were.

'They're fields down by the River Deben,' said Godfrey. 'Go for about twenty miles down the valley. Finbar and Barry rented forty or fifty acres between them. I've no idea what they're growing down there this year. They were both very secretive back at planting time, now I think about it.'

'Then that's where we'll look. First thing in the morning,' I said decisively.

The other two didn't seem that convinced.

'You said somebody had been snooping around, Godfrey,' I remembered. 'Were they snooping down towards the river?'

'No, it was around here. Somebody in the village told me they'd seen a car coming up here and I set off across the pig fields since Barry ran off with my Land Rover. I could see him taking an interest in that harvester outside but he was in his car and away before I got close enough to tackle him.'

'Maybe that was no bad thing. Did you see what sort of a car?'

'A Ford. Nothing special. I checked the combine. It didn't seem to have been tampered with.'

'And nothing to say where that came from?'

'No. It just appeared. It'll have been rented locally. I could ring round a few places.'

'Let's see what happens tomorrow. We may need it ourselves.'

Sophie held up a finger in 'back in a minute' mode and padded upstairs.

'Do you want to get into this, Godfrey? There are some bad people involved and it could get hairy.'

'Got to, Fitzroy, for Barry's sake. If it lets my son come home, count me in.'

Sophie reappeared with a bottle of Paddy Irish whiskey, another souvenir from the Duty Free shop at Zaventem.

'If we're going on a drug hunt, we might as well have a drink to get the expedition off to a good start.'

'Not for me,' I said. 'There's an old saying: twenty-four hours between throttle and bottle.'

I looked at my watch.

'Well, seven ought to be enough.'

# Chapter Sixteen

If you wear dark trousers and a dark blue sweater, preferably one with elbow patches, and carry a black briefcase, I reckon you could walk into any flying club in East Anglia and borrow the club plane without anyone even challenging you. Nip over to Le Touquet, a quick lunch and back, wave at the control tower and, unless the plane had been booked by a genuine member, you might even get away without paying for the fuel.

Of course, the trick is to know what you are doing and look as if you know what you are doing. So in our case, I thought it better to steal a plane when there was no one up and about to notice us. And at Shelton Green Flying Club, that meant just before six a.m., unless you counted the rabbits nibbling breakfast on the thousand-yard strip of grass which formed the runway.

'Are you sure you know what you're doing?' Sophie asked, stifling a yawn as she climbed into Armstrong's driving seat.

'Sure. If it's got wings, I can fly it,' I said cockily. 'Are you sure you'll be OK?'

'Hey, if it's got a handbrake, I can turn it.' She grinned, then saw my face. 'Don't panic, don't panic. I'll take care of your precious taxi. I've got my road map and my phone.'

She showed me both to prove it.

'And I've put my number into Godfrey's memory and shown him how to work it.'

'Good. Now go, you'll need a head start.'

'Aw, can't I stay and watch you get arrested?' she pouted.

'Sod off, Sophie, and try not to get lost.'

'Chocks away, Red Baron!' she shouted as she gunned Armstrong's engine.

The gate to the Flying Club was a metal pole affair meant to keep vehicles out, not pedestrians. (It would also serve to keep aeroplanes in, as joyriders had been known to drive them out on to main roads before now.)

Godfrey and I ducked under the pole and set off across the grass, still damp with the morning dew.

'You sure you know what you're doing?'

He just had to ask.

'Trust me, Godfrey. You must remember me and Finbar going for lessons when we were kids. I got my private pilot's licence before I got my driving licence. It's like riding a bicycle, you never forget.'

'I remember you used to fall off your bike when you were a kid.'

'OK, bad example, but you know what I mean.'

'And you never had to nick a bike . . .'

'Borrow, Godfrey, borrow. We'll have it back before they know it's gone.'

As long, that is, as we could find one unlocked and with enough gas for an hour's flying time. Oh yes, and as long as I could remember how to fly.

It was true that I had got my PPL before I could (legally) drive a car, but to *keep* a pilot's licence, they insist on five hours' flying experience a year, and recommend twenty. To be honest, the opportunities for a bit of crop-dusting or the odd hop over to France for lunch had been a bit limited living in Hackney and so I had sort of let things slide.

But as to the basic mechanics of borrowing a plane, of that I had no doubts. I had always said they were easier to hot wire than the average car.

Shelton Green was similar to a hundred other clubs: a control tower (which wasn't really a tower), a prefabricated hut or two and a couple of hangars where they would keep any vintage aircraft or did running repairs. Most of the aircraft were staked out around the concrete turning circle near the tower.

Godfrey, walking in a poacher's crouch in case the rabbits spotted him, pointed at a Beagle Pup, the first parked plane we came to.

'What about that one?' he hissed, looking furtively around.

'That's what I learned to fly on,' I said to reassure him. 'But it's a low-wing craft. We need a high-wing so we can see more of the ground below. Like that one.'

I pointed beyond the next plane, a flashy French Socata Trinidad.

'That'll do us.'

It was a Cessna 150 Aerobat in uniform white with a red stripe from propeller to tail, widening to show the call sign G-BECD. It was parked on the edge of the taxiway, tail into the grass, each wing anchored by a rope to a block of concrete, not an anti-theft so much as an anti-wind device.

The doors opened – few light aircraft are locked – and the interior of the Cessna smelled like the inside of a 1950s family car with plastic trim. There were headsets thrown casually in the back of the cockpit, which probably meant it was airworthy. Hell, it had two wings and three wheels. It was airworthy.

There were no keys inside, but I hadn't really expected there to be. I leaned in and flicked on the red masterswitch to the bottom left of the instrument panel. The radio came on and the gyros began to wind up. The fuel gauges registered both tanks three-quarters full, which would give us two hours' endurance. I turned the radio off, as we wouldn't need that, and then switched off the master and walked around to the front of the aircraft.

Godfrey was hopping from one foot to the other, glancing towards the control tower.

'Can you see a wind sock anywhere?' I asked, to give him something to think of as I ran my hands over the propeller and kicked myself for not bringing gloves.

'That thing up there?' he said, pointing to the tower.

'Probably. Which way is it blowing?' I said casually.

'That way. To the west.'

'Good, we can take off straight down the runway into it.' And I could wear my aviator sunglasses.

'Just check the air intakes, would you? Those things near the propeller,' I said as I moved around to the right-hand engine cowling and began to unscrew the fasteners.

'What am I looking for?'

'Birds' nests,' I said. 'Seriously. They'll catch fire in flight and it can be rather unnerving.'

I had the engine cowling up and it was a matter of seconds to undo the quarter-inch nut to the back of the right-hand magneto and disconnect the earth wire. The magnetos on an aircraft are always on, earthed to the switch in the cockpit. Disconnect the wire and the magneto is live.

I considered flying on just one, but then decided not to risk it and reached behind the engine to feel my way to the nut which held the earth to the left-hand magneto. It came away easily, which was just as well as they are buggers to get at with a spanner. Then I removed the dipstick just to check the oil level, which seemed fine, and shut the cowling.

'How you going to start it?' Godfrey asked.

'I just have,' I said. 'Well, more or less. Get in.'

I helped him into the right-hand seat and secured the four-point harness around him, thinking that it would have been more fun to have been doing that to Sophie. At least she would have said something as I strapped her down (she usually did), not just sit there gulping for air.

I jogged around to the pilot's side and climbed in. I checked the brakes were on by pushing on top of the rubber pedals while pulling the lock plunger, then fumbled between the seats to make sure the fuel tap was on. It was all coming back to me. Maybe I had been right about bicycles.

Check red mixture control knob to the right of the throttle set 'Rich' and the black carburettor heat knob on the left set to 'Cold'. Or was it the other way round? Primer – I pulled out the primer and pushed it back in four times to inject fuel into the manifold, aircraft not having chokes and needing a rich mixture to start. Four times ought to be enough as it wasn't a cold morning. The primer squeaked loudly and Godfrey whimpered.

'They always do that, don't worry,' I tried to reassure him. 'Nervous?'

'Never flown before,' he admitted.

'Safe as houses,' I smiled. 'And in case of trouble, the exits are here' – I pointed to his door – 'and . . .'

There didn't seem anywhere else to point to.

'Well, don't worry. It is going to get a bit noisy though.'

I jumped out and ran around to his door to make sure it was shut, giving him a thumbs-up as I did so, then I squared up to the propeller.

A Cessna 150 propeller weighs about sixty pounds. They are made of metal and sharp on both edges. They go round rather quickly and if you don't treat them with respect they will show you their well-known impression of a food mixer. But it didn't pay to let them dominate you, so I put my hands about three-quarters of the way along the blade and smiled at Godfrey in the cockpit. His face was whiter than the paintwork.

I swung down smartly, rotating my body so it carried me away from the aircraft as I had once been taught. When the engine runs, it draws air in and would like to take you with it. But this one didn't.

I swung again, trying to keep the action smooth and forget the sharp pain in my hands. Nothing. I swung a third time and again nothing. I swore at it and swung again and the engine caught and began to run up with a nice steady roar.

'There you are,' I shouted to Godfrey, 'nothing to it.'

He probably couldn't hear me, as he didn't look any more comfortable.

I ran to the pilot's seat and adjusted the throttle to idle at 1200 r.p.m.

'Let's go!' I yelled, then held up a hand. 'Ooops, silly me.'

I jumped out again and untied the aircraft from the concrete blocks holding down the wings. It could have been a short flight.

Back in the cockpit, I reached under my seat for the release bar and shunted my seat forward so I could reach the pedals and pulled on my straps, then closed the door. I remembered to switch on the electrics master as, though I had no intention of using the radio, the flaps were electrically operated.

I tried to remember the pre-flight checks I was supposed to do. The only one I should have done was to see if the area was in an MATZ (Military Air Traffic Zone). Still, you can't think of everything.

I took a deep breath, grinned broadly at Godfrey, who was staring rigidly ahead, released the brakes and then gently eased the throttle forward again. The Cessna moved forward and I steered with the rudder pedals until we reached the edge of the runway.

Brakes on, engine running up to 1800 r.p.m., set flaps to twenty degrees, check movement in the control column.

No reason to wait. Go for it.

I released the brakes, firewalled the throttle and steered with my feet in roughly a straight line, keeping an eye on our air-speed. At forty-five knots, I raised the nose so that the top of the instrument panel was level with the horizon. At fifty-five knots, the Cessna just lifted itself into the air and began to climb.

At 300 feet, I lifted the flap and remembered to exhale. Then suddenly we were at 1000 feet and cruising at 85 knots.

I turned and shouted at Godfrey over the hammering of the engine.

'Right then, where are we going?'

We flew by dead reckoning and Godfrey's local knowledge. Once he had realized that he could look out of his window without falling out of the sky, he began to shout off local landmarks. So-and-so's barn, Earl Shelton church, the Old Crown pub, his cottage and then Windy Ridge itself, with its new Dutch barn and a blue combine harvester parked next to it.

I also caught a glimpse of a black car on the road below. I wasn't sure it was Sophie, but there was nothing else on the road going in that direction.

'See if the phone works,' I yelled at Godfrey. I had forgotten just how noisy light aircraft were on the inside.

Godfrey put a finger in one ear and his mobile to the other and seemed to get through, as he gave me a thumbs-up.

'The river,' I shouted, pointing downwards. 'Start looking.'

'What am I looking for?' he screamed back.

'Something you don't recognize.'

I flew a long, gently banking right turn circle over the line of the river, rolling the Cessna so that Godfrey got a good view without feeling airsick.

He got it on the first run.

'There, down by the bend in the river,' he shouted.

I levelled the Cessna so I could get a better view. Between the river bank and the road Sophie was driving down was what looked like a water meadow, then a rectangle of a field with something green and rippling growing in it. Between it and the road were two more fields with golden-brown-coloured crops. There seemed to be no direct access from the road into the green field.

'You sure?' I asked.

He leaned against his straps to get near my ear. 'Well, it ain't grass and if it's barley, it's two months past ripening.'

'You may be wrong about the grass bit,' I said, but he didn't hear me. 'Get Sophie.'

I banked the Cessna into a turn and picked up the river and the road again. Godfrey handed me the mobile.

'Sophie, can you see me?'

'Yeah, you're just up ahead. Can you see me?'

'Yes, I can now. Keep going but slow down.'

I banked again and lowered the nose to come in over her.

'Hi there, Golf Bravo Echo Charlie Delta,' she said in my ear.

'If you can read the letters, I'm flying too low,' I said. 'Now slow when you come to the next field.'

I watched her do as I asked but by then I had to concentrate on turning the Cessna again. Godfrey wasn't white any more. He was going green.

'Now stop there. What can you see to your left?'

'A field of sweetcorn.'

'Good. Now look around and remember which field it is.'

'For Christ's sake, Angel, it's all fields around here. There's no dope growing here.'

'Oh yes, there is, you just can't see it from the road.' Which she had just confirmed for me. 'Now set the mileometer on the dashboard to zero and turn around. Meet us back at the Flying Club and try not to get lost.'

'I can find my way back, Red Baron. Can you?'

'I should know not to expect a civil word from a cab driver,' I said, then folded the phone and handed it back to Godfrey.

'Shall we go home or do you fancy a bit of a tour?' I mouthed at Godfrey.

'Home,' he said queasily. 'Just get us down.'

'No problem. Er . . . which way do you think it is?'

The one thing I knew about the Cessna was that it could be really banged down on landing, provided you landed on the main wheels not the nose wheel. And that was just what I did: bang it down. But nobody was looking except Godfrey and he was just plain relieved, so much so I thought he would do a

Papal impression on me and kiss the ground as I helped him out of his harness.

'Just keep an eye out and see if there's anyone about,' I told him, to give him an excuse to walk about and stop his legs shaking.

'What if there is?'

'Think of an alibi. Quick.'

I had taxied back to the spot where we had found the Cessna and it was easy enough to push the tail round to park it so I could refasten the wings to its concrete anchors. I checked the cockpit to make sure everything was off and as it had been before its unscheduled flight. There was nothing I could do about the tachometer which registered the time the engine had run, something which the club pilots were supposed to log in and out. But I counted on the fact that the discrepancy would be put down to bad arithmetic or just carelessness, as it usually was. There was also nothing I could do about the fuel usage, except hope that forty minutes' worth would be overlooked.

I lifted the engine cowling and, careful not to burn my fingers, reconnected the white earth wires to both magnetos. As long as no one came along and actually sniffed the engine in the next hour or so, I felt pretty confident no one would suspect she'd been up.

We were in the lane outside the club gate for about ten minutes before Sophie turned up. Godfrey had only had to nip into the hedgerow twice to relieve himself. It's funny how nerves affect some people.

Sophie jumped out of Armstrong and hugged me.

'You got down in one piece! I'm amazed! Yuk, your shirt's wringing wet. You're sweating like a pig . . .'


Armstrong's clock told us that Sophie had driven eleven and three-tenths miles, so that was what I did in reverse and I pulled off the road into the entrance to the field, Armstrong's radiator nuzzling up against the first row of six-foot-high maize.

'I love sweetcorn,' said Sophie as she climbed out. 'Is it ripe?'

She reached out for the nearest ear, halfway up the bamboo-like stalk.

'Nearly,' said Godfrey, 'but we call it maize and it'll go for animal feed. They chop the lot, leaves and all until it's like powder, then they press it and the cows'll eat it all winter.'

'Shame,' said Sophie, letting go of the hairy end of a cob.

'Don't tell the Jolly Green Giant,' I said. 'Come on.'

I led the way down the front edge of the field and then turned right and started walking down the side. The first maize field undulated gently upwards, something which had been difficult to spot from the air but explained why nothing but maize was visible from the road. The field extended over the rise and down towards the river valley. Its boundary was a hedge dotted every ten yards with small oak trees, a drainage ditch on either side.

The entrance to the second maize field must have been at the other end of the hedge. Rather than walk the length of the field, we pushed our way through the hedge and continued down the side. Looking back, we had no idea we were anywhere near a road. Birds sang, grasshoppers hopped out of our way, and in the distance we could see swans on the river. Not a pub or fast-food outlet in sight. It was a jungle out here.

Godfrey pointed to it, but we could all see long before we got there that the field nearest the river was growing something other than maize. It was taller than the hedge – about twelve feet – and it was green.

Again we scrambled through the thorny hedge and jumped down into the field to stand there, all three of us, as if hypnotized by the tall, thin reedy stems, the withered white flower heads (which produce very few seeds in the British climate) and the thin, curved leaves with serrated edges. There was hardly any breeze but still they seemed to sway hypnotically in front of us. Sophie and I both reached out to touch the nearest plant.

'Now that's what I call a stash,' she breathed.

'That's hemp,' said Godfrey.

'It might be hemp if you try and knit with it,' I said, not taking my eyes off the nearest plant, 'but it'll be Suffolk Gold once it's turned into resin.'

'No, that's hemp,' Godfrey insisted.

'Why don't you smoke some and then if you're still worried about it, it's hemp,' I said helpfully.

'Did you bring any cigarette papers, Angel?' asked Sophie dreamily.

'No, I thought you were in charge of provisions.'

'That's *bloody hemp*!' Godfrey shouted. 'That's exactly the stuff they grow over at Stortford. You could smoke that all day and bugger all would happen.'

We looked at him, then both Sophie and I broke off a leaf, crumpled it and sniffed it.

'Are you sure?' we said together.

'Sure as I'm standing here. I've seen it before. You cut it and let it ret on the ground for a week or two.'

'You let it rot?' Sophie was beginning to take this personally.

'No, it rets. It sort of toughens up once cut. Becomes more fibrous. That's why you grow it, for the fibre. Not for drugs.'

'Are you sure?' we both asked again.

'Yes, I am. This is probably all legal and above board.' Then he muttered: 'Needn't have gone up in that bloody aeroplane . . .'

I ignored that and counted to ten in my head.

'Think, people. This can't be right. There's got to be more to it. Finbar's running scared and Barry's done a bunk. There's a mad Dutchman with an impressive CV in drug trading involved and somebody has hired a combine harvester. There must be something going down.'

'Look, there's a harvester, right?' offered Sophie.

'Right.'

'And it's harvest time, right?'

'Thereabouts.'

'So if this isn't the crop to be harvested, where is it?'

'I don't know. We couldn't see anything else from the air.'

'So it's hidden somewhere, camouflaged somehow.'

It suddenly hit me: I was in love with Sophie.

'Sophie, you're a genius. Where do you hide a field of cannabis? In a field of hemp.'

Sophie pointed dead ahead with one finger.

'In there?'

'Bet you.'

We ploughed into the hemp plants, bending them aside like explorers in a patch of elephant grass. Within three paces I couldn't see Sophie any more, but I heard her well enough when she said: 'Christ, they could have filmed *North by Northwest* in here.'

A few more steps and Godfrey said: 'This is it.'

He was right. The plants here were smaller and their stems softer and juicier. The leaves were a lighter, more delicate green and there were seeds on the flower heads, the sort which explode gently like indoor fireworks when they are in a joint.

'Sure?'

'Well, I don't know what they call it, but it's a different strain to the hemp we've just come through.'

I looked behind me to compare the plants. Yes, there was a big difference, but you had to be this close to spot it.

'So they sow a few rows of real hemp all round the edge of the field and then put the good stuff in the middle?' I thought aloud.

'It'd be about two combine widths,' said Godfrey. 'You always go once round the field to give yourself room to move, then you cut in strips. Go round twice here and you can leave the hemp to ret on the ground while you pick up this stuff.'

'Wouldn't somebody notice a big empty hole in the middle?'

Godfrey shrugged.

'You could spread out the hemp with a tractor and rake, but who can see here? Mind you, if this is licensed, you'd have to explain away a pretty poor crop.'

'What do you mean?' Sophie asked, thinking I hadn't seen her stuff a handful of leaves into the pocket of her jeans.

'The hemp people will have targets for your yield per acre. I've read you can get twelve tons an acre in a good year, but you wouldn't get that if you took away the middle of the field. You'd have to explain a biggish shortfall somehow.'

'Just how big is this field, Godfrey?'

'I dunno. Can't see from here.'

Sophie and I followed him back through the hemp to the

hedge, where he stood on the roots of one of the oak trees and hauled himself up to get a view over the waving green crop.

'Nine or ten acres, I'd say,' he pronounced.

'And what, seventy per cent is probably very marketable smoking material?'

'Could be.'

'Fucking hell,' growled Sophie, 'that's a lot of stick to blow.'

'Yeah,' I agreed. 'You're gonna need an awful lot of cigarette papers.'

# Chapter Seventeen

'So what do we do now?' Sophie asked as she ate the last sausage.

We had finished the provisions we had bought on the way up and we were still hungry. Or at least I was. All this flying and drug-busting before breakfast didn't half give you an appetite.

'Well, we can stay here, in the middle of some of the best farming land in the country, and starve to death. Or . . .'

I had their attention.

'We could call the cops or Customs and Excise and report some naughty substances.'

'Wouldn't that get your brother into trouble?' Sophie was more worried about Finbar than I was, but then I'd met him.

'And my Barry,' said Godfrey, dead serious.

'That's right,' she said, and she'd never met him either.

'OK, I'm outvoted on that one. How about we harvest the stuff ourselves. Can you drive that thing outside?'

'If I could get into it,' said Godfrey. 'It's locked. They usually lock them these days. And I've no keys for starting it. Reckon you could jump start it like you did that aeroplane?'

'I'm not sure about that,' I said truthfully.

'And what would you do with it all?' asked Sophie with more than a touch of the headmistress in her voice.

'Burn it?' I suggested. 'Chuck it in the river, get rid of it.'

'Do we have enough time?'

'I don't know. Godfrey?'

He scratched his chin before answering.

'What I know is you don't hire a brand-new combine like that one out there, and not use it.'

'How long would it take you to cut that field?'

'Couple of hours, that's all.'

'And could they do it at night?'

'Yes, these new combines have lights. Might take a bit longer.'

'So how much time have we got?' Sophie persisted.

'I don't know,' I repeated wearily. 'Gronweghe could be here by now.'

'What makes you think he's not still in Brussels with his suit at the dry cleaner's?'

'Hey, don't get cocky. We were lucky over there. He'll be here, he won't leave it to his hired help. And he could have been on the flight out after ours. Come to think of it, Bumper probably sold him a ticket.'

'You mean he could be watching us right now?' She said it with an over-the-top melodramatic expression which had me going for a minute. She might well have a point but I didn't want to tell her so.

'I think we have a few hours in hand,' I said as confidently as I could.

'But if they turn up to start harvesting, you'll call the authorities?' Godfrey narrowed his eyes to make sure I knew where he was coming from.

'I don't want to drop Finbar and Barry in it, me old mate, but what do you suggest? Just let them drive away with it?'

'Why not?' he said, 'why not?'

Godfrey relaxed. Sophie tried to look shocked, but it didn't last.

'So we just hang around waiting for them to come? Maybe put the kettle on for them?'

'No,' I said forcefully, pretending I knew what I was doing. 'We make one last attempt to find Finbar. He will know what their plans are – or were before we crashed the party – and we know he's back in the country somewhere.'

'Unless he's gone on to another country,' said Sophie. Sometimes she was definitely not a team player.

'I doubt it. Where do you hide a gormless Englishman – in England. He hasn't been back here for clothes or money, and he's injured, remember.' Godfrey gave me a filthy look. I hadn't told him that bit. 'He's got a broken arm,' I said. 'So he'll be looking for help from someone.'

'You?'

'Probably not. I'll try my father and we can drive over to see if Mother's heard from him. Then we go through his desk again and –'

'Again?' said Sophie, but I ignored her.

'– and we ring everyone he has a number for, see if anything turns up. Friends, farmers, businesses he dealt with, garages . . .'

Which reminded me of something I had seen on Finbar's desk, a delivery note for a new BMW from a local garage. Could he drive with a broken arm? And where was the car, anyway?

'And we get some food in in case we need to hole up here,' I went on, beginning to enjoy my general's role. 'You never know, Finbar may be just daft enough to come here, or phone in. And phones – that's another thing. Have you got a charger thing?'

'Back at my cottage,' said Godfrey. 'I could get food and things from there.'

'OK.' I handed him the keys to Armstrong. 'Can you drive the cab?'

'I'll walk it across the fields. I'd feel a right prat going through the village in that. Never live it down.'

'Well, if that's your attitude, why are you still here? Get going, and don't forget the charger. We'll start on Finbar's office.'

I set Sophie on to going through Finbar's papers while I borrowed his phone and rang my father before he went to work.

'What does he do?' Sophie asked.

'As little as possible. He's just difficult to get at the office,' I said vaguely.

He was easy to get that morning, suspiciously easy, like he was waiting for the call.

'Where the hell are you now?'

'Windy Ridge, and good morning to you, dear pater. Has Finbar been in touch?'

'No, I was just going to ask you that. What's going on?'

'Nothing much,' I said airily, at which Sophie raised her eyes to the roof. 'Finbar's back in England and he's had a bit of an accident. Seems he's got a broken arm. We're doing a ring round of the usual suspects, see if he's holed up with an old mate or girlfriend.'

'Have you tried your mother?'

In the background, I heard him whisper, 'Thank you, Snuggles,' to someone. I thought it best not to ask.

'Going over there this morning. Shall we give her your love?'

'Yes, yes, whatever . . . Did you say "we"?'

'Yes, Dad, I have a friend too.'


We left Godfrey settled in a front-facing bedroom which he was rapidly turning into a sniper's nest. He had rested his shotgun with its butt on the bed and its muzzle on the window ledge. He had food, a kettle and tea bags and the mobile phone on its charging unit on the floor. From the window he could see the length of the track which led up to the house, as well as the Dutch barn and the shiny Claas harvester parked there. I thought about offering him my compact binoculars which were still in Armstrong, but then Godfrey had always been able to tell the sex of a pigeon at half a mile, so I refrained from making the offer.

I told him not to leave his post and to call us if anything happened.

'And if they come for the combine?' He held out a hand as if trying to stop me leaving, wanting a straight answer. Wanting instructions.

'Either call the cops or let 'em have it,' I said.

'I have to think of what's best for Barry,' he said slowly.

This the Barry who had left his old man to face a mad Dutchman and the Miller brothers when things had started to go belly-up?

'Sure you do. Just do the right thing and I'll worry about Finbar. Do not, on any account, get hurt. OK?'

I collected Sophie and piled her into the back of Armstrong. She had her phone with her and Finbar's address book and she worked her way through the numbers as I drove.

We were halfway to Romanhoe when she leaned forward to talk to me.

'Nothing. Twenty-eight calls and not one sighting of Finbar for over two weeks. He's overdue at his dentist's and he didn't show up for a haircut, and somebody called Maurice is very upset about that. I feel as if I know him. Is he like you at all?'

'Not in the slightest.'

'But you must have something in common.'

'Nah. He's in trouble. I'm not.'


I was indicating to turn right into Station Street in the old part of Romanhoe, when a figure leaped out into the road waving its arms frantically in front of its face.

For a second I thought it was a Squeegy Bandit of the sort who jump out at you at traffic lights in central London and demand money for wiping your windscreen with a filthy sponge soaked in cold, scummy water. Or alternatively, you can give them money *not* to clean your windscreen. But then I remembered that this was not London and not even the most desperate Squeegy Bandit would try it on with a black cab.

The figure jumped back on to the pavement, not totally certain that I was going to brake in time, then he pointed across the road to where there was a parking space behind a Ford Escort.

'Friend of yours?' Sophie asked from the back.

'Friend of my mother's,' I said.

Philip Ryder hopped up to Armstrong's door and opened it for me like an anxious commissionaire.

'Roy, I was hoping it might be you,' he said, as if he had been spoiled for choice from thousands of black Austin cabs.

'Hi there,' chirped Sophie, opening her door and surprising him.

'Oh yeah. Philip Ryder, this is Sophie.'

He nodded at her and she smiled at him and then he looked at me as if waiting for me to offer Sophie's surname. Once I remembered it, I would.

'I wanted to talk to you about your mother . . .' he started, dropping his voice.

'There's a surprise,' I said even more quietly. 'What's she done now?'

'Nothing as far as I know, that's the problem. She's become very reclusive, won't leave the house. She's hardly spoken to me since Saturday. She says she's working, painting, but I don't believe her. Is there any way you can find out what's the matter with her?'

His expression changed from one of sincerity to one of wide-

eyed amazement as he noticed Sophie's 'Just Because I Slept . . .'
T-shirt.

'You say she's been like this since Saturday?' I asked, sliding
a look towards Sophie, hoping she picked up on it.

'We were supposed to go out for dinner together, but she cried
off at the last minute and every time I've called round, she's
refused to come out with me. Won't invite me in, either.'

'And that was Saturday, was it?'

Sophie dodged eye contact. She knew.

'Yes, Saturday. Frankly, Roy, I'm getting worried. I really can't
think I've done anything to upset her.'

I sighed and rolled my eyes as if to say 'Women'.

'Leave it to me, Phil. I'll find out what's going on.'

'Would you?' He almost hugged himself, his waterproof
yachting jacket creaking under the strain. 'I'm not imposing,
am I?'

'No, no, this is purely a social call to let Mother meet Sophie
here.'

I felt rather than saw Sophie glare at me.

'Oh, I see,' he said, then turned to the Ford Escort. 'Wait, can
I give you something for Beth?'

He opened the back door of the Escort and leaned in. I felt
Sophie at my shoulder.

'So, I'm here to meet Mommy Dearest, am I? Have we set a
date, then? Is she helping us pick out curtains?'

'Shut up, you big girl's blouse,' I hissed. 'It was the first thing
I could think of.'

'Take more time in future,' she hissed back, but there was a
sickly sweet smile on her face when Ryder turned to us holding
an eighteen-inch-high plant in a plastic pot covered with tissue
paper bearing the name of the local florist.

'Would you give her this?'

As he held it out I noticed he had a large square sticking
plaster on the back of his right hand.

'Of course we will,' I said, taking it. 'You look as if you've been
in the wars.'

He examined the back of his hand as if for the first time.

'Oh that. Rope burn from the boat. Looks worse than it is. I'd
be grateful.' He held out the plant.

'Sure thing.'

'I'll wait here for a while, in case she wants to talk to me.'

Your choice, Phil, I thought, but unless Mother had changed, it would take more than a potted fuchsia to break her out of one of her moods.

I locked Armstrong, and as Sophie and I walked down the street, I gave her the plant to carry.

'You give it to her,' I said. 'She'll only be suspicious if I come bearing gifts.'

'Is it' – she paused, stifling a giggle – 'a *pot* plant?'

'Was that absolutely necessary?'

We reached the door of number five and I rapped on it with my knuckles and waited. And waited some more, then knocked some more.

There was an answering thud from the other side of the door, just one.

'What was that?' Sophie whispered.

'I don't know,' I said.

The thud came again, followed by a high-pitched whine.

'She's in trouble,' Sophie said urgently, bending at the knees and pushing open the letter box so she could see into the house.

Her face was an inch from the open slot when a hollowed sliver of flesh came out almost as if trying to kiss her.

'Jesus Christ!' Sophie went backwards, landing flat on her behind in a sitting position, but somehow managing to keep hold of Ryder's plant.

'No,' I said calmly, 'it's Elvis, actually.'

As I helped her we heard a voice from inside.

'Get in here, you mangy cur or your sweetbreads are history!'

Sophie glared at me while rubbing her right buttock.

'Mummy's calling you, Angel.'

'Ha, ha. Sorry, I should have warned you about Elvis.'

We heard a door slam inside the house and then footsteps and then the door opened. My mother stood there, wearing jeans and a T-shirt saying: 10% ANGEL, 90% BITCH.

She looked at me, then at Sophie, and at Sophie's shirt.

'Oh, it's you. You'd better come in, I suppose. Is that my birthday present?' She took the plant from Sophie. 'Thank you, how thoughtful. Love the shirt. Want to swap?'

'This is Sophie,' I said to her retreating back as she walked down the short hall and into the kitchen. I could see Elvis's snout pressed against the glass in the back door.

'Hi, Sophie,' she said over her shoulder.

'Hello, Mrs . . .' Sophie made claws of her hands and glared at me as if it was my fault she did not know what to call her.

'You can call me Bethany, most people do round here.' She put the plant down on the draining board of the sink and switched on the kettle. 'Coffee? I could use some.'

'Thank you,' said Sophie politely. 'No sugar for me.'

'I could tell that,' Mother said airily. 'Sorry about Elvis. He's a bit frisky for some reason. Best to keep him outside. Now, to what do I owe the honour? Two visits, one year. What's this? Bonding?'

I let her have that one for free as I remembered saying something similar to my father.

'I'm still looking for Finbar, Mum. Thought you might have heard from him.'

'Me? Why should I know where he is?'

She busied herself putting a fresh paper in the coffee filter and spooning coffee and banging cups. She wasn't looking at me, not even when I lounged against the fridge door and she had to push me aside to get the milk.

'I told you, he's probably just extended his holiday. He'll be enjoying himself somewhere and it would never occur to him that anyone might be looking for him. Specially not you.'

I used to pride myself on knowing when she was lying but now I was not so sure. I was out of practice.

Sophie tried to break the ice. She was standing by the back door mouthing endearments at Elvis through the glass.

'They're very intelligent, aren't they, the pot-bellies?'

'Yes, they are,' said my mother, hopeful of finding a kindred spirit. 'They're the ideal pet. Playful, distracting, big enough to be kicked if you want to take out your frustrations on them, guaranteed to get you noticed when you go for walks and they deter burglars and annoy the neighbours. And you can eat them.'

'Finbar's back in England,' I said, trying to get back to the subject. 'He flew in on Saturday and he's got a broken arm, so he'll need looking after.'

'Where had he been?' she asked, but still not looking at me, concentrating instead on wiping down a work surface with a kitchen sponge.

'Belgium. Brussels, actually.'

'Does he like being stroked?' Sophie asked, distracting her.

'Oh, he's harmless enough, but he doesn't know his own –'

'Aren't you interested, Mother?' I interrupted.

'Interested in what?'

'In how Finbar broke his arm. I thought you were supposed to take at least a passing interest in your children, and counting the number of limbs they have in working order might be a start.'

'I just assumed you were going to tell me whether I wanted to know or not. You always did get your own way.' She poured hot water from the kettle into the coffee filter.

'I'm sure he likes me,' Sophie was saying and from the corner of my eye I saw her reach for the door handle.

'He was run over, or rather, he ran into a car while running away from somebody and that somebody would like to do him some really serious harm. Me too, now I'm involved.'

'You're talking in riddles, Fitzroy. You always did. It was your way of being clever.'

'Hi there, Elvis,' Sophie was saying as she turned the handle.

'Exactly what sort of trouble is –?' She saw the back door opening. 'No! Don't do that!'

Sophie stopped dead, but the door was unlatched and Elvis had suddenly decided he didn't understand English. He put a shoulder to the door and with only a flick of the skin, Sophie was thrown backwards in another undignified sit-down, on the kitchen floor.

'Bloody hell!' cursed my mother, reaching for him but not able to make it without standing on Sophie.

Elvis veered away from her and set off down the hall, my mother sidestepping Sophie as smartly as he had and in hot pursuit.

I assumed he was heading for the front room, maybe looking to see if I had warmed a bed for him, but he shot by straight to the foot of the stairs, his rear hooves skidding and rucking the carpet as he did the pig equivalent of a handbrake turn.

I had never seen a pig go upstairs before. Elvis did it hoof-over-hoof and by that time my mother had reached him, but he was in no mood to listen to reason. He just levered himself upwards, my mother trying to get a grip on him and mostly failing, but when she did, he just pulled her along with him.

'You're bacon, you bastard!' Mother screamed as he reached the landing and turned to look down the stairs, flinging my mother against the wall as he did so.

Sophie was at my side and she flinched as we heard the thud of Mother's head hitting the skirting board.

'Now look what you've done,' I said to her.

Before she could reply, Elvis had our attention again. He put up his head and his snout quivered. He whined eerily, then snorted loudly. White saliva drooled from his jaw.

'Do pigs howl at the moon?' Sophie said, open-mouthed.

'He's not howling at the moon,' I said, my eyes following to where Elvis's snout was pointing.

Above his nostrils in the roof above the landing at the top of the stairs was a trap door giving access to the loft. The inner hardboard square suddenly moved upwards and inwards, leaving a black hole in the ceiling.

The blond, curly-haired head and the right shoulder of my brother Finbar appeared from the hole, upside down.

'Hello there,' he said cheerfully. 'I suppose the game is up, isn't it?'

Sophie and my mother held Elvis at bay while I helped Finbar lower the light metal ladder down from the loft so he could join us. With his left arm in plaster and strapped to his chest, not to mention three people and a pig on the landing anyway, it was a cumbersome and farcical procedure.

'Clever of you to find me, Fitzroy,' he said, looking at Sophie and trying out his wimpish smile.

'I didn't, the pig did.'

Elvis pushed his snout in between Finbar and Sophie. Good for Elvis.

'And the pig is standing on my sodding foot!' yelled Mother. 'Can we *please* go downstairs, for God's sake.'

'You go first,' I said to Finbar, 'and Elvis will follow.'

'Can you manage?' Sophie said to him. 'Lean on me if it helps.'

Finbar grinned inanely.

'Thanks awfully. That's a very funny T-shirt, by the way.'

'Funny?' she said, straight-faced. 'It's not meant to be funny.'

Elvis didn't want to go down the stairs, so we left him to work it out for himself, or call a cab or a chair lift.

Sophie settled Finbar in an armchair in the front room and plumped up a cushion under his injured arm. That was quite enough sympathy as far as I was concerned.

'So, scum-bag, you were just going to hide up in the attic until it had all blown over, were you?'

'Something like that,' he said. 'And what's wrong with that? No one asked you to get involved.'

'Oh yeah, fine, great. I knew it would be my fault.' I patted my jacket pockets for a cigarette. 'What about Barry Ineson? And his dad?'

'Godfrey?' he squeaked. 'What's it got to do with him?'

'He's worried about his son, who has taken a leaf out of your book and done a runner, leaving Godfrey to carry the can.'

'Now don't get on your high horse, Fitzroy,' Mother said. 'Finbar's told me everything and if we stay out of the way for a few days, it will all be over.'

'I don't think so, Finbar, do you?'

'What do you mean?' He began to redden about the cheeks and I knew I had him on the ropes.

'Assuming they harvest the dope, how are you going to explain your missing hemp crop?'

'Flooding,' he said lamely. 'The river margin fields always flood round about October. That's why we planted there.'

'Choosing the warmest, driest summer for fifty years. Have you seen how low the river is?'

He nodded sadly. I was glad he had, because I hadn't noticed.

'Is that why you lost your bottle and did a bunk?'

'I suppose that was the last straw. I tried to get de Bondt to see reason, that it was too risky. He's the one who came to me with the initial idea.'

'I didn't think it was one of yours.'

'Really, Fitzroy, don't underestimate your brother.'

'Sorry, Mummy,' I said nastily. 'Of course Finbar is capable of coming up with such a scheme. You screw the Common Agricultural Policy for a set-aside subsidy for land on which you then grow a controlled crop inside which you grow an illegal crop worth God knows how much and you expect a flooded river to cover your tracks. I bet you were going to claim for the flood damage on your insurance as well. Did you really think nobody would rumble you?'

'Nobody did until you came along,' he said petulantly.

'Just a minute, Finbar,' said Mother, moving towards him. 'This *crop* Fitzroy is talking about, just how big is it? You told me it was a few pot plants, a bit of market gardening, you said.'

'Well, actually, Mother, it's likely to be several tons . . .'

'It's a whole field,' said Sophie enthusiastically. 'Acres of it.'

'And I bet it's good stuff, too,' I said. 'Where did you get it?'

'De Bondt had a partner, a Dutchman.'

'We've met him,' chirped Sophie.

'Well, this Gronweghe had access to a new strain of seeds. They were developed hydroponically in Holland, designed for colder climates. They're supposed to give a plant with up to ten per cent THC.'

'What does that mean?' Mother asked me.

'It means it's a powerful leaf. Good street value.'

She reached for a cushion from the chair behind her and flung it at Finbar, aiming for his plastercast.

'You prat!' She was on her feet, pacing in small circles. 'He just turned up on Saturday off the London train and asked me to hide him because he'd got in over his head in something. Over his head? We're talking *Titanic* here, aren't we?'

'Now take it easy, Mother,' Finbar and I said together, then glared at each other for doing so.

Sophie was looking behind me and saying: 'Oh hello. Didn't hear you come in.'

I turned to see Philip Ryder in the hallway. He had a big bunch of keys in one hand and was pulling a snub-nosed revolver from his windcheater with the other.

# Chapter Eighteen

'This is really only for effect,' said Ryder, waving the gun casually in front of his chest. 'I don't expect to use it.'

'Good,' I said, turning my back on him. 'Then we'll ignore it.'

'No more jokes, Roy.'

'I see nothing remotely jokey, Philip,' my mother waded in. 'You've burst in on a perfectly good family argument uninvited and you seem to be threatening us. Well, I think it's rather sad. Now please leave.'

It was a good front and would have had me bowing gracefully out of the room. Ryder was made of sterner stuff.

'This is nothing to do with us, Beth. I'm only here because I've been waiting for Finbar. I thought he must come here eventually. There was nowhere else for him to go. We knew we could rely on Roy here to lead us to him.'

I put myself between Ryder and Sophie. I looked at the gun and then at the bunch of keys in his other hand.

'You could have got in here any time. Why now?'

'Until five minutes ago, I didn't know for sure that Finbar was here.'

My brain clicked into gear.

'The plant. There was a bug in the plant.'

'That's right. Only a little one, but effective enough over short range. I was told you were the smart one, Roy.'

Before I could ask, 'By whom?' the penny suddenly dropped on Mother.

'Are you saying you came here just to find Finbar? From the start, I mean?'

'I'm afraid so, Beth, though it was quite fun at times.'

'You bastard,' she said.

'Yeah, right, bastard,' echoed Sophie.

I tried not to be distracted.

'You were the one snooping around Windy Ridge, weren't you? Old Godfrey said he saw a Ford Escort and you've got one outside. You had one in London when you saw me. I should have known.' I looked down at his feet. 'And you were there when they dumped Barry Ineson. He said there was an intruder who wore canvas deck shoes. It was you, wasn't it? It was you who left him there, scared and trussed like a chicken.'

Ryder didn't deny it.

'So at least we know you're not working for Gronweghe,' I said.

'We do?' piped Finbar.

'Oh hello, brother, you still here? No, don't worry, Friendly Phil here isn't with them. The question is, who is he with, and what does he want?'

'That's two questions, actually.'

'Oh, shut it, Finbar,' said Mother. 'Come on, Philip, explain yourself or I'm going to shove that ridiculous little gun so far into your teeth you'll have to reload through your arse.'

Finbar and I looked at her in surprise. Sophie whispered, 'Yes!' to herself.

'I'm with what you might call the security services,' said Ryder, 'and I'm here to make sure Paul Gronweghe doesn't take his harvest home.'

'You're with MI5?' I asked, breaking the silence.

'Yes,' he said warily.

'Oh well, that's all right then. We can do a deal.'


The fact that the security spooks were looking for work now the Cold War had melted was no secret and had been the subject of acres of press speculation and investigative television journalism. And now that MI5 was supposed to have a more open, publicly accountable face (everyone knew where their London HQ was and the current boss was always getting her picture in the papers), they themselves contributed to the speculation.

The current debate about forming a national Police Squad was probably an MI5 proposal, ideally suited to keeping up the value of their pension funds. Part of the logic behind it was that MI5 officers could bring to bear all their vast experience of intelligence work on the current drug trade. Quite how five years of examining East German paperclips or studying local dialects in

Belfast equipped them to handle the average Brixton crack dealer was another matter.

The one thing I was sure of, if Ryder was telling the truth about being a member of Five, was that he hadn't told the cops anything yet.

'What sort of a deal?' Finbar asked me, as if Ryder wasn't there.

'That depends on what he needs to know,' I said, sitting down and pulling Sophie on to the chair arm, my arm round her waist.

'But you think we can trust him?'

From the staircase there came a loud thud, or perhaps three thuds close together, then a snort.

'Elvis,' said Mother. 'I'll just go see if he's hurt himself.'

She flounced up to Ryder and very casually moved his gun aside so that she could walk by him. Not once did she look at him.

'We might as well,' I said. 'The game's up as far as you're concerned, isn't it? Best we can do now is damage limitation. You don't want the dope and nobody wants Gronweghe to have it, so let's deal.'

'What exactly have I got to deal with?'

We were ignoring Ryder completely. It was a double-act Finbar and I had perfected as kids to use against other kids when we were feeling cruel, and against visiting aunts we had been told to be polite to.

'For a start, he seems to need you because he thinks you know something,' I said seriously.

'And do I?' said Finbar, just as straight.

'You might, like when Gronweghe is coming to harvest his crop. Or it might be just as simple as where it is. I found it, of course, but it was well hidden.'

'You mean I did something right? My dear brother, that's a rare compliment coming from you.'

Don't overdo it, Finbar, or I'll ask Ryder for the loan of his gun.

'So we have a "when" and a "where" to deal with, and what about a "where to"?'

'Where to what?'

'Where the stuff was going to go once it was cut.'

'Oh, that's why we had the Dutch barn built at Windy Ridge,' he confessed airily, then saw my expression. 'But of course they can't rely on that now, if I'm not around.'

'So they'll have made other arrangements and I've got one or two ideas about where they might be.'

Mother appeared in the doorway, ushering Elvis with her hands on his shoulders. He sniffed at Ryder in passing, then waddled over to Finbar and rested his chin on Finbar's knees.

'I think he just frightened himself,' said Mother. 'He's not good on stairs. Pigs aren't, usually.'

Sophie leaned over and stroked his back. Finbar fondled an ear with his good hand.

'Good boy, Elvis. Don't worry, I'm not cross about you giving me away.'

'He came straight for you, you know,' Sophie told Finbar. 'Just like a bloodhound.'

'He missed me. Probably thought Mother had locked me in the attic as a punishment. I gave him to Mother, you see.'

'Then you should have been stricter when he was a piglet,' I said.

At that point, Ryder cracked.

'Excuse me! Would everyone – someone – pay attention.'

'You still here, Philip?' Mother said.

'Is he a friend of yours, Mummy?' Finbar said innocently, not realizing the game was over.

'Christ, what a family,' breathed Ryder, the gun falling to his side in despair.

'Hey, I'm not one of them,' said Sophie.

'And I'm only related to him by blood,' I said, determined not to let Finbar have the last word.

'Shut up! All of you!'

Elvis turned around with much heavy breathing, then sat on his haunches, shuffled his bottom a bit into a more comfortable position, and stared at Ryder. He even cocked his head to one side like a curious Labrador. His jaws were on a level with – and less than twenty inches from – Ryder's crotch.

The four of us watched Elvis settle himself and then all looked at Ryder.

219

'You have our undivided attention,' I said. 'But put the gun away, Phil. I wouldn't want you to startle Elvis.'

He knew when he was beaten and tucked the pistol away inside his jacket.

'What is it with you lot and animals?' he said, almost to himself, but I understood.

'That plaster on your hand, it's not rope burn, is it? You did that at Windy Ridge when you were snooping about, didn't you?'

'A cat did it. A bloody great black panther of a cat. Came at me out of nowhere.'

Mother and Finbar looked at each other and said, 'Chuck Berry,' in unison.

Ryder put his hands in his windcheater's pockets and took a cautious step back away from Elvis.

'You are all in serious trouble, you know.'

'What have I done? This is nothing to do with me.'

Thanks, Mom, knew we could rely on you.

'Come on, Beth, you've been hiding Finbar since the weekend.'

'Is there a warrant out for him?' I asked. 'Or has anyone reported him missing?'

Ryder conceded that one. 'No, not exactly . . .'

'What, no one reported me missing?'

'Shut it, Finbar.'

'Look, you all know this is going to be a police matter at some point,' Ryder ploughed on. 'Cooperate with me and I can keep you out of it.'

'That seems jolly decent . . .' Finbar started.

'How?' I said sharply.

'You go down as confidential sources. As long as we catch Gronweghe in possession, bang to rights, we don't need to reveal our sources.'

'So it will look like you set the whole thing up and you get maximum credit.'

'Something like that.'

'Making MI5 look like the real business when it comes to doing the drug dealers, much slicker than the clodhopping cops in the Drug Squad. That it?'

'You've got a devious mind, Roy.'

'You can say that again,' said Sophie.

'So, are you ready to do a deal?' said Ryder, and he was talking just to me.

'How good are your guarantees to keep us clear?' I asked, even as Finbar started nodding enthusiastically.

'You may have to sign the Official Secrets Act, so we can always get you on that later if we need to.'

'I meant what guarantees do *we* get?'

'You're sharp enough, Roy. You know we're not interested in prosecuting for possession, that's not our game plan. Anyway, you'd get off with a caution these days.'

'Sure, if you've got an ounce of weed stashed about your person. I think we're talking an entirely different scale of things here.'

'It's not in anybody's interest to show how this can be done, is it?'

I looked at Mother and she shrugged her shoulders. I looked at Finbar and he shrugged his good shoulder. Sophie sighed noncommittally and her T-shirt went up and down.

'OK, Phil, what do you want to know?'

'First thing is the "when". What's the likely time of the harvest?'

'Any day now,' I said. 'The plants look ready and they rented a harvester a couple of days ago. My guess is this week.'

'I'd go along with that. What are they going to do with it?'

'The original plan was to stack the bales at Windy Ridge,' Finbar volunteered. 'Then stack rolls of winter silage round the outside to hide it. I thought that if I wasn't around, they would have to find somewhere else.'

'I think they have,' I said. 'Gronweghe has hired in some local talent. A couple of small-time hoods from Ipswich, a pair of brothers called Miller. I'll bet you they've got a place lined up, maybe rented somewhere on another farm somewhere between Windy Ridge and Ipswich.'

'Miller, you say? Thanks, we didn't know about them.'

'We? How many of you are there?'

'There are three of us, but I'm the Case Officer. We've had one at Stansted Airport watching Finbar's car in the long-term car park for God knows how long.'

'I came back through Heathrow.' Finbar smiled weakly,

holding up his plastercast. 'Sorry, couldn't drive. Is the car all right?'

Ryder ignored him.

'The third one is based at Felixstowe, keeping an eye out for Gronweghe and liaising with Customs and Excise. I can call them in now. All we need is the "where". We haven't been able to spot anything yet, so somebody will have to show us where the stuff is.'

'Didn't you think about hiring an aeroplane?' asked Sophie with an unbelievably sweet smile.

'We have to watch our budgets,' said Ryder seriously, 'but we were coming round to the idea. But now one of you can show us where the stuff is growing, can't you?'

'And I suppose it'll have to be me,' I said.


It had to be me. Finbar couldn't drive and I squashed the idea of Sophie driving him in Armstrong on the grounds that I valued Armstrong too much. Mother didn't know where the stuff was growing and didn't have a car of her own, so she would have had to travel in Ryder's car. I didn't think even I could get her off a murder charge if I let that happen, given the way she had started to glare at him.

I suppose I could have given Ryder directions, but then he would probably have shown up at Windy Ridge and Godfrey would have shot him. I felt I ought to give Godfrey a chance to get free and clear. I saw no reason for Godfrey to even get involved as one of Ryder's 'confidential sources' – if such an A-list actually existed – unless his dutiful son Barry grassed him up.

Ryder wanted to head off immediately. I wanted to get something to eat. Finbar wanted to take Sophie to lunch. Mother wanted Ryder out of her house. That sort of clinched it, so we hit the road again, Sophie lounging in the back of Armstrong and Ryder following us in his Escort, a carphone glued to his ear for most of the first twenty miles.

'He's probably rounding up his troops,' I said when Sophie asked me what he was doing. 'We should do the same. Give Godfrey a ring and warn him that we're on our way back and that we've got company.'

Sophie busied herself with her mobile phone and in my mirror I saw her put it to her ear, then take it away, look at it and shake it and start dialling again. When that didn't work, she smacked it on the seat and then shook it some more.

'Angel,' she whined, 'you know you said you thought I'd bought a cloned phone?'

'Yes,' I said slowly.

'What happens when they find out you've been cloned?'

'I think you get cut off.'

'I think you're right.'

'Oh shit.'

'So what do we do? Borrow Ryder's carphone?'

'No, I don't want Ryder to know Godfrey was involved. Let's just press on. We'll be there in twenty minutes. Godfrey'll be all right.'

Wrong.

I put my foot down and we were zipping through Earl Shelton within fifteen minutes. Another two and we were the other side of the village and turning off the village road and on to the track which leads up to Windy Ridge.

Even as we turned on to the track I could see that the combine harvester had gone from the Dutch barn.

Halfway up the track, I could see that the front door of the house was open.


'Keep your head down,' I snapped at Sophie in a tone which made it clear I didn't want to debate about it.

'Whatsamatter?' she shouted, from somewhere on the floor.

'They've been here, but I hope they've gone.'

'If they've gone' – she yelped as Armstrong went over a rut in the track – 'why am I hiding? By the way, this floor is *filthy*.'

'I said I hope they've gone. If they've left someone in the house, maybe they'll think I'm a cab somebody's ordered.'

'What about Ryder?' She coughed, probably from dust in the floor mats which one day I really must get around to cleaning.

I looked in the mirror. Ryder's Escort was a hundred yards behind us, going slower than we were as he was not used to the potholes.

'What's he supposed to be?' Sophie cried. 'A back-up mini-cab?'

'Look, I didn't say it was a good plan, just a quick plan. Stay down.'

We were fifty feet from the house when I veered over the farmyard to the right and then swung down hard left on the wheel, putting Armstrong through almost a hundred and eighty degrees, facing back towards the track and Ryder's oncoming Ford. I hit Armstrong's horn and blew three short – and one long – toots for the benefit of the house, at the same time flashing my headlights at Ryder in the hope he would take the hint and slow down, if not stop.

There was no response from the house. I had a perfect view of the open front door in my wing mirror. Nothing moved in the doorway, none of the curtains twitched. I still sank down in my seat until I could just see the mirror and, over the dashboard, Ryder's car pulling to a halt to the side of the track.

I hit the horn again. Nothing stirred. I saw Ryder open the door of the Ford very slowly. He seemed to be as low in his seat as I was.

'Anything happening?' Sophie hissed.

'How many times do I have to tell you to keep your head down?' I snapped back.

'Normally only the once, darling, but I thought we were in trouble.'

'Very funny. There's no sign of anyone.'

'Is that good?'

'Yes and no. It's good that no one is actually shooting at us, but where the fuck is Godfrey?'

I saw Ryder easing his way out of his car, then stop and put his head rapidly above the door. He had his right hand inside his jacket. His head bobbed back down as if he had seen something.

My eyes flashed back to the wing mirror.

'It's OK, Sophie,' I said. 'I think we're safe.'

I had just seen Chuck Berry walk slowly out of the front door and trot across the yard.

I switched off Armstrong's engine and climbed out, opening the back door so Sophie could crawl out. Down the track, Ryder got out of the Ford, his right hand still inside his jacket, looking like an anxious Napoleon.

I waved to Ryder, beckoning him on.

'Are you sure it's safe?' Sophie said, sounding as if lying on the floor of Armstrong maybe wasn't such a bad idea.

'Pretty sure. Chuck Berry wouldn't be prowling around if there were strangers here, he'd be lying in ambush somewhere.'

Sophie grabbed the back of my left thigh with her right hand and squeezed.

'You're saying this based on a cat? There could be a psycho Dutchman in there with a grudge against you and a mega dry-cleaning bill for me, and you're going on the prowling of some mangy cat?'

'It's the way of the countryside, Sophie.'

'Bollocks.'

'OK, let Ryder go in first, just in case.'

Ryder was in earshot by now.

'The harvester has gone and the house has been left open. There was an old boy, used to be a farm labourer, keeping an eye on the place for us. He should be here.'

'Let me take a look,' Ryder said, taking the lead.

Sophie and I exchanged glances then followed at a suitable distance.

By the time Ryder reached the open front door, he had the snub-nosed pistol out and was holding it in a two-handed grip. He went down into a crouch and pushed the door all the way open with the barrel of the gun, then he leaned in as if feeling for something with his left hand.

He drew out Godfrey's shotgun by the barrel, or what was left of it. It must have been lying on the hallway floor. Someone had walloped it against the doorstep, at least twice, once to bend and buckle the barrels, once to smash the wooden stock. I guessed it hadn't been Godfrey.

Good guess.

Godfrey was in the kitchen on the floor. He was lying on his back, his arms behind him. The bruises around his eyes and on his cheeks were already dark and I couldn't see where his lips ought to be for the blood. I was grateful for the blood, which formed an obscene bubble from his nose, though, as that told me he was still breathing.

I knelt beside him and only then realized why he was lying scrunched up with his arms behind and underneath him.

'Bastards! Get a knife.'

'Where . . . what . . .?'

'It's a kitchen!' I shouted at Sophie. 'Find a fucking knife.'

'Here.'

Ryder was holding out a Swiss Army penknife. They were probably standard issue to all M15 boy scouts these days.

It took me three goes to get the main blade out, my hands were already slippery with blood. Then I felt around Godfrey's neck until I located the slip knot, inserted the knife and began to saw as gently as I could. The baling twine frayed then snapped. There was an instant bubbling rasp of breath from the old man and his body seemed to relax. Then I cut the twine where they had run the noose down to his wrists, which were in turn tied to his ankles.

Sophie had found a towel and I folded it and slid it under his head. She helped me straighten him out.

'I think he's got broken ribs,' she said.

'You done first aid?'

'Enough to know he needs a hospital.'

'Why did they beat him?' asked Ryder. He still had the gun in his hand for some reason.

'He probably tried to phone us and when we didn't answer, he tried to stop them. Must have thought we'd left him, like Barry and Finbar.'

'Would he have told them where the stuff was growing?'

'No,' I said firmly. 'In any case, he wouldn't have to. They knew all the time. It was only when Finbar lost his nerve, and then Barry did, that they got worried. Gronweghe more or less told us in Brussels that he didn't *need* Finbar, just needed him to stay out of the way. He'd made other arrangements by then, with the local talent, the Millers.'

'If they are there and cutting the crop, I've got to be there. You'll have to show me.'

'We need an ambulance here.'

'I'll use my carphone for you.'

He waved the gun towards the hallway and I saw what he

meant. Finbar's phone had been ripped from its mounting and thrown against the wall.

'I've got a map in the car. Come and show me. Now.'

He wasn't exactly pointing the revolver at me, but he was thinking about it.

'Do it,' said Sophie. 'Don't let those bastards get away with it. I'll get Godfrey cleaned up.'

I caught her eye and stared hard.

'OK, I'll go with Phil here and use his phone to call for an ambulance.' As I said it, I emphasized 'phone' and raised my eyes upwards, meaning upstairs, hoping she'd got it.

'Come on, get your map out,' I said to Ryder as I got to my feet and began to hurry for the door.

Once on the blind side of him, I folded the Swiss Army knife and palmed it into the pocket of my jacket. By the time we were outside and jogging for the cars, I was wiping my hands on my jeans and apart from Godfrey's blood, they were empty.

Ryder reached the Escort first and tore the door open. He leaned in and pulled out a large-scale Ordnance Survey map which he must have had open as he had been driving. He spread it on the bonnet of the car.

'Show me.' He tapped the map with his pistol and metal clunked on metal.

I smoothed the map and ran a bloodied finger along the line of the road to Earl Shelton then out to Windy Ridge.

'We're here. Follow this road for almost exactly seven miles. Here, where it bends to the right you'll see the river on your left. Just here' – I stabbed with my finger – 'there's a field of maize. The entrance to the field is here. Field, ditch and hedge, a second field of maize, then another hedge. Then between there and what's marked here as river-bank marsh, that's where they'll be. You won't see anything from the road, but you should be able to hear the combine.'

'Good.' He pulled the map away from me and bundled it into the Ford, backing off around the driver's door.

'Now let me use your phone.'

'I'll do it on the way, Roy. Trust me.'

'Won't take a second. Let's do it now.'

Finally, the gun came up.

'I need some time to get the lie of the land, Roy. The first thing the paramedics will do when they see the old man is call the local Plod and I may not be ready for them. I will call, but I need a bit of time. My back-up can't get here for an hour or so.'

'That's your problem, you fucker!'

'Now, Roy, don't get – oh, I see, you were thinking of me and your mother . . .'

I didn't say anything. I didn't have to.

'Sorry, that was uncalled for. You'd better give me the keys to your cab. I don't want you screwing things up.'

I glared at him for five seconds, then reached into my pocket for Armstrong's keys and threw them to him. He caught them easily.

'Now back off.'

'You will call?'

'Yes, I will.'

I turned on my heels and ran back to the house. By the time I reached the front door, Ryder had turned the Ford and was bouncing down the track towards the road.

'What the hell was all that about?' asked Sophie. She was on her knees by Godfrey's head, using a towel and a washing-up bowl of water to clean him up.

'Is Godfrey's mobile still here?'

'It was upstairs.' She held it out for me.

'Call an ambulance. Tell them it's Windy Ridge Farm going west out of Earl Shelton. God knows how long it will take them to find it.'

'Where are you going?' she cried.

I stepped over Godfrey and began to unbolt the kitchen door.

'There's bound to be something I can use in the shed,' I said, mostly to myself.

'What the bloody hell are you doing?' she yelled as I ran out into the yard.

'I'm going to screw things up,' I shouted over my shoulder.

# Chapter Nineteen

This was ridiculous. Farms were supposed to be the most dangerous places excluding Irish pubs at closing time, outside of an active war zone, but could I find anything useful? There were empty cans and jagged bits of metal on which I managed to cut two fingers, but nothing I could identify as readily flammable. I already knew that Finbar didn't keep a supply tank of diesel, unlike most farms, and cursed Big Mac McCandy. I could really have used one of his missing tankerloads.

Then my foot stubbed something under the workbench and I bent down to look. There was an open yellow plastic sack under there, and two other unopened ones. I dragged the open one out. It looked like fish food, small white and granular, except fish food wasn't white and this didn't smell like an old fish tank.

I straightened up the sack and read the printing on the front. AMMONIUM NITRATE, it said, 45% NITROGEN. Then, in smaller letters much lower down: CAUTION – ASSISTS FIRE.

'Assists Fire'. I liked that. Yes, that would do nicely.

I pulled out the two unopened bags and dragged them to the entrance of the shed. They were fifty-kilo bags and I wasn't up to carrying them round to Armstrong, so I decided to bring him to them and carry just the open one, swinging it two-handed over my shoulder like a burglar's swag bag.

Sophie was in the kitchen doorway as I staggered across the yard with my load.

'Ambulance is on its way. I just said there was someone badly hurt and it was a farm. What the hell are you doing?'

'Taking out some insurance,' I said, hurrying round the corner of the house with her in hot pursuit.

'What? What's going on?'

'Just stay with Godfrey, will you?'

She ran in front and put herself between me and Armstrong, holding her arms out like she was going to make a defensive tackle.

'Hold it right there, Angel, and tell me what you're doing.'

I sidestepped her and she made only a token attempt to stop me.

'I don't trust Ryder not to blow it,' I wheezed, out of breath. 'And if he blows it, any guarantees he made are blown too. If that happens, I'm going to light up the biggest fucking joint you've ever seen.'

She got in front of me again and slapped her hand on Armstrong's door handle. Looking up at me from under her blonde fringe, she said:

'Do you want me to call the fire brigade?'

'Only if you see smoke,' I said.

She opened the door for me and I threw the first bag on to the back seat.

'Thanks.'

'You take care, OK?' She took my face in her hands and dived in for a kiss. 'Can I help?'

'No, you keep an eye on Godfrey. I'll drive round the back for the rest.'

She ran back into the house and I dropped to the ground under the rear of Armstrong and felt for the spare key I carried on a magnetic pad welded near the exhaust pipe. I had to scrape the mud from it before it would fit, but then I had Armstrong fired up and I reversed around the house into the cobbled back yard up to the outbuildings.

I pulled on the pair of ancient black leather gloves I keep in Armstrong's boot to protect my hands as I ransacked the shed for anything else I could use.

I found a tin of white spirit and shook it. The can was less than a quarter full, but every little helped. I put it with the fertilizer and ran a hand along the jars and tins on the shelf above the workbench, knocking things off and smashing them as I did so. Nothing. I had never seen a shed or garage so *safe*.

Then, at the end of the shelf, I saw a reel of garden hose hanging from a nail in the wall and I kicked myself. As I took out Ryder's penknife, I tried to work out how many miles Armstrong had done since I had filled him up. His tank held just over sixty litres and I guessed he had forty left in there if I was lucky. I didn't bother consulting the fuel gauge. That hadn't worked properly for years.

I pulled the hose off the wall and cut off a four-foot length, then I started loading.

From on top of the shed, Chuck Berry lay and watched me with mild curiosity and, I would like to think, approval.


Ryder had parked his Ford in the entrance to the first maize field, which had been made wider by the combine and, judging by the tracks and the amount of maize knocked over, at least one other vehicle.

I turned Armstrong off and got out to listen. I could hear engines from down by the river. Definitely one, maybe two.

There was plenty of room down the side of the field for me to drive and the ground seemed solid enough, the tyre tracks of the combine hardly more than an inch deep. I decided to risk it.

Armstrong groaned, or his springs did, as I bumped along in first gear. He was no four-by-four.

As I judged I was nearing the top of the natural rise in the field, I stopped and let the engine idle. I hugged the edge of the maize crop, being whacked in the face more than once by cobs of corn as the plants sprang back at me.

From the top of the rise I could see down as far as the river. On the other side of the second maize field, the hemp field had been shaved around the edges, the real hemp plants left on the ground to dry out or ret or whatever it was it did. The serious crop had been cut and tied into oblong bales which dropped from the rear of the combine as if it were a giant metal insect laying a string of eggs.

There were three of them working the field. One driving the combine, one driving a tractor with a forked shovel on the front which loaded the bales on to a flat-back trailer where the third man stacked them. I couldn't tell at that distance which one was Gronweghe.

The combine had cut the cannabis in a decreasing square pattern and at least half the field was already baled. The trailer was almost full. They'd be taking it somewhere to store it soon.

Ryder had the same thought.

He had been hiding in the hedge bordering the second maize field. When the tractor driver and the man on the trailer were stacking a load and the combine turned towards the river, he broke cover and ran across the cut hemp into the remaining rectangle of cannabis.

'Shit,' I said aloud, and ran back to Armstrong to get my binoculars out of the boot.

With them, I could see the tops of the cannabis plants move as Ryder made his way through them towards the tractor and the trailer. By this time, the combine was on the opposite long side of the rectangle, parallel to the river, and making ready to turn right and cut the shorter side towards the tractor, towards me, and towards Ryder.

I focused the glasses on the two men loading the trailer and didn't recognize either of them. I couldn't tell if they were brothers or not but I was going to count them as the Millers.

I flashed over to the combine, now turned and heading in my direction. It was impossible to see clearly into the cab but if that was Gronweghe, then Ryder was in trouble.

'Don't do it,' I said to myself.

But he did.


As the combine approached, its whirling jaws chewing up the plants in front of it, Ryder stepped out of the cannabis. He held his pistol at arm's length, aimed at the men on the tractor and trailer and used his other arm to flag down the combine, like a policeman on traffic duty.

I had no chance of knowing what he was saying, but the sight of the gun seemed to make an impression on the Millers. They stopped what they were doing, the one standing on the trailer even going as far as to put his hands up.

Ryder stepped further out into the cut field so that the driver of the combine could get a clear sight of him. He even swung the gun towards the harvester. Surely the driver could see now. He probably could, he just wasn't going to stop.

When the combine was twenty or thirty – it was difficult to tell – feet away from him, the combine veered off its line of cutting and went straight for Ryder in the open field. Ryder put both hands on the gun and fired, the shot barely audible above the engine noise.

The door of the combine's cab flew open and the driver leaned half out. Through the binoculars I could see the driver was Paul Gronweghe, and he had a gun which even at this distance looked a lot bigger than Ryder's. And he was using it.

I had no idea how many times he fired, but one shot knocked Ryder almost into a backward somersault. He stayed down for no more than a second, and you couldn't blame him as the combine was still heading straight for him.

On his feet, clutching his chest, Ryder staggered back into the uncut cannabis. He must have offered a perfect target at that stage, but Gronweghe was back inside the cab, swinging the wheel to turn the combine in chase.

I stomped the accelerator and Armstrong roared into life. Fastening my seat belt took three attempts, partly because I wasn't used to wearing it and partly because I still had my gloves on and I could feel my hands sweating inside them.

We bounced over the rise and down the hill in the ruts made by the combine and the tractor. Something went in the suspension on the front offside wheel, advertised by a loud juddering noise.

By the time we hit the entrance to the second maize field, Armstrong was doing thirty miles an hour but something very bad was happening to his rear axle.

There was a Range Rover parked near the hedgerow, which I hadn't spotted before, but I didn't stop as by then I was fighting for control of the steering wheel as we thundered into the hemp field, smashing my head twice on the roof as the cab bucked and jumped under me.

Something flashed by me – a figure with a white, startled face. In the mirror I saw it move again. It was one of the Miller brothers, almost as scared as I was, running out of the field.

Armstrong hit a bale, sending it spinning into the air to land on the bonnet and burst in a cloud of leaves and dust. I hit the wipers to clear the windscreen but nothing happened. I tried the horn to signal Ryder; again nothing. Then the front offside wheel sank suddenly, the tyre blown, metal grinding on metal. I kept my foot on the accelerator, the engine howling.

Gronweghe was swinging the combine in a figure of eight, the cutting blades whipping the plants up and to the side, the baler either switched off or broken. It was producing a dust cloud like a smokescreen.

Then Ryder was ahead of me, lurching out of the plants, his gun in one hand hanging by his side, his other hand clutched to his chest, his windcheater stained red.

I wasn't sure what to do next, all I knew was that if I stopped to pick him up, I would probably not get Armstrong started again. He was already skewing sideways, a drunken crab on three and a half wheels.

Ryder raised the gun.

'Not me, you idiot!' I shouted, though I could hardly hear myself.

Then I realized he was pointing, not shooting.

The combine was coming out of its dusty smokescreen, right up behind me.

Ryder was ten yards away, straight in front of me. Gronweghe was closing fast behind me. Ryder raised his gun again, but the effort must have proved too much. He fainted, or maybe he died on me. Either way, he fell over and lay face down in the field.

Great. If he wasn't dead, he would be when I hit him with Armstrong and if that didn't kill him, Gronweghe would make sure.

I swung the steering wheel over to the right and it took all my strength. Armstrong crashed into the uncut cannabis, plants whipping across the windscreen.

I got to full lock and held it there, trying at the same time to fumble open my door and spot where the combine was. They used to say that a black Austin cab could turn on a sixpence, but since no one knows what a sixpence is these days, they usually just say it can turn in its own circle. Of course, they are normally referring to a nice, level, metalled London street, not the middle of a field.

'Come on, boy, you can do it.'

Above the grinding and clanging that was going on inside Armstrong, I could hear the roar of the combine. I could hear the damned thing even though I couldn't see it for the plants and the dust and what looked like steam coming out of the front of Armstrong's groaning engine.

But Gronweghe had taken the bait and followed me instead of mowing up Ryder. I knew he had because the combine was there in front of me as Armstrong completed his turning circle. And Armstrong was heading directly into its rotating blades.

When we hit, Armstrong was doing no more than five miles an hour and the combine perhaps ten. The impact was still enough to throw me against the windscreen, cracking my forehead.

I think I blacked out for a second or two. Or maybe I just sat there bemused, watching the combine's blades trying to chew their way through Armstrong's radiator and engine block, the bonnet buckling, almost rippling as if liquid, and then springing open, the final downstroke of the paddle cutters ripping it away completely.

Then the blades stopped turning, shorted out. But the combine didn't stop, it kept coming, slowly pushing Armstrong backwards.

I hauled on the handbrake but it made no discernible difference. It was time to get out, if I could. I had the door open but I couldn't move for some reason. Then I remembered the seat belt which held me in place, although the damned thing hadn't prevented my face from bouncing off the windshield. Still, no time now to go back to the makers and complain.

I got it unclipped and threw myself out, landing on one foot and one knee, stumbling, crashing through the plants. One of them tripped me and I spun round, getting a full view of the combine as it juggernauted by me.

In the cab above the wreckage of the cutting cylinder, there was Gronweghe struggling with the controls, trying to stop the combine from climbing up and over Armstrong. He saw me and reached down under his seat, bringing up a big automatic.

I stumbled backwards, wanting to get out of the plants but yet knowing they were at least something between me and him. Then Armstrong did me a last good turn, digging his wheels into the earth and refusing to be pushed any more.

The combine shuddered and more metal screeched. I don't think Gronweghe was trying to crush Armstrong, I think he just couldn't stop it. The harvester shuddered again then jolted as something gave way and Gronweghe was tossed around the cab, the steering wheel hitting him in the stomach and his shoulder bashing into the cab frame.

I saw the gun drop from his hand but then a sheaf of plants

put a curtain between us and I was waving my arms, chopping at the others to get away.

I fell out into the mown field no more than a yard from where Ryder lay inert. Across the field I could see the Range Rover four-wheel-driving it up the side of the maize field; the Miller boys making a tactical withdrawal. Behind me, I heard the combine's engine roar as Gronweghe revved for more power. Unlike the Millers, he didn't seem to want to give up.

I crawled to Ryder on my hands and knees. It seemed easier.

He was breathing, but there was a lot of blood on his chest and it was seeping through the fingers of the hand he had clutched to his jacket. In his other hand was his gun.

I prised it out of his fingers and gripped it tightly with my gloved hand.

'I'm just borrowing this,' I explained to the back of his head. 'I have an old friend to avenge.'

Then I got to my feet and strode back into the cannabis plants which towered over my head.


Gronweghe was struggling two-handed with the gears, trying to reverse the combine. What was left of Armstrong was being shaken like a rabbit in the jaws of a dog. The noise was that of a waste-disposal unit on overdrive.

I was no more than fifteen feet from the cab, at an angle to his left, when I parted the cannabis plants and let him see me.

He reached behind him in his seat, levering himself up so he could clear his gun, showing more of himself.

I put up Ryder's pistol and fired.


I climbed the metal ladder of the juddering combine and pulled open the cab door so I could lean in and kill the engine. The silence was deafening.

Gronweghe was slumped half on, half off the driver's seat, wedged semi-upright by the other side of the cab. I didn't touch him. There was a hole in his cheek, quite a neat hole, actually, just below his right eye. I could tell from the rear of the cab that the exit wound was probably less neat.

I'm not a particularly good shot. Just lucky.

I left Gronweghe's gun where it lay on the cab floor, then jumped down and walked around the wreckage of Armstrong.

I took my binoculars and slung them over my shoulder. The glove compartment yielded an empty quarter-bottle of vodka (which had not been quite empty before Sophie drove him), my emergency pack of cigarettes and a book of matches. I looked at the cigarettes and then at the plants around me.

Nah. There wasn't time.

I patted Armstrong's roof.

'Now for the Viking funeral.'

No time for sentiment. Ryder might die on me. His back-up might arrive. The Millers might return. Somebody might have told the cops that they'd heard a gunfight in the middle of the afternoon and wasn't that a bit early even for Suffolk?

I climbed into the back of Armstrong and opened Ryder's knife. I used it to slash open the bags of ammonium nitrate until the back seat was covered in the small white, odourless pellets. Then I ripped into the seating itself, exposing the spongy padding.

My chemistry was rusty but I knew that diesel needed help to get it going and that ammonium nitrate fertilizer had been a traditional ingredient in homemade bombs for many years. I wasn't building a bomb, I just needed to get a good blaze going.

I unscrewed Armstrong's fuel cap and inserted the length of hosepipe I had taken from Finbar's shed. Crouching down, I put the other end in my mouth and sucked until the vacuum pulled up the diesel. I managed to get a thumb over the end of the pipe before I got a mouthful. That I had done before.

I took my thumb away and squeezed the hose so that a stream of diesel sprayed over the fertilizer and soaked the seat.

I let the hose run and walked backwards through the plants to where Ryder was, digging my right heel into the ground to make a crude channel. When I got to the last row of cannabis, I ran back to Armstrong and pulled the hose out and laid it in the channel. The diesel still flowed and fumes filled the air.

Gradually, the fuel began to form a small river, trickling down the channel I had made.

I held my breath and reached into Armstrong for the last time to grab the can of white spirit. That at least I knew would go up easily, but I still wasn't sure I had enough makings for a big enough fire.

The answer was staring me in the face. I had guessed that Armstrong had about forty litres of diesel in his tank. The combine was a big, new model and these big new combines had big new fuel tanks, didn't they?

It was easy enough to find, along the right-hand side of the machine, and it was big enough to hold a hundred litres or even more. I had no way of knowing how much was still in it, nor any means of finding out, short of climbing back into the cab and trying to find a gauge. That, I decided, was not an option.

I pulled Ryder's gun from my pocket and stood back, took aim and fired at where I guessed the bottom of the tank was. Red agricultural diesel poured out of the hole even before the echo of the clang of the bullet on metal had faded from my ears.

I put the gun away and picked up the white spirit and crashed back through the jungle of stalks to Ryder.

The tractor the Miller brothers had abandoned was on the other side of the field, its engine still ticking over. Attached to it was the trailer of bales.

I ran across the cut field to it and climbed aboard. It had been a long time since I had driven a tractor, but once you stop panicking at the massive choice of gears, they're not that difficult. I drove over to the uncut rectangle of plants and followed the path made by Gronweghe's charge on Armstrong until I reached the combine, parking the trailer alongside it.

I unhooked the trailer and left it there, its rear wheels already inches deep in a spreading pool of diesel. I avoided looking at the combine's cab.

I swung the tractor round the sad, sunken shell of Armstrong and ploughed out of the plants and put the brake on.

Loading Ryder on to the tractor damn near finished me but I got him wedged over the right wheel arch eventually. My diesel river hadn't quite reached the end of my channel, but I couldn't wait any longer.

I pulled up a cannabis plant and folded it into a crude torch, dousing it with white spirit and letting what remained in the can pour into the channel. I fumbled the book of matches – not easy wearing gloves – and struck one and put it to the torch.

It caught immediately and I touched it to the diesel. And not much seemed to happen at first, then I could see that the orange-red flames were spreading and darkening and black smoke was snaking through the plants towards Armstrong.

I held on to Ryder's jacket collar with one hand and steered the tractor up the hill with the other. I had balanced him on the mudguard of the large rear wheel. It was hardly the most comfortable way to travel but I wasn't worried about that. I was more worried about the amount of blood still soaking through his clothes.

As we topped the rise in the first maize field, I turned my head. The smoke stack was now over fifty feet high and I could still hear the crack of glass breaking and the pop of pressure caps as filters and cooling systems exploded.

I took a deep breath of the smoky air.

Even this far away it was very interesting.

I abandoned the tractor in the maize field near Ryder's Ford. He groaned as I pulled him over my shoulder in a fireman's lift and staggered to his car.

I had to lie him down on the ground and go through his pockets to find his keys and as I did so, I found Armstrong's keys as well. I put them back in his pocket. I wouldn't need them again and if anyone had to explain what a burnt-out black London cab was doing in a field in Suffolk, then it had better be him.

I got the Ford open and hauled him on to the back seat. He groaned but didn't move.

Carefully, I unzipped his windcheater and then took his pistol from my pocket, slid it into his jacket and rezipped it.

Let him explain that as well.

# Chapter Twenty

I used Ryder's carphone to call Sophie on Godfrey's mobile, hoping I had remembered the number correctly.

'Angel? Are you all right?'

'Yeah, so far. And thanks for asking. How's Godfrey?'

'The ambulance is here now. They're fixing him up so he can travel.'

'Tell them not to leave, I've got another customer for them.'

'Angel, I can see smoke. Do I ring the fire brigade?'

'When you've a minute,' I said.


By the time I pulled in to Windy Ridge, there was more than an ambulance there. There was a blue Transit van, a black Rover and two of the most obvious unmarked police cars I had ever seen.

The unmarked cars had two men in each of them and they made no effort to get out. By the Rover, a large, thickset man wearing a leather jacket was standing at the open door talking into a radio handset. I nominated him as the one in charge and drove the Escort up to him.

I could tell he recognized the car and his face creased in puzzlement as he saw me driving it. I jerked my thumb back over my shoulder as I drew level and he looked into the rear window.

He was still holding the radio when he looked.

'Fuck, somebody's shot Phil!' he yelled into the handset.

'You should see the other guy,' I said.


That was the start of it and it was six hours before Sophie and I were left alone.

They left us alone because we couldn't go anywhere, we had no transport. We were also tired, hungry, probably in shock and certainly shell-shocked from answering so many stupid questions so many times.

The one with the Rover did seem to be in charge after all. He said his name was Bingham, but didn't say whether it was his first or his last. He wanted to know what had happened, so I told him.

I told him that Ryder had prevented me from calling the police or an ambulance for Godfrey. That he had taken my keys but that I had a spare and followed him because I thought he was in league with the bad guys. That I had arrived in time to see him shooting it out with Gronweghe and how I had driven to the rescue, smashing into Gronweghe and the combine with no thought of personal safety. It was only then I realized that Gronweghe was dead and how my sole concern was to get Ryder to a doctor and how the fire started, I hadn't a clue. Oh yes, and the other men there? No idea who they were.

The guys in the unmarked cars turned out to be Customs and Excise, not police, and they wanted a word with me too, but Bingham kept them at arm's length. The real police arrived eventually, but the advance guard was a solitary traffic cop who said he'd had a report of illegal stubble burning in a field near here. Bingham put an arm round his shoulder and walked him back to his police car, explaining the facts of life as they went.

More senior cops turned up later, including a couple of CID men in plain clothes. You could tell they were CID; they wanted to interview Sophie, not me.

Bingham fobbed them off, but that took a stand-up row in the yard, out of earshot. Sophie nipped upstairs and returned with a bag of groceries: Godfrey's emergency rations. The bag contained a huge pork pie and a bottle of Scotch. It may have had other things too.

Eventually the questions came down to where would we be over the next few days, were these addresses correct (they had three for me) and did we have any plans to leave the country? That sort of thing. Oh, and we wouldn't mind signing the Official Secrets Act, would we?

Bingham produced two forms from a leather document wallet. I didn't bother to read it, I just scribbled 'R. Maclean' and hoped he wasn't a graphologist. I think he was so relieved I had signed without screaming for a lawyer that he didn't check.

I noticed that Sophie signed hers 'S. Baudaire'.

Baudaire?

So that was her surname.


We slept late in Finbar's bed and woke slowly. I wanted to fool around again but Sophie said I badly needed a shave and I still stank of diesel.

'Is that a "No"?' I asked, and she punched me in the stomach.

Over coffee in the kitchen (with both of us stepping around the spot on the floor where we had found Godfrey, but neither of us mentioning it) she asked how we were going to get back to London.

'We could go into the village and con someone into giving us a lift into Ipswich and catch a train,' I suggested.

'I've gone off trains,' she said.

Fair enough. I took Godfrey's mobile off the overnight charger and dialled Stuart Street, though I was far from certain anyone would be in so late in the morning. To my surprise, Fenella answered.

'Why aren't you at work?' I asked, not wasting a 'Hello' on her.

'I've been let go!' she wailed. 'Oh Angel, it was . . . Where have you been, anyway? People have been asking about you.'

'Such as?'

'Well, there was a very nice policeman this morning, one of those who wear a suit, you know, not the uniform. He wanted to check that you actually lived here and I said yes, you did, but only *occasionally* and that you treated the place like a hotel. Then that perfectly horrid big person turned up only a few minutes ago. The one who was here before, the really really big, gi-enormous bloke –'

Domestos.

'What did he want, Fenella?' I cut in.

'Wanted to know why you hadn't returned Mr Mac's phone messages.'

'What messages?'

'They're all written down here by the phone!' She reeked of indignation as much as I did of diesel. 'He's rung three or four times and he can't get through on that other number you left.

Says he has to talk to you urgently. What was it you wanted, anyway?'

'It doesn't matter. Thanks, Fenella.'

I pressed the END button and looked at Sophie.

'Are you sure you don't fancy a few more days in the country? It might be safer.'


'You want me to *what*?'

'I want you to grass my son Nigel.'

'You want me to turn him in to the Old Bill? Your own son?'

'And his mates; the whole shooting match,' said Big Mac reasonably. 'Well, I can't, can I? I'm not a grass.'

'Neither am I,' I protested.

'But everybody knows I'm not. I have my position to think of.'

'So you want *me* to inform on *your* son? I've got this straight, have I?'

'Got it in one, Roy, preferably catch 'em red-handed, so there's no point in having expensive lawyers.'

'They send people down for smelting these days, Mr McCandy. The breweries have got it together and they press for prison sentences. It's not just a fine and a slap on the back of the legs any more.'

'I know that.' He sounded dreamy, almost philosophical. 'Prison was an education for me. It taught me how to manage people, how to plan ahead, diversify, watch your stock control, expand your options, how to make the best of a static market. I think of it like other people think of school: maybe the best days of your life. Doesn't mean you want to go back, though.'

I gulped.

'You are absolutely sure about this, Mr McCandy?'

'Yup. When I think of what I've spent on Nigel's education and he's still daft enough to think he can cross me . . . A spot of stir will be the making of the lad. He'll thank me for it one day, but he mustn't know it was me. That's why you've got to do it. I don't care how. I need twenty-four hours to clean out the Plumstead yard, make sure we don't have any of his metal there.'

243

I held the mobile away from my ear and pulled a face at it.

'But I can't, Mr McCandy. I'm stuck up in Suffolk without wheels.'

'Anything to do with the Miller brothers? I hear there are certain people looking for them.'

They say good news travels fast and somehow it didn't surprise me that McCandy's intelligence network was better than MI5's.

'Not really, but my cab's a write-off.'

'Get it repaired and send me the bill. I'll find a good garage for you. Where are you, exactly?'

'It's beyond that, Mr McCandy, it's burnt out, totalled.'

'Oh dear. I suppose I'd better send a car then.'


'He's big, isn't he? Isn't he big?' said Sophie for about the nineteenth time.

We were in the back of McCandy's Mercedes, heading southeast towards Romanhoe, with Domestos driving. The radio was tuned to Classic FM and was playing Elgar. Loudly. Domestos drove with both hands on the wheel, but conducted the music with both forefingers.

I had asked him to detour to Romanhoe and he had grunted in agreement. I wanted to check on Mother and Finbar, to make sure they were keeping their spirits up and not under house arrest.

When we reached Station Street, Sophie said she would stay in the car and talk to Domestos as I probably wanted it to be a family affair. Possibly quite emotional, as Mother would have been worrying about me, especially if the forces of law and order had been round. I wondered who she was talking about for a minute and was about to demand all the help I could get when Domestos grunted again, which I took to be agreement that he would like to have Sophie stay so he could grunt at her.

There were no policemen outside Mother's house, no snipers on the roof, no sign of the Riot Squad. I knocked on the door and heard a thump as Elvis hit the other side, his snout snuffling at the letter box.

I knocked again and when there was no answer, I bent down and carefully pushed open the letter box flap.

'Nobody home, boy?'

Elvis grunted. Maybe I should introduce him to Domestos.

Perhaps they had been arrested and carted off to chokey. Then I noticed the sheet of paper rolled into a cylinder and stuffed into the top of a milk bottle. I knew it was a clue: it had FITZROY written down the side in green ink.

I unrolled it and read: 'Everything cool. The bogies have been and gone so we've gone sailing. Love, Mum.'

Obviously Mother was worrying herself sick.

Back at the Mercedes, Domestos was telling Sophie how underrated Offenbach was.

'Sorry to interrupt, music fans, but could we just drive round by the Quay?'

We did so and when Domestos parked, I got out and walked along the edge of the Quay, looking at the boats bobbing gently on the full tide. There was a young lad working on one of the boats, applying varnish to the roof of a cabin. I asked him if he knew where the *Direct Star* was moored.

'Just over there,' he said, pointing with his paint brush. 'But she was taken out this morning.'

'A middle-aged woman and a guy with his arm in plaster?'

'Yeah, that's right. I didn't know it was their boat.'

Neither did they.

What a family.

I started to get back into the Mercedes, then I spotted the ship's chandler's on the corner next to the pub.

'Hang on a minute,' I said to Domestos. 'I've just remembered a bit of shopping I've got to do for Mr McCandy.'


Back in London, I had to borrow a pub. Preferably one of McCandy's but not one run by son Nigel. That was no problem, but I had better take Domestos along with me to smooth the way.

As it turned out, having Domestos with me was better than having a warrant card.

Norman Reeves, the manager of the Shadwell Arms, the farthest-flung pub in the McCandy empire, was also the longest-serving employee of Big Mac. Without Domestos there, he would have had me out on my ear for saying 'Good morning' let alone demanding to go into the pub's cellar.

The Shadwell was a backstreet boozer within a stone's throw of the Tower of London but few tourists were encouraged to find it. Even though we called round an hour before opening time, Norman gave the impression that he was far too busy to be spending time doing a guided tour of his cellar.

'How many kegs do you get through in a week?' I asked him, just to show polite interest.

'Usually two or three kils or twenty-two's and, say, six firkins or elevens or tubs, whatever we've been selling most of,' he answered carefully. He had been told to cooperate with me, but not why.

I knew enough from my own days as a barman to decode what he'd said. Beer came in casks or pressurized kegs, a keg being a type of container, not a type of beer as many think. They were graded by the amount of beer they held: a 'kil' was a kilderkin (eighteen gallons) and a firkin was half that (nine gallons), all the old imperial measures being in multiples of nine up to a barrel (thirty-six gallons). Metric containers were measured in hectolitres but most publicans referred to them by their nearest imperial equivalents: twenty-two or eleven gallons, or just 'twenty-two's'. A 'tub' was slang for anything which wasn't a regular size, say a ten-gallon keg or even smaller, which would be used for slow-selling beers or cider.

'And when do they collect the empties?'

'Tuesdays. Crack of dawn so they don't screw up the traffic.'

'Do you stack them up on the street?'

'Not allowed to, round here.'

'OK, thanks, Norman. I'm going to take a couple of empties with me if that's all right by you.'

Reeves looked to Domestos for instructions. Domestos nodded.

'Take your pick. Can I get back to work now?'

'Sure. Oh, just one other thing. What do you use to unscrew the spears?'

He pretended to look stupid. He was a gifted impressionist.

'Don't know what you mean. Them's sealed containers, you can't tamper with them.'

'Now, Norman, you and I know you *shouldn't* tamper with them, doesn't mean to say you can't.'

He looked at Domestos again and when Domestos grunted, he reached behind a stack of crates and produced a long-handled tool adapted from an adjustable wrench.

'Just lock on to the pressure seal and turn anti-clockwise,' he said.

'Thank you. Shall I get Domestos to return it when I've finished?'

'Don't bother, I've got a spare.'

I hefted the wrench on to my shoulder.

'I'll need a couple of those kegs in the back of the van,' I said to Domestos.

I had told McCandy I needed a Transit van or similar for the weekend if I was to do what he wanted. That too had been no problem.

I scanned the pub cellar and read some of the fading notices stuck on the walls in no apparent order. There were the regulation safety notices about carbon dioxide, no heavy lifting and electrical circuits in cellars and one, newer than the others, which said: KEG THEFT HOTLINE – TO CLAIM YOUR REWARD.

I pulled it off the wall and folded it into the back pocket of my jeans. Behind me I heard Domestos grunting up the stairs to the saloon bar above.

He was climbing the stairs sideways as he had an eleven-gallon keg under each arm. I could see that they still had green plastic caps on the syphon head where you plugged in the beer pipe.

'No, Domestos,' I said gently. 'Empty ones.'


The balloon went up, so to speak, just after ten past ten on Sunday morning.

It wasn't a balloon, of course, it was a large cloud of noxious orange smoke which even the fans they had fitted to the smelter chimney couldn't cope with. Short of a big arrow coming down from heaven and pointing 'Here They Are', there wasn't a better way of spotting the smelter. And the assembled hordes of policemen and brewery security men took the hint and smashed through the door in the fence, driving their vehicles across the waste ground to where choking, crying smelters were staggering out of the smoke.

Big Mac McCandy and I were watching from the Transit he had loaned me. We were parked at a discreet distance so as not to attract the attention of the forces of law and order.

'What were those things?' he asked me.

'Distress flares. I got them from a ship's chandler's out on the coast.'

'They poisonous?'

'Don't think so.'

Once I had removed the spears from the empty kegs from the Shadwell Arms, I had experimented with sheets of bubble-wrap plastic so the flares wouldn't rattle around or fall out when the smelters removed the spear. They were so light I doubted they'd be noticed. When I was satisfied, I replaced the spears and it had been easy enough to slip them into the stack awaiting collection outside the Jubilee late on Friday night.

'Well, that's that, then,' he said.

'You don't want to see any more?'

'No. You've done what I asked, Roy.'

'I didn't mean that,' I said. He was staring out of the van's window, not looking at me, not looking at the figures running around in the orange smoke in the distance.

'Can I ask you something, Mr McCandy?'

'Yeah, if you like.'

'What's Mrs McCandy going to do when she hears that Nigel's been arrested?'

He turned to me and a slow smile ignited his face.

'She'll be mortified. Absobloodylutely gobsmacked. She'll have to resign from about five hundred committees and stop putting on airs and graces. Probably won't leave the house for a year.'

It suddenly dawned on me that there were other families like mine.

McCandy picked up his Mercedes from Stuart Street and said he would have taken me for a drink but he really ought to be home when the solicitor rang.

'You OK to hang on to the van?' he asked.

'Sure,' I said, and saw him remember.

'That's right, your cab's written off, isn't it? What happened?'

'It sort of caught fire,' I said vaguely.

'I'll see what I can do about that,' he said in the tone of a Greek with a Gift Token.

'Er . . . don't put yourself out, Mr McCandy.'

'No, I owe you one, Roy.'

'Really, don't . . .'

'Did you get your problem sorted? A family problem, you said, didn't you?'

'That's fine. Or it will be. I'm having lunch with my father tomorrow and that should sort it, I hope.'

'That's good, Roy. That's encouraging. Fathers and sons should stay close.'


To my horror, McCandy came round to Stuart Street the next day, just before noon.

'I was just passing, Roy, thought I'd collect the van.'

'Yeah . . . er . . . whatever suits you, Mr McCandy. I was just going out, actually.'

'Lunch with your dad, right? I'll give you a lift if you don't mind turning up in the Transit. Going anywhere posh?'

'Westminster. But I can get a bus . . .'

'Won't hear of it. Let's go.'

He didn't say anything about Nigel or what had happened when the family solicitor or the cops had phoned, or what Mrs McCandy's reaction had been to the news. I think he would have if I had asked, but I decided not to intrude on private grief. I had enough of my own.

Instead, he talked about Armstrong.

'I've been thinking about that cab of yours, Roy. Now, the way I see it, you drove that old cab because it suited you for some reason. Now, you have your reasons, but if you fancied another one – 'cos you'll need a set of wheels, won't you? – it just so happens that I know this cabbie, lives out at Upminster, who's coming up for retirement. He's got a Fairway and I might just be able to get it for a fair price. He says it's got 190,000 miles on the clock but it's in exceptional nick. Would you be interested?'

I did some arithmetic. A possible insurance claim on Armstrong, whatever I could screw out of my father and the reward money for phoning the keg theft hotline.

'I might very well be interested. Can I give you a bell at the end of the week?'

''Course you can. I think he'd take four grand for it.'

The ex-cabbie was either sunstruck or deeply in debt to Big Mac.

'Four grand?' I must have sounded startled.

'OK, I'll knock him down to three.'

And I might find his hands still attached to the steering wheel.

'Now, where do you want dropping?'

'There.' I pointed to the Houses of Parliament. 'Just round the corner. St Stephen's entrance.'

'I didn't know there was a restaurant in there,' he said sulkily.

'There isn't. My dad works there.'

'Fuck me, I didn't know your dad was an MP.'

'I never said he worked in the House of *Commons* . . .'


We ate in one of the smaller dining rooms. People would nod and smile at my father as they went by our table. Waitresses called him by his first name. Nobody said anything to me.

'You could have put a tie on,' he told me.

'But then I would have had to wear a shirt.'

Over the lamb cutlets he finally broached the subject.

'Everything seems to be in hand up in Suffolk. Amazingly enough.'

'No nasty headlines? No questions being asked?'

He chewed meat before he answered.

'Not really. Too many vested interests, it appears.'

'You can say that again. How's Philip Ryder?'

'Sick leave, of course, but he'll survive. He doesn't remember very much, but there'll be an internal enquiry which will vindicate him. He took too much responsibility on himself but it all seemed to work out in the end.'

'And the body they found?'

'Police matter,' he said dismissively. 'Unidentified as far as I'm aware, and likely to remain so.'

I helped myself to some more wine, despite a filthy look from a hovering waitress.

'How long did you know about Ryder?' I asked gently.

'I'm sorry?' he said, all innocence.

'You were in touch with him, you must have been. He was waiting for me in Romanhoe when we found Finbar. No one else knew I was going there.'

He didn't miss a beat.

'There were pressures, Fitzroy. A word was whispered in my ear about what was going on. Better if I helped. Family farm, family name, that sort of thing. Soon as I heard, I knew Finbar couldn't cope.'

'But I could?'

'Oh yes. I had every confidence that you would stir up so much shit that we would provoke a result one way or the other. Which is exactly what you did, wasn't it?'

Thanks, Dad.

'Heard from Mother?' I said savagely, to get my revenge.

'No, I haven't. I have heard that she has taken up sailing, though. There's a small matter of a rented yacht which seems to be missing.'

'You're on your own there, Father.'

'Did hear from Finbar, though,' he went on. 'He may come out of it quite well, actually. Compensation, that sort of thing.'

'Now I'm glad you raised that,' I said, 'because I'm looking for compensation for a written-off black cab. An insurance claim might embarrass a few people.'

'I'll have a word. See what can be done.'

That was nice. Old Godfrey Ineson gets put in hospital standing up for his son. Big Mac McCandy gets his son sent down because it will do him good. Mine has a word with somebody.

'Do it quick, Dad, would you? You owe me on this one.'

He looked at his plate.

'And next time there's a family problem, put me out for adoption, would you?'

251

'Ah. Funny you bringing that up,' he said, and I felt ice form in my stomach.

'It's about your sister . . .'

'No! No way!' I shouted, pushing my chair back and knocking over the wine. 'Not my sister!'

She was bloody dangerous.

# Other titles available from Robinson Publishing

*Lights, Camera, Angel*                Mike Ripley                £6.99 [   ]
Streetwise Jack-the-lad Angel is bored, so his fashion designer partner, Amy, gets
him involved in her new project – working on a big-budget American movie at
Pinewood Studios. With his unerring nose for trouble, Angel soon discovers that
the mishaps dogging the set are anything but accidental and the handsome star
of the film seems to be in particular danger. Angel gets stuck into life on the
celebrity A-list, mingling with the sexiest actresses. It's a dirty job, but someone's
got to do it.

*Bootlegged Angel*                Mike Ripley                £6.99 [   ]
Recently hitched Angel is supposed to be cleaning up his act. However, his new
job in the fashion business, is not all it's cracked up to be. He's offered a job
working undercover for a brewery in darkest Kent, where bootlegging cheap
beer from France is a growth industry. Angel manages to infiltrate a gang of
smugglers and finds himself in charge of a run-down country pub. Plus a
crooked American couple are preying on unsuspecting publicans in the area . . .

*Thus Was Adonis Murdered*                Sarah Caudwell                £6.99 [   ]
His was a body to die for . . .
Reduced to near penury by the iniquitous demands of the Inland Revenue,
young barrister Julia Larwood decamps on an Art Lovers holiday to Venice. But
poor, romantic Julia – how could she guess that the ravishing fellow Art Lover
for whom she conceives a passion is himself an employee of the Inland Revenue?
Or that her night of love with him would end in murder – with her inscribed
copy of the current Finance Act discovered next to the corpse . . .

Robinson books are available from all good bookshops or can be ordered direct
from the Publisher. Just tick the title you want and fill in the form below.

TBS Direct
Colchester Road, Frating Green, Colchester, Essex CO7 7DW
Tel: +44 (0) 1206 255777
Fax: +44 (0) 1206 255914
Email: sales@tbs-ltd.co.uk

UK/BFPO customers please allow £1.00 for p&p for the first book, plus 50p for
the second, plus 30p for each additional book up to a maximum charge of
£3.00.

Overseas customers (inc. Ireland), please allow £2.00 for the first book, plus £1.00
for the second, plus 50p for each additional book.

Please send me the titles ticked above.

NAME (block letters) ......................................................................................................

ADDRESS ............................................................................................................................

...............................................................................................................................................

POSTCODE .........................................................................................................................

I enclose a cheque/PO (payable to TBS Direct) for ...................................................

I wish to pay by Switch/Credit card

Number ...............................................................................................................................

Card Expiry Date ..............................................................................................................

Switch Issue Number ......................................................................................................

# Other titles available from Robinson Publishing

***The Mammoth Encyclopedia of***
***Modern Crime Fiction***      Ed. by Mike Ashley     **£9.99 [ ]**
This affordable and comprehensive new reference for the world of crime fiction
is the only one in the field. Amongst other things, it has a historical introduction,
showing the background and development of crime fiction from its earliest days
to the present. It also has an author A to Z, covering 500 entries on the major
crime writers in the crime fiction field.

***The Mammoth Book of***
***Comic Crime***      Ed. by Maxim Jakubowski     **£6.99 [ ]**
This terrific anthology offers the best from this very popular genre. Here is old
and new comedy crime writing in an explosive barrel of wit and wisecracking,
featuring cack-handed villains, accident-prone good guys and a host of criminal
characters who range from deadpan to dead stupid, often in pretty surreal
circumstances.

***The Mammoth Encyclopedia of***
***Locked Room Mysteries***
***and Impossible Crimes***      Ed. by Mike Ashley     **£6.99 [ ]**
For the first time ever, the biggest collection of such stories. They included how
a man can by stabbed in the open countryside surrounded by plenty of witnesses
who saw nothing, and the women who were shot from a theatre's stage when the
only people on it were male strippers – with no visible weapons! These and 30
other stories will stretch your powers of deduction to the limits.

Robinson books are available from all good bookshops or can be ordered direct
from the Publisher. Just tick the title you want and fill in the form below.

TBS Direct
Colchester Road, Frating Green, Colchester, Essex CO7 7DW
Tel: +44 (0) 1206 255777
Fax: +44 (0) 1206 255914
Email: sales@tbs-ltd.co.uk

UK/BFPO customers please allow £1.00 for p&p for the first book, plus 50p for
the second, plus 30p for each additional book up to a maximum charge of
£3.00.

Overseas customers (inc. Ireland), please allow £2.00 for the first book, plus £1.00
for the second, plus 50p for each additional book.

Please send me the titles ticked above.

NAME (block letters) ................................................................................................................

ADDRESS ......................................................................................................................................

..........................................................................................................................................................

POSTCODE ...................................................................................................................................

I enclose a cheque/PO (payable to TBS Direct) for ......................................................

I wish to pay by Switch/Credit card

Number ..........................................................................................................................................

Card Expiry Date .......................................................................................................................

Switch Issue Number ................................................................................................................